D0465883

More praise for
KATHERINE SUTCLIFFE

"The incomparable Katherine Sutcliffe is in top form with her trademark blend of passion, pageantry, and thrilling romance."
—Susan Wiggs,
bestselling author of *The Charm School*

"Sutcliffe is a marvelous talent and a treasure of the genre."
—Laura Kinsale,
New York Times bestselling author

"Sutcliffe entertains. She hits a home run every time!"
—Kat Martin, *New York Times*
bestselling author of *Perfect Sin*

"One of the best writers of romance . . . today."
—*Midwest Book Review*

"A powerful, sensual thriller. Only a true master can pull off a story like this one!"   —*Romantic Times*

"The suspense will peel your socks off!"
>—Gayle Lands, *New York Times*
bestselling author of *Mesmerized*

"A wonderful, exciting, suspenseful book with multidimensional characters."   —Romance-Central.com

"A must-read. Five stars."   —*Fiction Factor*

"An exciting chiller."   —*BookBrowser*

Notorious

"Stunning . . . this is by far the best historical romance I've ever read . . . and I can't recommend it highly enough."
>—*Rendezvous*

"Dark and dangerous . . . and exactly what makes Katherine Sutcliffe's novels classics in the purest sense. This is absolutely one of the most compelling historical reads of the year."
>—Jill Barnett, *New York Times* bestselling author of *Wicked*

"*Notorious* has everything I expect from a Katherine Sutcliffe novel: breathtaking action, an exquisite hero, very vivid and evocative prose . . . Edgy and intense."
>—*The Romance Journal*

"With a touch of a master storyteller, Katherine Sutcliffe mesmerizes readers from the very first word by weaving an intense story of exquisite passion and deep emotions. A luminous love story that shines brightly in your heart."
>—*Romantic Times*

Praise for the novels of
KATHERINE SUTCLIFFE

Bad Moon Rising

"What a stupendous talent! Sutcliffe has given us another winner, even better and more chilling than her last. *Bad Moon Rising* is going to be the talk of the literary world for a long time to come."
—Sue Hartigan, *All About Murder*

"Probably the most chilling murder mystery this reviewer has ever read. If you love fabulous, riveting romantic suspense rife with true-life danger, you'll be crazy about *Bad Moon Rising*."
—Beth Anderson, *Rendezvous*

Darkling I Listen

"The most riveting contemporary suspense novel this reviewer has read in a long time. Sutcliffe has set a towering new standard for romantic suspense—one so high, I can't imagine anyone else ever coming close."
—*Rendezvous*

"You won't be able to put it down, and you won't be able to sleep after you've finished this on-the-edge-of-your-seat romantic suspense, full of unexpected twists and turns . . . [Her] best work to date."
—*About.com*

"Her many fans will embrace this edgy romantic thriller."
—*Publishers Weekly*

"A full, complex read: a mélange of wry, down-home wit; dark eroticism and good old-fashioned suspense with some Hollywood glitz thrown in for good measure."
—*The Romance Journal*

"Well-written, rich in detail, erotic, sexy, darkly complicated and touching and sad, this is one of the best romantic suspense novels I've ever read."
—*All About Romance*

continued . . .

Bad Moon Rising

KATHERINE SUTCLIFFE

JOVE BOOKS, NEW YORK

If you purchased this book without a cover, you should be aware that
this book is stolen property. It was reported as "unsold and destroyed"
to the publisher, and neither the author nor the publisher has received
any payment for this "stripped book."

This is a work of fiction. Names, characters, places, and incidents
either are the product of the author's imagination or are used fictitiously,
and any resemblance to actual persons, living or dead, business
establishments, events, or locales is entirely coincidental.

BAD MOON RISING

A Jove Book / published by arrangement with
the author

PRINTING HISTORY
Jove edition / June 2003

Copyright © 2003 by Katherine Sutcliffe
Cover design by Marc Cohen

All rights reserved.
This book, or parts thereof, may not be reproduced in any form without
permission. The scanning, uploading, and distribution of this book via the
Internet or via any other means without the permission of the publisher is
illegal and punishable by law. Please purchase only authorized electronic
editions, and do not participate in or encourage electronic piracy of
copyrighted materials. Your support of the author's rights is appreciated.
For information address: The Berkley Publishing Group,
a division of Penguin Group (USA) Inc.,
375 Hudson Street, New York, New York 10014.

ISBN: 0-515-13487-2

A JOVE BOOK®
Jove Books are published by The Berkley Publishing Group,
a division of Penguin Group (USA) Inc.,
375 Hudson Street, New York, New York 10014.
JOVE and the "J" design
are trademarks belonging to Penguin Group (USA) Inc.

PRINTED IN THE UNITED STATES OF AMERICA

10 9 8 7 6 5 4 3 2 1

GRATEFUL
ACKNOWLEDGMENT

As always, my sincere appreciation to my editor, Christine Zika, for her belief in my books and her uncanny ability to keep me on track. To my agent, Evan Fogelman, whose encouragement keeps the torch of hope burning brightly.

And to a few brilliant individuals who helped along the way.

Maureen Williamson, investigative reporter and reserve officer for the San Jacinto Police Department, who was always ready and eager to answer any and all questions. Love you, Sis!

Natalie Collins, incredibly talented author of *SisterWife,* who came to my rescue when I needed her the most. (www.nataliercollins.com)

And a very special, heartfelt thank-you to retired New York Detective Dennis J. McGowan, who patiently took me under his wing through the writing of this book and educated me on the particulars of police work. The highly tal-

ented author of *False Stature,* Dennis took time away from
his own writing to hold my hand through it all and assure
me I could pull it all together.

Always remember, Dennis: I've got your back!
(www.dennisjmcgowan.com)

To my readers. Thanks for your continued support!
You're appreciated more than you know.
(www.KatherineSutcliffe.net)

PROLOGUE

The bitch is harder to kill than most others.

Her wide eyes stare up at him—whites showing around the stark blue of irises that are fast being eclipsed by her expanding pupils. He's seen enough women die to know just how much longer he will need to wait before getting down to business.

He smiles and settles back in the chair, crosses his legs and checks his watch, first nudging down the surgical glove from the watch face—quarter of two. Ten minutes at the most and she will be a goner.

Tyra isn't her real name, of course. Hookers never use their real names—like the dancers and waitresses over on Bourbon Street, the sluts who take care of their high-roller clientele back in the VIP and champagne lounges of the tittie clubs.

She looks like a Nicole. Perhaps an Amanda. Definitely the cheerleader type. Long blond hair, long legs, and *collagen-puffed lips that make her look as if she's taken a deep suck off a green persimmon. Better looking than most paid whores, granted.*

But, a whore is a whore is a whore.

A parasite deserving of extermination.

"Would you like to scream?" he asks. "Go ahead. I won't stop you."

She opens her mouth and gurgles. The blood would be filling up her throat by now, what hasn't drained out around the ice pick in her neck, just below the jawline. There is an art to such a wound—the precision of it so masterful a surgeon would be tempted to applaud him. The thrust had been deep and clean, puncturing the windpipe and vocal chords. She hadn't seen it coming. He'd simply yanked back her head and slid the pick into her throat—careful to miss the jugular.

She can't scream, of course. But he does so enjoy teasing them. It helps to pass the time.

Ten of two.

On the floor near his feet is Saturday's newspaper, the Times-Picayune. *He nudges it carefully with his foot so he can better read the front page . . .*

SERIAL KILLER SCHEDULED
TO DIE MONDAY

Angel Gonzalez, a Mexican drifter who was convicted for the murders of seven women and two children, will be put to death Monday. . . .

"*Poor bastard.*" He chuckles and shakes his head. "*Imagine how they're going to feel when they find out you were innocent.*"

Oh well. The scum sucker had admitted to child molestation and if anyone deserved to get burned, it was child molesters—short circuit them until their brains bubble out of their ears.

He reaches for the backpack on the floor and hefts it into his lap, unzips it, and digs out the scalpel and hacksaw, peels aside the red felt in which he has so carefully wrapped them—a master of his trade must always take special care of the tools of his craft—sets them aside, then begins to undress. First, the Nikes. He tucks them into the backpack—no socks, they are just one more piece of evidence that he will have to dispose of. Then, his jeans—no underwear, of course—and his Mardi Gras T-shirt; fold them all neatly and tuck them into the backpack as well, zip it closed for safe measure, unzip the coin pocket and withdraw a condom packet, collect the scalpel and saw, then walk to the bed, careful to avoid the growing pool of blood on the floor beneath the mattress.

Lifting the foil packet up for her to see, he winks. "*Ribbed for pleasure.*"

She struggles weakly. The wires around her wrists and ankles have already cut through her flesh. Tyra obviously isn't doing herself any favors, but it's certainly enough to get his juices flowing. Oh, yeah.

"*See this?*" He lifts the scalpel. "*I'm going to cut you open with this, Tyra. Yes, I am. I'm going to lay open your flat, pretty stomach and eviscerate you. Do you know what that means, cutie?"*

She thrashes. Her eyeballs are starting to swell and quiver.

Oh, yeah. Having fun now. His blood is warming. Head a little dizzy. The aroma of death hangs in the sweltering air like the titillating scent of a horny woman.

He glances down at the penis. Almost there.

Then he raises the hacksaw. *"Tyra, are you paying close attention, dear? Now, don't die on me yet. Hang on for just a moment longer. You wouldn't want to miss all the fun, would you? I'm going to cut off your head. I'm going to put it in that backpack, then we're going to take a ride out of town where I'll toss the backpack with you in it into the river."*

Feeling good now.

The penis is aroused and jutting from between his legs like a crowbar. Despicably ugly thing—engorged and painful—a constant source of trouble.

Big deep breath. Remove the condom from the packet and put it on. Careful, careful—oh, yes. Stroking himself now. Pumping gently. Sweat rising.

Her eyes begin to glaze and her chest rattles. She makes a pitiful attempt at squirming, which excites him more, and he strokes himself harder. *"Come come, Tyra,"* he says through his teeth. *"You can do better than that."*

The psychologists who had profiled him four years ago had termed him a "Domineering Serial Killer"—a killer who enjoys seeing his victims suffer. *Correct. He gets off on inspiring fear. Correct again. He gets more enjoyment from the victim's fear, from feeling a sense of control and power over another human being than he does from the actual killing.* They were off a little on that one, but hey, no one is perfect. *This murderer does not suffer from delusions, visions, or voices. He is totally aware of what he is doing and may be very well versed in the laws and penal codes of his area.* Nailed it. *He had been tempted to send the team of head shrinkers a "booby" prize for their extreme intelligence but mutilating a woman's finest assets had been a little too distasteful, even for him.*

The somewhat disconcerting idea occurs to him that perhaps Tyra isn't afraid to die—even embraces the idea. Not that he blames her. Surely death is preferable to this sordid life of whoredom, night after night of spreading her legs for any disease-infected creep who has a hard on and is willing to pay for his satisfaction.

Suddenly Mick Jagger's voice rings inside his head— Can't get no satisfaction—*as if good old Mick had a problem with that. Yeah, right.*

What was it about women who didn't give a flying frog about how ugly a man is as long as he has money and acclaim? Let some dude get his name on Entertainment Tonight *and he is grade A number one prime beef. Fame and success are aphrodisiacs to the female species. He's willing to bet that Jerry Hall wouldn't have looked twice at Mick had he been a CPA or, better yet, the mechanic who changed the spark plugs in her Ferrari.*

He realizes then that Tyra is dead. She hadn't so much as given a shudder. Her eyes are frozen open and void as two copper pennies.

Looking down at his penis, he watches it shrivel and the condom droop like a deflated balloon.

Damn.

1

Holly Jones drifted on the edge of sleep, too exhausted to fight it, yet too happy over the day's events to give in yet to her dreams. She wanted to relive every wonderful moment. Cherish them. Exalt in the pleasure she had experienced surrounded by people who loved her. She could still taste the sweet marzipan icing of her birthday cake. Hear the joyous, if not slightly off-key, rendition of Happy Birthday, Holly! Candles glowing. Presents stacked high with bright ribbons and cards that declared her friends' love and devotion. At long last, life was good. Life was wonderful! How long had she dreamed of this?

Bright balloons formed a dancing wall around her and overhead. They made her laugh as she batted them aside, the chorus of Happy Birthday, Holly resonating in the air as tears rose in her eyes.

When had she last been this happy? She felt as buoyant

as the shimmering balloons that glowed with a strange iridescence from inside, and when she looked harder she realized that within each colorful globe burned a birthday candle, and within each tiny flickering flame she saw the faces of her friends. Peggy Sue Milligan, whose bouffant hair could withstand hurricane-force winds. Fred Kenopensky, a retired Air Force captain who had been injured in Iwo Jima and who considered her as precious as the granddaughter he had lost to breast cancer ten years ago. Clarence McCarthy, who had taken her under his wing and trusted her enough to manage his prized gift shop and hinted that soon she would be capable of running the entire motel so he and his wife Lou Ann could at last retire and enjoy this bit of Shangri-La in the Ozarks.

She held up her wrist to display the watch Clarence had given her for her twenty-eighth birthday—a Timex whose face was emblazoned with the likeness of the Orange Blossom Inn, not the finest watch she had ever owned, far from it, but the best because it had been given to her out of love.

Suddenly she stood outside of the gift shop, looking back through the glass doors into Peggy Sue's smiling, wrinkled face, which was bracketed by a revolving rack of Branson, Missouri, postcards and another of plastic key chains.

"Careful 'round them corners, hon!" Peggy Sue shouted.

No chance of taking any corners on two wheels. Not in the Ford she had picked up for a whopping thousand bucks before settling into bright lights, big city Branson— Live Entertainment Capital of the World.

Holly pumped the accelerator three times before the Taurus started. It humped its way out onto the highway, hesitated, gulping for gas like an animal gasping in death throes.

Holly struggled to open her eyes. Something had awakened her. She turned her head and looked at the glowing bedside lamp. She'd fallen asleep before turning it off.

The phone rang. She glanced at the bedside clock. Two A.M.

Few people had her number—just those she had worked with after arriving in Branson six months before. She thought of Captain Fred and his bad heart, and the fear that something had happened to him since she had left her birthday party hours ago, or Peggy Sue whose diabetes too often sent her to the hospital in a near coma.

She slipped from the bed and hurried to the phone, rubbing her eyes, and froze as she looked down at the caller ID: OUT OF AREA.

Only one person outside of Branson had her phone number, and she had been cautioned never to call Holly unless there was an emergency. Cautiously, she lifted the receiver to her ear. Too late. Whoever called had hung up.

Releasing her breath, Holly gently replaced the receiver. A wrong number perhaps. Sure. That was it.

She glanced around the dimly lit apartment. Sofa, chair, and formica dining set provided by Lonesome Dove Apartments, as was the fridge and the bedroom suite. She preferred it that way. No ties. If she needed to up and leave again at short notice, she needn't worry about moving anything but a few pots and pans, linens, and clothes. All could fit neatly in the backseat of the Taurus.

The kitchen was a narrow rectangular jut off the dining area. Standing on the kitchen threshold, she dug a cigarette out of the package she retrieved from the countertop and lit it with a disposable lighter advertising Owen's Theater, famous for their celebrity impersonators of Elvis and Liberace.

Taking a deep drag from the Slim, she allowed her gaze to shift around the small room, lit only by the night-light she had plugged into a socket over the stove.

She wasn't much of a decorator, but had made the room as homey as possible, a few culinary gadgets hanging from plastic hooks on the walls, a wire basket of onions, another of ceramic eggs dangling from the ceiling.

She was so damn proud of the cozy apartment—the first place she had allowed herself to call home for more than a few weeks. Branson, Disney World of the retired set, had become a refuge where she could disappear from the ghosts of her past. No reminders here of the bad, old days, and of the mistakes she had made with her life. They only existed in her nightmares.

Take a deep breath, she told herself. It had only been a wrong number. She was absolutely sure of it.

Holly opened the fridge and extracted a Fuzzy Navel Cooler, flung the screw cap in the general vicinity of the overflowing garbage can, and returned to the living room.

Her stomach hurt, as it always did when she allowed her overactive imagination to get the better of her. Which wasn't often—at least not as often as she used to. Her long hours of selling Mel Tillis key chains kept her mind off of too many what-ifs. Still, the occasional cataclysm did manage to worm its way into her thoughts when she let her guard down. Like now.

She drank deeply of the Fuzzy Navel, then smoked again, and stared at the phone. She could hear her Blossom Inn Timex ticking in the quiet.

She crushed out her cigarette and poured the remaining drink down the drain, returned to the bedroom, and climbed into bed. She took a deep breath and told herself again it had been a wrong number. Nothing to worry about. Life was good, right? No memories allowed. Not today.

Holly flipped off the light and nestled down, focused her thoughts on her plans for tomorrow—her day off. Once a week she volunteered at a local church's Mother's Day Out. She relished every second of the children's company. Drooling babies and precocious tots. Their innocence somehow purified her.

Her heavy lids drifted closed.

She lit a cigarette as an odd, gray haze enveloped her. As she drove down Highway 76, the Vegaslike marquees of the theaters formed halos of muted colors that melted like streams of watercolor into fog. A niggling of confusion made her dizzy and, for a moment, it seemed the car was floating. Balloons surrounded her, drifting like airborne bubbles around her head.

She turned on the radio and a familiar voice boomed out at her. "This is KRLA Radio, New Orleans. Shana, baby, you can run and you can hide, but eventually we're going to find you. Dr. Yah Yah is going to find you and when he does—"

The stations changed as if by magic, racing from one to another, a cacophony of country western, classical, and jazz until it settled on one that blasted loudly enough to make Holly grab her ears.

"And when he does, Shana, baby, he's going to make you very sorry, sorry, sorry."

She turned off the radio and clutched the steering wheel, her heart pounding in her ears and the balloons moving rapidly around her, thumping against the windshield so she couldn't see. They glowed with a red, pulsing heat. She thrust her cigarette at them, popping each one, but no sooner did they explode than they were replaced with others, each one stenciled with the name Dr. Yah Yah.

Jumping from the car, she found herself in the parking lot of the Lonesome Dove Apartments. As she sprinted up the three flights of wrought iron stairs, she heard a phone ring and froze.

Suddenly she stood in her living room, cautiously lifting the receiver to her ear.

"You can run and you can hide, but Dr. Yah Yah is gonna get you, baby."

A sound came from behind her and she spun around, a scream working up her throat.

Holly sat up in bed, gasping for breath, her gaze flashing around her small bedroom, to the clutch of helium balloons drifting along the ceiling. They didn't glow, just shifted from the gusts of air rushing from the vent near the ceiling.

A dream. Just a dream—a nightmare. And the phone

call had simply been a wrong number. No need to panic. No point in allowing in all the old fear. She had locked that away since settling into Branson. Still . . .

Leaving the bed, she crossed to the closet door and slid it open, stooped, and studied the pair of Samsonite suitcases partially visible behind her measly grouping of dresses and an impressive collection of different-colored wigs. The cases were there, all right, calling to her. *Just say the word, girlfriend, and we are out of here.*

Paranoia was back. It seeped from her pores in big drops of sweat that beaded over her lip and between her breasts. It crawled over her scalp and slid down her spine like cold fingers.

She slammed the closet door and hastened to the bathroom, hit the light that exploded through the tiny room from a humming, flickering fixture over the sink. She bent over the sink and turned on the water. Splashed her face. Took a fortifying breath. Finally, she lifted her head and focused on her reflection in the mirror. Her blue eyes were wide and frightened. Her long hair fell in black waves around her unnaturally pale face. "Get a grip, Holly, or you're going to lose it."

No, she wasn't going to lose it. Not again. She'd worked too hard these last few months to put all that behind her.

Almost desperately, she thrust her fingers through her hair, black as spades with a touch of natural curl that became a bit too wild to manage in the humidity of New Orleans. Once, while she was living in Charleston, soon after leaving New Orleans, she had considered cutting it. But a man named Randy, whom she had dated briefly, had convinced her against it. Thank God. She could cut off her hair, disguise herself in her many wigs, but if Dr. Yah Yah wanted to find her, he would find her.

And she would be a dead woman.

The phone rang.

It rang again.

Holly slowly turned for the door. She had the feeling that she was still asleep, that this was yet another twist of her nightmare. She had a disembodied sensation of floating out of the bedroom into the living room where light from the porch lamp spilled through the open drapes. A collection of moths and june bugs, buzzing as loudly as the bathroom bulb behind her, swarmed around the yellow porch light and slammed with kamikaze determination against the window.

Again.

She moved to the phone: OUT OF AREA.

Hand trembling, she picked up the receiver, breath caught in her lungs, and lifted it to her ear.

"Shana, is that you?" came the weak, quivering female voice.

She closed her eyes, felt the room begin a slow spin that made her wobble from side to side.

"Shana," came the urgent, horrified whisper, barely audible in her suddenly short-circuiting brain. "He's back. Oh, God, Shana . . . the monster is back."

2

J.D. Damascus had one hell of a hangover.

Not that such an occurrence was unusual. Hell, no. Since his thirty-third birthday, seventy-five percent of his time was spent bumping around in a fog of extreme head pain.

Therefore, the ache stabbing through his temples at the moment was nothing new or unexpected.

Wearing dark-tinted Ray Bans to diffuse the sunlight from his throbbing eyes, J.D. slouched on a bench under a sprawling oak tree, legs outstretched, left ankle hooked over the right, and watched the group of little girls dash like frolicking puppies over the well-manicured lawn, batting balloons emblazoned with HAPPY BIRTHDAY AMBER!

J.D. grinned.

"John, I'm so glad you could make it."

Only one person, besides his mother, called him John. Sliding the Ray Bans down his nose, J.D. looked over the glasses at his sister-in-law. Beverly Damascus, former Miss Louisiana, smiled and handed him a paper plate heaped with pink-and-white birthday cake. "Wouldn't miss it for the world, darlin'. You know that."

She smiled and sat down beside him. Her scent stirred the hot, still, summer air: Estee Lauder's Pleasures. He should know. He'd bought it for her at Christmas.

"The kids are thrilled, of course. First thing Amber asked this morning was if her Uncle J.D. would be here." Beverly looked into his eyes. "I told her it depended on your schedule."

He put aside his drink and dug into the cake with a pink plastic fork. "My nine o'clock never showed. Wasn't a problem."

"I'll warn you; Patrick is going to hit you up again about coaching his soccer team."

He nodded and ate.

She glanced down at the glass of Smirnoff. "Would you like some coffee?"

"No thanks. Too early in the day." He winked at her.

She frowned and brushed a tendril of hair back from her brow. She didn't even have the good grace to perspire in the damned suffocating heat and humidity. Beverly Sinclare Damascus always looked as cool as an ice sculpture. Which is what made her the perfect politician's wife. Fires could be raging out of control in the furnace, but damned if she would show it—except in her eyes. She had the kind of eyes that, if a man had any heart about him at all, would turn him inside out with a solitary blink.

"You don't look so good, John."

"I've felt better."

"That drink isn't going to help your ulcers," she pointed out gently but sternly, or as sternly as the former Miss Louisiana ever spoke. In all the years he had known her— since the days they attended Tulane together—he had never heard her raise her voice, even to her children, in the slightest irritated manner.

Not that she didn't have backbone. God, no. He suspected she had a spine as dense as a steel girder. Must have to have survived the last eighteen years of marriage to his brother, Eric—God's gift to government.

He didn't want to discuss his ulcers at the moment, though they were hurting like hell.

"You look tired," he said, changing the subject. "Everything okay?"

She sank back into the bench and crossed her long, denim-clad legs—legs that were still deserving of miniskirts and string bikinis, as was her body. He was certain she didn't weigh a pound more than she had when they were friends their junior year at Tulane. Her only signs of aging were the faintest hint of crow's feet at her eyes and a sprinkling of gray in her short brown hair.

Finally, she shook her head, and for a moment appeared to work up her courage. When her voice finally came, it was breathy with emotion.

"No, I'm not okay. It's Patrick. I just don't know what to do with him anymore. It's like I don't even know my own son any longer. He's just so . . . angry all the time. He stays holed up in his room at night. That's not like him, John. We've always been so close." She took a shaky breath. "I even caught him smoking the other night."

"Did you kick his butt?" He grinned.

She didn't, just turned her big green eyes, pooling with tears, to his.

"Hey." He put his hand on her shoulder, a mistake, he realized, but too late. She wrapped her fingers around his wrist, gripping it fiercely, and laid her cheek against his hand. He swallowed. "Kids are going to experiment, Beverly. He's sixteen years old. Think hormones."

"First it's cigarettes, then it's booze, then drugs." She nuzzled his hand, lifted her head, and swiped a tear from her cheek. "It gets worse. I got a call from the school. Seems he got into an altercation with his teacher. She caught him cheating on a test. And do you know what he said to her? 'Fuck you. Expel me and my dad will get you fired.' " She gave a dry laugh and shook her head. "The sorry thing is, he's probably right."

"Have you talked to Eric about it?"

"You're joking. I haven't had five minutes alone with your brother since the Senate recessed, not since Jack announced his bid for the presidency. They're holed up in the house now—he and Jack and your father. They should be out here. It's Amber's birthday, for God's sake."

"Would you like for me to talk to Patrick?"

"Would you? Oh, John, that would be great. You know how much he loves you. Maybe coming from you—"

"It's not a problem."

"It's that—Eric is so involved—"

"I understand. No problem, really."

"He so desperately needs a father figure now." She froze and her face blanched of color. "Oh God, John. I'm so sorry. God, I'm so sorry. What a stupid choice of words."

He put down the plate of cake. "Forget it. You're right. He does need a father figure."

She reached out and touched his cheek with her trembling fingertips. "I'm so stupid sometimes. Yesterday was Lisa's birthday—"

"I really don't want to talk about it."

He nudged the Ray Bans up to his eyes and watched Amber take a ballerinalike twirl on her tiptoes. "I'll have a word with Eric before I go. Tell Patrick I'll give him a call tomorrow night. Maybe we'll catch a movie or something."

She touched him again, her fingertip lightly brushing against his earlobe. "John—"

J.D. stood and moved up the brick walkway, through the hot August sun that diffused the color of the flowers flourishing in the well-tended beds along the path. Last spring, the house and gardens had been featured in *Southern Living* magazine as one of the finest restored landmarks south of the Mason-Dixon line, all thanks to Beverly, of course, and her fine eye and great appreciation for historical detail. Eric wouldn't know the difference between an azalea and a Venus's-flytrap.

He dug two Tums from his jeans pocket and popped them into his mouth. Entering the house through the back French doors, he arrived in the den just as Eric, his father, and Jack Strong, the Democrats' brightest hope for the presidency, filed into the room, their expressions buoyant and their eyes burning, as always, with steely ambition.

Eric glanced at J.D. and smirked. "You look like hell."

"Screw you." He glanced at his father. "Hello, Dad."

Charles Damascus, former Governor, ignored him and

proceeded to the door where he paused and looked around at Senator Strong. "Golf tomorrow. Seven sharp."

Jack Strong flashed Charles his best John Kennedy smile and gave him a thumbs-up.

J.D. moved to the French doors and watched his father walk down the path toward Beverly, who remained on the bench just as he had left her.

"Hello to you too, son. How nice to see you. How are you, by the way? I'm fine, Dad. *Terrific, son, how would you like to join us in a round of golf in the morning?* Love to. *Great. Seven sharp.* Wonderful. See you then. My best to Mom." He gave a thumbs-up and turned back to his brother. "Son of a bitch can kiss my ass."

While the senator made himself comfortable in a chair, helping himself to Eric's stash of expensive and illegal Cuban cigars, Eric planted himself on the edge of his authentic Louis XVI desk and crossed his arms, waiting.

"We need to talk," J.D. said.

"Busy."

"So I gather. It's important."

"Make it quick."

"This is private."

"You need money, right?"

"Since when have I ever come to you for money?"

"Maybe if you'd rope in a better clientele than hookers and whiplash victims, you wouldn't be on the verge of rolling belly up." He looked over his shoulder at Jack. "Right, Senator?"

Senator Strong smiled around his cigar. "I'm staying out of this. Wouldn't want to lose the vote of one of my constituents, after all."

J.D. gave a sharp laugh. "I wouldn't vote for you if you were the only candidate on the ballot. I rank your ethics just one rung above Sammy 'The Bull' Gravanno."

Jack's eyes narrowed and his bright smile dimmed. "Careful, J.D. Although I highly respect your daddy, I wouldn't hesitate a minute in pulling a few strings to get your law license rescinded. Such as it is."

"What's that supposed to mean?"

Jack shrugged and took a deep drag on his cigar before replying. "You ain't been worth a damn as an attorney since you left the D.A.'s office. Fact is, *boy*, you're nothing more than a laughingstock anymore. A sleazy ambulance chaser whose clients are nothing more than a lot of derelicts and prostitutes. It's no wonder your daddy has disowned you."

"You son of a—"

"Here now." Eric placed himself between J.D. and the senator. "If you'll excuse us, Jack, my brother and I will just step into my office for a few minutes."

Eric took a hard, warning hold on J.D.'s arm and ushered him out of the room, into his office, and slammed the door. His face beet red, he said, "Just what the hell do you think you're doing coming to my house and insulting my guest?"

"In case you aren't aware, it's Amber's birthday."

"And your point is?"

"I think your wife would appreciate a few minutes of your time."

Eric walked to the window and looked out at his wife. "I saw the two of you talking. If I was a suspicious man, I might believe you had a thing going on."

"Patrick is having problems."

He turned away from the window. "Is that so?"

"He needs his father."

"I wasn't aware that you had, between your vodka binges, gotten your shrink's shingle."

Trying hard to rein back his temper wasn't easy—just ask the judge he'd slugged when the jury had cleared Marcus DiAngelo, of the Lucky Lady, of gambling corruption. He had never slugged his brother, but he was as close to it in that moment as he was ever going to be.

His hands fisted, he stared into his brother's eyes. Eric was a chip off the old block, no doubt about it. If cloning human beings had existed forty years ago, J.D. would happily wager that Eric had been spawned in a petri dish. The amount of compassion Eric and their father had squirming around in their hearts would fit on the tip of a straight pin.

"There's no use in talking to you," J.D. said. "There never is."

As he turned for the door, Eric slammed one hand down on J.D.'s shoulder. "I'll forgive you for coming into my house and insulting my friend. And I really don't care what you think about Daddy. But you keep your sanctimonious nose out of my family life. My kids are none of your business, J.D. And neither is my wife." Eric jammed one finger into J.D.'s breastbone and finished, "You best remember that if you know what's good for you."

It was probably a mistake coming here, considering his mood. But often, the serenity of the place

brought him as much peace as it did heartache. And it
was definitely preferable to drowning himself in the Smirnoff bottle he had tucked away in the Mustang's glove
compartment. His ulcers simply wouldn't tolerate it at the
moment, and he was out of Tums.

J.D. parked the classic 1966 fire-engine red Mustang
convertible in the shade of the three-hundred-year-old oak
trees, collected the red and blue balloons by their dangling
strings, and exited the car.

No matter how hot the temperature soared, the air was
always cool here; no traffic noise, screaming sirens, or rap
music blasting from jacked-up pickup trucks driven by the
newest generation of juvenile delinquents.

Here, the air was still and fragranced by jasmine, the
grass glossy green under the sunlight and emerald black
beneath the wide, spreading limbs of the ancient oaks. As
he walked down the manicured, winding path, the only
sound was the gentle *bump bump* of the balloons dancing
above his head. A pair of squirrels dashed across this path,
scratched their way up a tree, and chattered at him from
their perch overhead. An egret lifted from a lily-pad-
covered pond, wings popping before it glided in a circle
above the trees and settled somewhere over the line of
mausoleums in the distance.

Would this ever get any easier?

He didn't think so.

There were three graves side by side—smoke gray
granite, highly polished, their bases surrounded by sprays
of iris and daffodils. .They weren't blooming at the moment—only during spring—but the tall, green growths

were well tended, as was the lush, broad-blade Saint Augustine grass.

J.D. sat on a bench, propped his elbows on his knees, and looked from one name to the other.

WILLIAM DAMASCUS
1992–1999

LAURA DAMASCUS
1966–1999

LISA DAMASCUS
1994–1999

He tried to take a breath. It wouldn't come.

"Hi, funny face." He smiled at Lisa's headstone. "Sorry I didn't make it out yesterday. I was"—*drunk and contemplating suicide*—"busy. Aunt Beverly sends her love. She sent balloons. It was Amber's birthday today. Cute kid. Looks just like you, pigtails and all."

He straightened and closed his burning eyes. His throat convulsed and his stomach responded with a hot spear of pain that made a groan swell in his chest. The heat of the day pressed down on him, making his body break out in sweat. Christ, he was going to be sick.

The tremors were there, crawling along his arms and stinging like fire ants. No point in willing them away. Since the dawn of August 10, 1999, they had become as natural to him as breathing, surging up from the pit of his stomach twice a day, first thing in the morning and last thing at night before he fell into his waiting nightmares. They came, too, when he visited Mother of Grace Cemetery, only here, the tremors enlisted not just over-whelming grief but fury—cold, mind-obsessing hate. The kind that whispered revenge. The sort that impelled a nor-mally rational man to empty a loaded semiautomatic into the chest of a murderer, which he fully intended to do.

The day would come. Oh yeah. Because no matter that his ex–best friend, Jerry Costos, former District Attorney, had convinced a jury that Angel Gonzalez was a cold-blooded serial killer, J.D. didn't buy it. He was going to find the son of a bitch who'd slaughtered his children, and his wife, and he was going to blow his head off, and then—

The cell phone on his belt began to twitter, wrenching him from thoughts of vigilante murder and suicide. He fumbled for the phone, and swallowed twice to ensure his voice was steady enough to answer.

"Where the hell have you been?" shouted May Kraft in his ear. May was a sixty-year-old black woman with two perforated eardrums that made her mostly deaf. She'd worked as his secretary for the last two years, initially to work off her attorney's fees for a contested divorce. But she had made herself indispensable and stayed on, lending a minimal amount of sanity and structure to his floundering law practice, such as it was, according to Jack Strong.

"May, you're shouting again." He held the phone away from his ear. "You're deaf, not me. Remember?"

"I done tracked down your nine o'clock no-show. Cherry what's-her-name."

"Brown," he reminded her.

"Whatever. I done found her."

"Yeah? What's her excuse this time?"

"She's dead."

3

The police had barricaded the premises around Cherry Brown's apartment located in the deep black heart of New Orleans's red-light district, which flanked the Mississippi River: one square mile of honky tonks, strip bars, and old warehouses that had, some thirty years before, been renovated into sleazy dance clubs, illegal backroom gambling establishments, and cheap apartments. Here, hookers sold their assets by the hour, and business was good. Not just for the girls, but for scumbag lawyers like himself.

J.D. was forced to park his Mustang a half block away, behind the string of patrol cars and an EMT unit, lights still flashing. The team of medics smoked as the ambulance radio squawked with conversation and static.

Uniformed cops lined up along the walls, conversing while they waited for the crime scene unit to do their thing. As J.D. ducked under the yellow tape, they made a move toward him, then stopped, their initial concern turning into recognition. He knew them all from his days as New Orleans's top assistant district attorney—destined to replace Jerry Costos when he aspired to higher governmental ambitions. Too many times he had worked the crime scenes with them, dogging them for evidence. They had cursed him and revered him.

While they would have tackled any other intruder to the ground, they relaxed, Officer Michaels flashing him a grin as he said, "You can take the D.A. out of the office, but you can't take the office out of the man, right, Damascus?"

"Right," he said, wading through beer cans, cigarette butts, and discarded condoms.

Inside the apartment, the initial walk-through to examine the scene for potential evidence had been completed, as well as the photo snaps. The forensic investigators were already at work, the technicians carefully isolating and securing possible evidence by bagging each individual item so it would not be contaminated or lost on the way to the laboratory.

The coroner stood back, arms crossed over his chest, sharing what J.D. assumed, from his ear-to-ear grin, was a humorous conversation with one of the detectives assigned to the case. Though the detective's back was to him, J.D. would have recognized that bald head and bulldog neck anywhere: Detective Enoch P. Mallory.

J.D. turned his back to the conversing duo, slipped around a technician who was intent on logging in his evidence, and stopped short upon the sight of Cherry Brown's body. Or what was left of it. Good Christ.

"Damascus!"

J.D. turned away from the corpse, vomit crawling up his throat, and came face-to-face with Mallory. He wasn't certain which was more stomach-turning: the bloody massacre on the bed or the investigator's pan-faced, double-chinned countenance thrusting into his own face so closely the smell of Mallory's breath, tainted with garlic and cigarettes, rushed over him in a noxious wave.

"Mind telling me what the hell you're doing in here?" Mallory growled.

"My client," he managed.

"Was your client. In case you ain't noticed, she's dead and you're trespassing on a crime scene. Need I remind you that you're not an A.D.A. anymore?"

He couldn't argue the point, so he said nothing, not that he could if he wanted to.

Mallory looked away and planted his fists on his hips. The action distorted his suit coat, exposing his big belly and the .38 he had tucked into his shoulder holster. Massive sweat stains splotched his shirt and coat beneath his armpits. As he regarded Cherry Brown, his mouth worked from side to side.

"Offers a new meaning to giving head, don't it?"

"You're an ass, Mallory." J.D. blinked the sweat from his eyes and moved for the door. He needed air. Fast.

The alley offered little respite. The fumes of sour beer and urine only exacerbated his need to puke. He made it as far as a garbage Dumpster before losing it. He heaved up the coffee he'd purchased on his way to Cherry's. It was tinged with blood.

"I see your ulcers aren't any better," Mallory said be-

hind him. "I had an ulcer once. As they eat into the muscles of the stomach or duodenal wall, blood vessels are
damaged, which causes bleeding. Over a long period of
time, a person may become anemic and feel weak, dizzy,
or tired. You look damned anemic to me."

J.D. fell back against the wall, face sweating. His gut
felt as if it would incinerate at any moment. He dug into
his pocket for his new supply of Tums.

"When did this happen?" he said between his teeth.

"Between midnight and eight this morning."

"Who found her?"

"A friend. Calls herself Honey. Cherry was supposed
to meet her for breakfast. She didn't show and the gal
came 'round to check on her."

"Where's the friend?"

"With Stakouski. You know the drill. She's pretty upset."

"I want to talk to her."

Mallory glanced over his shoulder, then moved in
closer. "Look, I can appreciate how this might look—"

"Save it. I don't want to hear anymore of the pat
bullshit I've been hearing for the last four years."

"Leave it alone, J.D. The force doesn't need any more
crap out of you about Angel Gonzalez. I'm warning
you—"

"The force can kiss my ass. Angel Gonzalez didn't
butcher my family or those prostitutes. The state fried the
wrong man and we both know it. He was convicted on
circumstantial evidence and had any judge besides Shanks
been presiding, it would never have been allowed to happen."

"You're just pissed at Shanks because he screwed your case with DiAngelo. Get over it. This homicide is nothing more than a copycat killing. It happens. If there weren't maniacs roaming the streets, we'd be out of business."

"Yeah?" J.D. gave a short, dry laugh that caused a fresh spear of pain to cut through him. "I guess we'll see soon enough, won't we?" He shoved by Mallory and moved up the alley.

"Get some help for those ulcers!" Mallory shouted.

Although the sweltering night air was rife with fear and tension—not to mention suspicion over every sex-starved male who cruised slowly by in search of companionship—J.D. had no problem locating Honey. Most of the hookers prowling the district at midnight had been his clients at one time or another, and they were fairly certain he wasn't capable of decapitating and eviscerating a woman whether he approved of her morals or not.

Honey occupied an apartment on the second floor of a renovated warehouse that had, at the turn of the twentieth century, been the Jamieson Cottonseed Oil Mill. However, a devastating fire on June 23, 1925, had consumed one-half of the warehouse district along the river, and the extent of rebuilding the Jamieson Mill had extended only to its redbrick walls when the owner declared bankruptcy and left the warehouse to fall back into decay.

Marcus DiAngelo's father, Mitchell, had purchased the properties and rebuilt. Marcus had inherited it all upon his father's untimely death, which had shown evidence of a mob hit. But that, too, had been swept under the city's ever-spreading carpet of See No Evil.

Honey had greasy platinum-blond hair with black roots, breast implants that must have set her pimp back a bundle, and tattoos over her arms and down the outside of her legs. Her nails were painted black, the polish peeling off in chips. Each ear was studded with five dangling bobs and on each finger was a silver ring, the kind the tourists bought at a booth in the market. They were staining her skin green.

She looked fifty, but J.D. suspected she was more like thirty. The business was hard on the girls . . . so were the drugs she was apparently shooting. The insides of her arms were scarred with tracks, and her nose looked as if it had been scoured with sand paper. However, at the moment, she appeared to be semilucid, if not totally traumatized over Cherry's demise. She paced her apartment, pulling at her hair one minute and crying the next.

As a defense attorney, J.D. knew from experience that before he could hope to secure the kind of information that he needed, a relationship of trust had to be developed. Patience was necessary. Except he wasn't feeling very patient at the moment. What little patience he held on to these days had vaporized the instant he'd seen a headless Cherry Brown laid open like a gutted pig.

"I already told the cops all this. I don't want to talk about it again."

"I understand."

"It was horrible." She covered her face and whimpered.

"I understand."

"He cut off her head!"

She was losing it. Time to back off a little. Think sympathy.

He walked to her and took her in his arms. "It's okay. Calm down, sweetheart." She shook against him and he stroked her hair. Her tears bled through his T-shirt, warm against his skin. "Take a breath and try to relax."

She gulped several deep breaths and sagged against him.

"We'll talk when you're ready." He scoped the apartment, noting the many voodoo emblems hanging from the walls—gris-gris against evil.

"Cherry was a really sweet girl, you know? I mean, she didn't deserve this."

"No one does."

"She was only twenty-one. And special. Real special."

"Have you any idea who her midnight john was?"

She pulled away and began pacing again. "That's the thing. She wasn't supposed to work last night. She hadn't worked all week." Wringing her hands, she turned to face him. Black mascara had melted around her brown eyes and streaked her right cheek. "She wanted out of the business. Wanted to move home, back to California. The man was really pissed about it."

She needn't explain who "the man" was to J.D. The simple thought of Tyron Johnson encouraged fresh pain to coil in his gut, along with hatred, not to mention suspicion that made his heart slam against his ribs.

Tyron controlled girls in three states, but made his home in New Orleans. He lived in the penthouse suite of the Lucky Lady Casino—ten thousand a month including all the champagne he could drink and all the caviar he could eat. He had a nuclear temper and his girls paid the price big-time for crossing him.

During his four years with the District Attorney's office, J.D. had attempted to bury him in prison several times for assault with deadly intent and drug-related charges. In each case, the girl he had carved up during one of his tantrums had refused to testify, or he'd gotten off on some technicality. Case closed. Again and again and again. The last time they had met, that being on the courthouse steps on a beautiful June morning, 1999, Tyron had declared in front of eight witnesses that J.D. was going to live to regret his harassment. Two months later, his wife and children had been murdered.

Tyron had had an alibi for the time of the murders. Marcus DiAngelo.

"It's starting again," Honey said. "Just like before. They were wrong, weren't they? About that Gonzalez creep. He wasn't the killer at all."

"It's too early to jump to those conclusions." Christ, old habits were hard to break. He was sounding like Mallory, but no point in exacerbating the woman's panic. Not yet. "Could be some freak copycat. One murder is a long way from a serial killing."

She stopped pacing and turned to face him. "She's not the first."

"What the hell are you saying?"

"You wouldn't have heard about it. The state don't want the public to know it put an innocent man to death."

*   *   *

Patrick Damascus, sixteen and a half, going on thirty, or so his mother declared, sat at his desk crowded with schoolbooks and assignment sheets that he had not so much as glanced at, though the hour was growing late. He hated the "alternative school year" that came with the private school his mother had insisted he attend. It was supposed to provide him a better education, because he was "gifted" and public schools couldn't afford him the opportunity to utilize his genius.

That was a lot of crappola. She simply didn't want him hanging with normal kids because, according to her, they were a bad influence. That, too, was a lot of crappola. The kids attending St. Elizabeth's Boys' School were the worst. Those who weren't geeks were freaks, but there wasn't any reasoning with her. Once she set her mind to something, there was no changing it.

Opening the bottom drawer of his desk, he dug deep beneath several spiral notebooks labeled GEOMETRY SUCKS THE BIG ONE and ENGLISH LIT IS FOR FAGS, withdrew a magazine, and carefully, as if it would detonate at any moment, placed it on his desk. He arranged the lamp closer, adjusting the shade so it cast a spotlight on the glossy, colored photographs of naked couples.

Certainly, he was well aware of the facts of life, birds and bees and all those clichéd stupidities adults termed "fucking." But the photos presented here were highly enlightening, in short, leaving nothing to the imagination. His curiosity of the female anatomy had been assuaged within the covers of this encyclopedia of smut. Couples, threesomes, men and women, women and women, men and men emblazoned the photos with a boldness that made a knot form in his stomach and a heat center in his groin that flushed his entire body, not just with the stirrings of his awakening hormones, but with an anger that made him grit his teeth so hard his jaw hurt.

So engrossed was he at the moment, he didn't hear his bedroom door open. It wasn't until he heard his mother's horrified gasp that he realized he had been caught with the goods.

"Oh my God."

He stiffened.

As his mother snatched the magazine from the desk, Patrick leaped from the chair and spun around to face her.

"Oh my God," she repeated, her face blanched of color and her eyes wide with horror as she stared at the photographs in her shaking hands. "What in God's name—"

"What happened to knocking?" he shouted, embarrassment turning his face red.

"Where did you get this trash?"

He glared at her, a gazillion excuses scrambling in his brain.

"Answer me, Patrick. Where did you get—"

"None of your business," he finally managed, unable to come up with anything more appropriate at the moment. It was a kid's right of birth to turn the tables on his parents when caught with his pants down, so to speak. To acknowledge one's own guilt went against the laws of nature.

"I beg your pardon? None of my business? I find my son with a pornographic magazine and it's none of my business?"

"What's it matter? I got it, okay?" He shoved by her

and walked to his bed, flopped onto his back, and stared at the ceiling. Genius or not, there were times when playing stupid was essential to pubescent survival. "What's the big deal, anyhow?"

She sank into the chair. "The big deal is, you're sixteen years old—"

"Sixteen and a half."

"You've got no business looking at this kind of perversion."

He might have continued the argument had his mother's voice not begun to tremble. She obviously was on the verge of crying, and if anything could stop him cold and fill him up with raw, ragged, and bloody regret, it was his mom crying. Anger and rebelliousness took a backseat to guilt when it came to disappointing his mother. And although he seemed to be doing that a lot these days, he just couldn't help himself. Just like he couldn't help not destroying the piece of smut that intrigued him as much as infuriated him.

His mother rolled the magazine into a tube while her gaze continued to bore a hole into him. He wondered if this would be the impetus for her to finally lose control and start yelling like most parents when they got pissed at their kids. Often he listened to his friend's tales of parental terror with envy. They were normal, and normal intrigued him. Life in the Damascus household had never been normal.

"I just don't know what to do with you anymore," she said.

He watched a model of a stealth fighter slowly rotate above him.

"What's happened to us, Patrick? We used to be so close. You used to talk to me."

"Guess I don't have anything to say."

"Why are you so angry? What have I done?"

Come into my room without knocking, for one.

"First I get this call from the principal at your school, now this." She tapped the tube on the desk. "I suppose I should speak to your father—"

"He won't give a damn. Why bother?"

"Stop cursing."

"Everyone curses. Even the geeks. What's the big deal?"

"Because you're only—"

"Sixteen. God, why can't I be eighteen? Then I could get the hell out of here." He rolled to his side, offering his mother his back. "It sucks here. I hate it. I want to go live with Uncle J.D. He's cool."

His mother crossed the room and sat on the bed beside him. She touched his shoulder.

"J.D. comes to my soccer games," he continued. "We watch videos together when I'm at his place. He doesn't treat me like I'm a stupid kid."

"I'd miss you," she said softly.

He rolled again to his back and focused on her eyes. "You could come, too. And Amber."

She forced a smile. "Move in just like that, huh?"

"Why not?"

"Because I'm married to your father."

"So get a divorce."

Her eyebrows lifted.

"Why not? You two don't love each other. Not anymore."

A deep red flush crept up her face.

"You're not denying it," he pointed out.

"Because it's ridiculous."

He gently placed his hand on her back, felt her stiffen. "It's okay, Mom. I don't blame you. He treats you like shit."

Leaving the bed, she paced to the window and looked out. "I can't believe I'm having this conversation with my son. I can't believe you would welcome a divorce—"

"You'd be happier. And so would I. Besides, Dad doesn't deserve you."

She turned again to face him. "Is that what all this anger is about? Your father?"

"I hate him." There. He'd said it. Lightning didn't bolt out of the sky and incinerate him.

"Patrick!"

"I do. I hate his guts. He doesn't love you, and he doesn't love me and Amber."

"That's not true."

"He's a creep and I wish he was dead."

"That's enough. I won't have you talk like that about your father."

"If you don't divorce him, I'm going to run away from home. I'll move in with Uncle J.D. whether you like it or not."

"I won't listen to any more of this nonsense."

As she always did when she found herself unable to cope with the momentary crisis, his mother moved toward the door, gripping the porno tube so tightly in her hand it bent in the middle.

"Mom," he said as she reached the door. She paused and looked back, her eyes so full of anguish he felt punched in the stomach. "Please . . . don't tell Dad about the magazine." He swallowed. "Please."

She left the room, closing the door behind her.

He felt certain that she wouldn't tattle. She never did. Because she knew as well as he did that bad news regarding Eric Damascus's kids would float in one ear and out the other. Normally, Patrick wouldn't have bothered with the request to keep this type of perverted news from Louisiana's distinguished legislative director, but this was an exception. This shocking revelation would have caused consequences he wasn't ready to deal with at the moment. Not yet. In time, but not now.

He locked his door. Something he should have done before pulling out the porno magazine, but he wasn't accustomed to needing to. His mother had always respected his privacy, but lately she'd been slipping. Since she'd caught him smoking, it seemed he was always finding her popping up out of nowhere.

He retrieved his portable disc player with earphones from his bookshelf, along with his favorite CD—both of which J.D. had given him the last time they'd gone out together. He prized it as highly as the soccer ball, autographed by David Beckham, that J.D. had given him last Christmas.

Crawling under his bed, he extracted his hidden stash of cigarettes and matches the freak Raymond Dillworth had provided him at school. Raymond had offered him weed sprinkled with crack as well, but he was genius enough to know that if he was caught with a juice joint, his mom wouldn't have been just rattled to tears, she would have gone apoplectic. Couldn't have Senator Strong's legislative director having a son who walked around baked. Might cost the asshole a vote or two.

Easing up his bedroom window, Patrick crawled out on the roof, carefully working his way along the gable until he settled down beside the chimney. Then he leaned back, positioned the headphones on his ears, and hit the play button before lighting up his Marlboro Light. As Credence Clearwater Revival exploded against his eardrums singing about a bad moon rising and trouble being on the way, he gazed at the sky, inhaled deeply from the cigarette, and studied the moon overhead.

There was definitely trouble on the way, he thought. It was only a matter of time.

4

The nights were always the worst, when memories clawed their way to the forefront of his mind and arranged themselves like a slide show in chronological order.

Laura on their wedding day dressed in a beige suit, loose-fitting to hide her pregnancy, their vows spoken to a justice of the peace while Vegas lights flashed on and off against the fake chapel windows.

His holding her hand as she gave birth to their son six months later. He'd kissed her and whispered, "We're going to make it. Things will only get better now."

He'd wanted to believe it, if for no other reason than to spite his father, the honorable mayor of New Orleans at that time, who felt J.D., his shining hope for the future, was throwing his life away by marrying the daughter of a used car salesman.

No, he hadn't been in love with Laura any more than she had been in love with him. But neither of them believed in abortion, and both believed that, eventually, they could come to love one another, for the sake of the child, if nothing else.

For a while, the hope had sparkled like new diamonds. William Damascus had been a dream child, healthy, happy, a bundle of pleasure that filled J.D. with enough love that he didn't miss the void of affection he shared with his wife. But, little by little, the glimmer had eroded as he was forced, thanks to his father cutting him off financially, to work a night job in order to pay his way through his last year of law school.

The pressures of school and mounting bills had corrupted their home life. There had been talk of divorce. But again, the thought of his father's "I told you so" had been the impetus to hang in there. He had been certain, once he passed the bar and landed the A.D.A.'s position, that he and Laura could start fresh. William was everything to him. The idea of weekend visiting privileges seemed intolerable.

Yet, despite the immense love he had felt for his son, he found himself burying himself more deeply in his career. *Avoidance,* a marriage counselor had termed it. A failure to communicate. If he would be more attentive to his affection-deprived wife, perhaps she wouldn't need to drown her sorrows in American Express Platinum cards and daily jaunts through the Neiman Marcus catalogues. J.D. had snidely remarked that if she backed off the Am Ex and Neiman Marcus catalogues, perhaps he wouldn't have to put in twenty hours a week of overtime.

It hadn't helped that, thanks to hourly threats from the criminal element, he was forced to start wearing a gun.

In a space of two short years he had become The Man Most Likely to Be Snuffed.

The prediction had almost come to fruition when someone unloaded a shotgun through his bedroom window. In order to keep Laura from collecting Billy and hightailing it to her parents in Milwaukee, he had taken a leave of absence to try to save their marriage. They'd rented a condo in Gulf Shores, Alabama, and tried to revive their nonexistent love for one another—romantic walks on the beach in the moonlight, champagne and candlelight, and sex like horny teenagers. Two weeks later, they had driven away from the love nest with the absolute certainty that they had no future together. Three weeks later, Laura had informed him she was pregnant. So much for condoms.

He couldn't imagine that he could ever love another child as much as he loved Billy. Not possible. But the moment he held Lisa in his arms, he had been gut-punched, brought to his knees by her cherubic face, awash with such heartrending responsibility and protectiveness, he had been willing to sell his soul to the devil to keep the marriage together. He cut back his workload, lived for the moment when he could sprawl on the floor and allow the children to jump on his belly as if he were a trampoline. Never mind that he and Laura existed in an emotional vacuum where they rarely spoke and slept in separate bedrooms. The love he felt for his children was his cup that runneth over.

Lisa with her wispy, blond pigtails bouncing around her shoulders as she chased butterflies in the park.

Billy on the first day of school looking back over his

shoulder, eyes full of tears, as J.D. stood on the sidewalk
with his hands crammed in his pockets and a knot the size
of a goose egg in his throat.

Birthday parties, tooth fairies, Santa Claus.

Then they were gone.

As J.D. lay in the dark in his bed, the nearby buzz fan
doing little to assuage the heat that made his naked body
sweat, he stared at the ceiling that faintly reflected the
distant neon of the Lucky Lady Casino. Occasionally, he
reached for his glass of Pepto-Bismol and milk, a mixture
that he had grown accustomed to over the last few years.
The radio in his room played softly. A classical station
that often soothed him to sleep.

Tonight, however, sleep was elusive. Every time he
closed his eyes, the image of Cherry Brown was right
there in all its gory detail . . . superimposed over those of
his family.

He'd spent three days in Shreveport, business that had
kept him out of town longer than anticipated. He had spoken to Laura Thursday night, late, to let her know that he
would be home Friday afternoon. She had been testier
than usual. They had argued and she had refused to let
him speak to Billy and Lisa—already in bed, she had lied,
though he could hear them playing in the background.

Something in the way she had behaved had caused caution and suspicion to niggle at him long after he'd hung
up the phone. Something wasn't right. Not that it ever
was right between them, but that particular conversation
had set his every instinct on edge. He hadn't become a
kick-ass A.D.A. without being able to sniff out the un-

dercurrents of brewing trouble, and Laura's nervous, evasive attitude had reeked of it.

He'd canceled his meetings for the next day and taken a late flight, arriving in New Orleans after midnight. In the airport, he had bought Lisa a doll and Billy a T-shirt.

He had arrived home to an empty house. Standing there with sweat running down his temples, the fear that she had left him at last, taking his children, rushed like acid through his blood.

At four in the morning, he had fallen into bed, exhausted from pacing the floor all night, repeatedly calling her cell phone and getting no response.

At six-thirty the doorbell had rung. He'd known, the moment he looked into the detectives' faces, why they were there.

He'd held it together in the car, even walking down the long corridor to the morgue. Avoidance, again. There was always a chance that the bodies a jogger had discovered were not those of his family. Laura wasn't a prostitute. No reason that the serial killer who was slaughtering prostitutes would suddenly turn on a housewife and kids. They didn't fit the victim profile.

He'd held it together until the medical examiner, Janice, Mallory's wife, had pulled the sheet back to reveal Billy's face.

After that, it had all been a blur. Like he was fighting his way out of a nightmare that wouldn't end. First Billy, his throat cut from ear to ear, then Lisa, her blond pigtails soaked in blood. Then Laura. He'd identified her by the birthmark on her right hip, and, of course, the wedding ring on her finger.

Like the prostitutes who had been killed, they never found Laura's head.

He couldn't recall much of the following months. They were spent in a fog of tranquilizers and antidepressants. Downers to make him sleep without dreaming, uppers that allowed him to stumble through the day. He'd finally unraveled before a judge and jury and half the New Orleans press corp. It hadn't been pretty. Jerry Costos had tackled him to the floor, and he'd been wheeled out of the courtroom strapped to a stretcher by men in white coats. So much for promising careers.

He'd withdrawn from life—family, friends—holed up in his empty house full of memories, surrounded by photographs of his children. Six months after his breakdown, he'd been forced to move out of the house and file for bankruptcy. Only one thing had kept him from putting a bullet in his head. Anger and the need for revenge. It raged in him.

He had become a short fuse on a keg of dynamite, one fizzle and spark away from complete detonation. He was certain that Tyron Johnson had been his family's killer and was convinced that their murders had not been connected with those of the hookers. The son of a bitch had actually sent flowers to the funerals, attached with a card: *Have a happy life, asshole.*

Angel Gonzalez had a sheet of priors as long as his arm, including child molestation and arrests for solicitation and assault on prostitutes. Swabs taken from the vagina of the last murdered hooker had matched Gonzalez's DNA. But when he heard Jerry Costos's shitty, circumstantial evidence, J.D. had known in his gut that Angel was innocent, a man at the wrong place at the wrong time—just as his family had been, according to the investigators who wanted like hell to close the books on his wife's and kids' murders. It was one thing for prostitutes to be slaughtered. It was another for a mother and her kids to be murdered. Their deaths had sent panic through the city like a wildfire.

There was no doubt in his mind now that Angel Gonzalez had not been the monster who had murdered his family—or the prostitutes who had undergone the most brutal slayings in Louisiana history.

The state had not prosecuted Gonzalez for all the crimes, only one of them, but that had been enough to get him the death penalty from a jury who had been shaken to tears during a trial the entire country had watched with morbid fascination. After all, as Governor Damascus had proclaimed, "You can kill a man only once. No point in bleeding the state's budget any more than necessary."

Never mind that three of the victims had been the governor's daughter-in-law and two of his grandchildren.

With Gonzalez's conviction, the case had been closed on his wife and kids, all tied up in a neat little package with a few grumbled words of sympathy from Jerry Costos. Never mind that Laura's, Billy's, and Lisa's deaths did not fit into the victim profile. His wife was not a prostitute and the children had not been decapitated—the killer had been kind enough to only slit their throats.

Honey, who had discovered Cherry Brown's body, couldn't have been more correct. If the public got wind that the state could have—had, in fact—executed the wrong man, there would be hell to pay. The repercussions would be felt all the way to the White House. The advocates against the death penalty, NCADP in particular, would burn the state's politicians on every cable network news station in the country.

Rolling over, he hit the replay button on the telephone answering machine beside his bed. The message had come in at eleven-thirty.

"John . . . it's Beverly. I need to talk to you. Desperately. It's Patrick again." Pause. She cleared her throat. "I found him with . . ." Pause. "I don't want to talk about it on the phone. I need to see you as soon as possible. Call me. Please."

As the machine kicked off, he left the bed, wandered to the kitchen nook, opened the fridge and extracted a Coors Light, then returned to the bed where he slid his hand between the mattress and box springs and withdrew his gun, a Beretta Model 92 9mm automatic boasting a fifteen-round magazine and weighing less than three pounds fully loaded. As he balanced it in his hand, he glanced down at the phone. The clock beside it glowed two forty-five in bright red numbers.

He walked to the open sliding glass doors, stepped out on the rickety balcony that overlooked the river and the Lucky Lady Casino. Lights from Tyron Johnson's penthouse winked in the dark.

He imagined Beverly pacing the floor, waiting for him to call. Beverly, with her soulful green eyes and floral fragrance. Beverly who, over the last years, had become a balm to his decomposing soul. She was in love with him, though it had never been spoken aloud. It was evident in the trembling touch of her hand, her quivering smile, in her gaze that pierced to the very heart of him. He suspected that her problems with Patrick were only an excuse to reach out to him, though she probably didn't realize it herself.

There had been moments, over the last four years, when he had come close to saying to hell with it and taking her to bed. They had been friendly in college. She'd hinted more than once that she was interested in more than friendship. But he had had only one consuming passion in his life at that time. Law. There simply wasn't room in his life for both. So they had drifted apart, lost touch the summer between his graduation and starting law school. Months later, he had received an invitation to her and Eric's wedding.

Still, there were times when the loneliness, the emptiness of his life threatened to erode his self-restraint. When the pain boiled up inside him, ripping at his heart, gnawing at his belly. When he felt as if he were tumbling back into the madness of grief. When the faces of his children paraded through his mind's eye and the memory of their laughter sent a dagger through his raw, bleeding soul.

The phone rang. He didn't answer. If it was Beverly again, he might suggest that she come over . . . to talk. About Patrick. But he was feeling too damn needy at the moment. And she was too damn vulnerable.

The machine kicked on. It wasn't Beverly.

"Damascus? J.D. Damascus?" A woman's voice, a little sultry. Definitely nervous. "My name is Holly." Pause. "Holly Jones." A sound, as if she had dropped the phone. There was loud talk in the background. "Okay, ah . . . I found your number on the bathroom wall. I think I need a lawyer. I've been arrested. . . . I think I might have killed someone."

The phone went dead and the machine cut off.

J.D. remained on the balcony, the rank, muddy smell of the river as cloying as the hot, August night. Raising the gun, he pointed it toward Tyron's window and looked down the site. "Bang," he said through his teeth. "You're dead."

After a night spent in hell cell ten listening to two dozen prisoners howl about their civil rights, Holly wasn't in the best frame of mind by the time Damascus showed up at ten A.M. looking like death warmed over. He wasn't at all what she expected or remembered from her days of living in New Orleans, and she wondered, briefly, as she stared at him through the cell bars, if the name and number she had found on the ladies' bathroom wall had been another J.D. Damascus. The unshaven middle-aged man, wearing jeans and a threadbare sports coat over a T-shirt, shaggy, dark brown hair to his shoulders—not to mention a small, gold loop in his right ear—could hardly be compared to the Versace-suited shark who had once made the area's criminal element shake in their shoes.

"Holly Jones?" he asked in a slightly husky voice as he stared at her with bloodshot eyes. He was *that* J.D. Damascus, all right. While his appearance might have gone to hell, there was no mistaking that voice and the steely eyes that had the uncanny ability to crawl into a person's psyche.

Not good, she thought. Definitely not good. But she was in no position to be picky. Not by a long shot.

As the cop beside him opened the cell door, Holly stood up and willed the strength back into her legs. She nodded.

Damascus waited until the cop had departed, then entered the cell, his gaze looking her up and down, eyes narrowing as if assessing her guilt or innocence.

She swallowed and ran her sweating palms up and down the butt of her jeans. "Look, I shot him, okay?" she blurted. "But it was in self-defense. The creep was dressed like Darth Vader and came at me with a knife."

He nodded and dug into his pocket, withdrew a couple of white tabs, and popped them into his mouth. "You're a hooker," he said as he chewed and continued to study her.

Her face began to burn. "No."

One dark eyebrow lifted and his mouth curved. "I guess you just happened to be in the wrong place at the wrong time, huh? Just cruising that warehouse because you had nothing better to do at two in the morning."

"I was . . . looking for someone."

Again with the grin that made her face burn hotter. "Obviously."

"That's not what I meant." She cleared her throat in an attempt to keep her voice steady. Any other time and she would be tempted to slap the condescending smirk from his face, but she was in no position to allow her temperament to get the best of her. J.D. Damascus was the only defense between her and a possible murder conviction. "I was looking for a friend who was supposed to meet this . . . creep. She's the hooker. Not me."

"Right."

"Hey, I thought an attorney was supposed to believe in his client's innocence."

"Did you or did you not shoot a man?"

"He had a knife."

"Did he attack you?"

"He had a knife."

"Did he attack you?"

"When a man who is dressed in a black hood and cape pulls a knife from said cape, one has reason to suspect that he intends to use it. I had every right to defend myself."

"So who's the friend?"

"Melissa Carmichael."

He nodded and glanced around the cell. "I know Melissa. She's a client of mine. Specializes in kinky." He shifted his weight to one hip and crossed his arms over his chest. "So what were you doing there?"

"Looking for Melissa. She was . . . frightened. The girls always look out for one another, so I was concerned, okay?"

His mouth curved. "So you *are* a hooker."

She looked away. "No."

"So what's a young lady such as yourself doing walking around with a .38 in her possession?"

"Why does anyone own a gun?"

"To shoot someone?"

"For protection."

"So where is Melissa?"

"I don't know. She didn't show."

"How did you know where she was to meet this particular john?"

"She left a message on my cell phone. If you don't believe me, listen to it."

His gray eyes narrowed again. It was that look that could unnerve the most cold-blooded killer to the root of his black heart—as could the silence that filled up the space between them. The eyes, the condescending smirk on his mouth, at another time in her life might have made her confess to a crime she didn't commit. It was a look that could convince a soul they were guilty whether they were or not.

She swallowed and tried to keep the tremor from her voice. "Look, I shot him. I don't deny it. But I'm telling you—"

"Self-defense." Again with the smirk, a tip of the head, the gaze that slid over her from head to foot, then back to her eyes, his own narrowing even more. She could almost hear his brain shifting through the files in his memory. Damascus's cutthroat courtroom techniques weren't the only reason defense attorneys had too often floundered in their representations. The former assistant district attorney had a photographic memory that could make a computer blow its circuits.

"Do I know you?" he asked.

There it was.

"We've never met."

"You look familiar."

"Our paths might have crossed." She cleared her throat. "But we never met."

He slowly nodded, his inspection of her still intense. "I know you."

"Hey, what difference does it make? I need a lawyer, okay? I killed a man—"

"No, you didn't."

She blinked. "No?"

"No." He shook his head. "He'll be sore as hell for a few days, but he'll survive to grate on my nerves yet another day." He stepped to one side, away from the cell door. "You're free to go, Miss . . . *Jones*."

She blinked again, disbelief and relief rushing through her in a hot wave. "Free?"

He nodded, still smirking.

"I don't understand."

"No charges are being pressed against you."

"Just like that."

"Just like that."

"But—"

"Don't look a gift horse in the mouth, Miss Jones. Just go and don't look back."

Her gaze still locked on his lean face, she slowly moved by him. He was still assessing her, she could tell.

"You can retrieve your personal belongings, including your weapon. That is if it's registered and you have a permit."

"It's registered and I have a permit."

He reached into his pocket and withdrew another couple of tablets, popped them into his mouth, and followed her out of the cell, eyes still narrowed, gaze moving slowly up and down her body. As she opened her mouth to again question this somewhat miraculous turn of events, he cut her off.

"Good-bye, Miss Jones."

*   *   *

He had a major bone to pick with the chief of
police regarding the murders of two prostitutes, but obviously that was going to have to wait considering Travis
Killroy's shoulder had been laid open with Holly Jones's
.38. The chief's recent forays into kinky with the local
hookers was a hush-hush point of controversy on the
force, but like many other covered-up scandals, it wasn't
high on the list of the department's priorities at the moment. The last thing they wanted was for such information
to become public knowledge, so obviously they would
want Holly Jones cut loose as soon as possible. J.D. would
sure as hell like to be a fly on the wall as the chief tried
to explain to his wife how he was injured. In the line of
duty just wasn't going to cut it. Had the chief of police
been injured in a shoot-out with a suspect, it would be
blasted over the local papers and he would be up for a
medal. Alas, there were no medals for wounded in the
line of blow jobs.

As J.D. hit the elevator button for the morgue floor in
the basement, he continued to run Holly Jones through
the files in his brain. The woman was a looker, no doubt
about it. And she was lying through her teeth. He had
always had the uncanny ability to sniff out deceit as
adeptly as a bloodhound on a scent. She hadn't squirmed,
exactly, when she'd denied she was a hooker, but damned
close. And while the department had found no priors on
her, not so much as a traffic ticket, she was clearly hiding
something.

And he had definitely seen her before. A man simply

didn't forget her kind—not that sort of exotic beauty. Had his mind not been so fogged from lack of sleep and cluttered with the recent murders and the implications thereof, he might have given more thought to her. Might have even asked her out for a drink, just so he could assuage the niggling in his head that he had, at some time, done more than simply crossed paths with her.

But she looked too damn good in her jeans, and a simple cocktail might have led to dinner, and he had always avoided getting involved with his clients. He had enough personal problems of his own without getting emotionally tangled up with people whose lives were in a mire. His gut instinct told him that Holly Jones—babe or not—could be trouble in more ways than one.

Besides, his stomach was hurting like hell.

"Hey, Damascus!"

He looked around as the elevator door opened. Holly Jones ran down the corridor toward him.

"Wait up," she shouted, her pretty face set in grim determination. He didn't like the looks of it and suspected what was coming.

He stepped into the elevator and punched the Close Door button.

Too late. She leapt into the elevator just as the door was sliding closed.

She glared at him, breathing hard. "You'll never believe what they told me."

He punched the basement button. "Try me."

"They aren't going to pursue charges on that creep. I mean, he had a knife—"

"He didn't attack you, Miss Jones."

"This is unbelievable. There should be an investigation at least—"

"If the department investigated every freak out there, there would be no time to investigate the significant crimes—"

"Murdering hookers is not significant? Is that what you're saying, Damascus?" Her blue eyes flashed.

The elevator stopped and the door opened. She followed him into the hall, her stride lengthening as he walked faster.

"So who's to say that he wouldn't have attempted to kill me?"

"You don't arrest people on supposition, Miss Jones." He stopped so suddenly she nearly plowed into him. Her face red, she stood toe to toe with him, visibly shaking with anger, her body language confrontational. Withdrawing a paper from his jeans pocket, he handed it to her. "I almost forgot."

She forced her gaze away from his and looked at it. "What's this?"

"My bill."

Her mouth dropped open. "Three hundred dollars? Oh my God. You're joking, right?"

"One hundred an hour. You can drop by my office Monday morning and pay it. I don't take checks, FYI."

He turned and entered the morgue through wide, double doors, leaving Holly staring at the statement in her hand. The reception desk was empty, so he continued down the long, pale green corridor, the intense cold biting through his coat and T-shirt and the odor of formaldehyde making him a little queasy.

Once he had traipsed these corridors with regularity, shadowing the medical examiner during murder victims' autopsies looking for evidence that could nail a suspect and make his case. He had eventually become desensitized to the sight of corpses, though he was continually shocked over what human beings inflicted on one another.

As he entered the exam room, the medical examiner glanced away from the cadaver she was working on, grunted, and mumbled behind her nose and mouth shield, "Figured as much. Enoch mentioned you'd probably be snooping around. Cherry Brown, right?"

He nodded and held his breath, the stink of gastric acids making his eyes water. Obviously, Janice Mallory was on the back end of the autopsy. The room was swimming in blood. It dripped from the hanging meat scales used to weigh the organs and was smeared on the chalkboard where she had written organ weights. The deceased's organs were scattered over tables and the brain had been hung by a string in a large jar of formalin.

"Grab yourself a coffee and make yourself at home. I won't be a minute."

He poured himself a black coffee and joined her at the table. The cadaver looked to be a teenaged girl.

"Another damn drug overdose." Janice shook her head. "I'm telling you, if the schools would haul the kids' delinquent asses into this room so they could see what waits for them on the other side of slamming, we might see less of these."

She tossed the pick ups into a tray of disinfectant and barked an order at the diener.

"You shouldn't be here, Damascus," Janice pointed out.

"You know I'm not supposed to talk to you about Cherry Brown."

"But you will because you adore me." He sipped the hot coffee.

She glanced at the diener and nodded at the body. "Close her up and make it neat. The parents have enough grief to deal with without their baby coming back to them looking like Frankenstein's monster."

Turning her back on the assistant, she looked at J.D. and rolled her eyes, lowered her voice. "Guy's a rookie, and a shit one. Someone at the university was asleep at the wheel when they turned him loose." She pulled the double layer of rubber gloves from her hands and raised one gray eyebrow. "How's the ulcers?"

"Don't change the subject, Janice."

"Mallory says you were vomiting up blood."

"It comes and goes."

"Get it taken care of. I'd hate to have to cut your cute ass open when a trip to your doctor could easily prevent it."

He followed her to a table where she proceeded to label the specimen cassettes. "I understand Cherry Brown wasn't the first."

"Yeah? Who told you that?"

"A source. And she's reliable, so don't give me any of your famous Mallory double-talk."

She scribbled on a cassette, then picked up another. "A woman was brought in last week. Tyra Smith, or so she called herself. Body's still in the cooler if you want a peek."

"Same mutilation?"

"Identical. Evisceration and decapitation. Both women were dead before the mutilations. Thank God for small favors, huh?"

"Cause of the actual death?"

She shrugged. "Possible head injuries. Could have been strangled or had her throat cut. But since the decapitation included the neck to the shoulders, it's impossible to say for certain. Considering the amount of blood loss before death, I'd be willing to wager my reputation that her throat was cut."

"Evidence of sexual activity?"

"Nope. Not before or after death. I don't think it's sexual appreciation that's giving this guy his jollies."

"Did the CSI team pick up any evidence?"

She grinned and continued labeling. "That's not my job description, J.D."

"Your husband must have said something."

"Don't ask me to go there. My husband would chew my butt good if he knew I'd told you as much as I have." Janice tugged the shield from her face and tossed it onto the table. "Let the department do its job, okay? Stay out of it. It's none of your business."

"It damn well is my business, and you know it."

She finally turned her gaze up to his. Her eyes showed sympathy, the deep lines in her brow concern. "We're dealing with a prostitute, J.D. God knows how many men have been in these women's apartments."

"What about the bodies?"

"Clean as a whistle. No latent prints, hair, or seminal fluids." She rested one broad hip against the desk and pinned him with her eyes. "Look, I can appreciate how you're feeling—"

"I'm getting pretty tired of hearing how everyone appreciates how I feel. My wife and kids are dead, Janice, and a man was executed for murders he didn't commit."

"We don't know that. Yet."

"The M.O. is identical."

"It was a well-publicized crime. Gonzalez wasn't the first nut to cut off women's heads. It happens. Two months ago, some freak decapitated a woman and hung her head from a flagpole on Jackson Square. Why? Because she cut him off at a traffic light. The world, unfortunately, is full of weirdos."

He reached past her and retrieved Cherry's exam report from the desk, scanned it briefly before focusing again on Janice's face. "Hacksaw. Evisceration wounds by probable surgical type blade."

"All public record, you know that." She sighed. "J.D., those murders were well documented. Three books were written on the crimes that I know of. Hell, have you had a look on the Internet? It's there in all its gory detail, including photos."

He looked away. "I've seen them."

She put a comforting hand on his arm. "Why do you insist on doing this to yourself? It's eating you up. You've let it destroy your career and your health. It's been four years. At some point you've got to move on."

"If I thought the right man had been executed, maybe I could."

A door opened and a woman peered in, her eyes brightening as she noted J.D. "Hey, gorgeous. Long time no see. We've missed your harassment around here."

He grinned. "Hi, Connie. How's the family?"

"Great. My daughter is still single, by the way. Hint, hint."

He laughed.

Janice elbowed him. "She's pretty, too. Just what you need right now. Or are you still dating that gal from records?"

Shrugging, he tossed the report back onto the desk. "Off and on. Nothing serious."

"Great," Connie said. "Maybe there's hope yet. Doc, you have a phone call. Sounds important."

Janice smiled. "Sorry. Duty calls. Maybe we'll do lunch soon?"

J.D. nodded.

He followed Janice out of the exam room and watched as she strode down the corridor, her bloodied scrub suit flapping around her legs. As she disappeared around a corner, he moved down the hallway, passing several empty exam rooms, and paused at the closed door of the file room. He entered and moved swiftly to the wall of files, to the "D" storage. When he located the folder labeled DAMASCUS, LAURA, he withdrew the file and made his way cautiously through the reception area and back out through the wide, double doors, coming face-to-face with Holly Jones.

Stopping short, he glared down into her irate blue eyes. "Why the hell are you still here?"

"I can't pay this." She waved the statement under his nose. "I'm not made out of money, you know."

"If you couldn't afford a lawyer, you shouldn't have called one."

"I suspected any lawyer who advertises on the wall of the women's bathroom wouldn't charge his clients out the yin yang. You're not exactly Johnny Cochran, you know."

"If I was Cochran, you'd be paying six hundred bucks an hour." He stepped around her. "Call my office Monday. Set up a payment plan."

Exiting the building into the heat, J.D. paused, checked his watch. He was to meet Beverly at twelve sharp for lunch. He would just make it if he hurried.

"You could at least give me a lift to my car," Holly said as she moved up behind him. "Or will you charge me for that as well?"

Christ, the woman had attitude, and if there was anything he wasn't in the mood for at the moment, it was attitude. He glanced over his shoulder, prepared to tell her to get lost. In the harsh light of the August sun, she looked pale, her face pinched by stress and concern. Pretty. Too damn pretty. Keep walking and don't look back. Holly Jones had trouble stamped all over her.

5

The traffic along Royal Street was typically heavy as J.D. maneuvered his Mustang through the tourists and cars parked bumper-to-bumper along the curbs. He could almost read their minds as the sightseers looked at French Quarter maps, mopped the sweat from their brows, and stared up at the sun as if it had no right to beat down on their miserable shoulders. Yeah, the heat and humidity were a bitch, but what did they expect from New Orleans during the heat of summer? If they wanted cool, they should have gone to Alaska.

He checked his watch—quarter of twelve—and glanced at Holly, who had remained quiet the last ten minutes, eyeing the statement in her hand. J.D. suspected he'd never see a red cent from Holly Jones. Nothing new. Half of his clients never paid him. Filing suits against them did little good, even caused him to be in the hole. His grandmother often said, "You can't get blood out of a turnip."

Holly Jones could hardly be labeled a turnip, but he knew the look of financial woes.

For the third time in the last ten minutes, Holly called Melissa's number and didn't get an answer. Returning her cell phone to her purse, she slumped into the Mustang's leather seat, then stared out the passenger window. Her slender fingers drummed the console with impatience.

"So, if you aren't a hooker," he said, breaking the stilted silence between them, "how do you know Melissa?"

"What difference does it make?" She shook her head and searched the faces of the pedestrians lining the sidewalks. There was an intensity in her perusal, as if she expected to recognize someone. There was also avoidance. Each time a face swung her way, she turned. "Something's wrong. I know it. She didn't show for her john this morning. She's not answering her phone or returning my messages."

"Maybe business is good."

She turned to face him. "What do you mean?"

"She's occupied."

"Why do I get this feeling you've got a hump on for hookers? What happened to you? Get fed up terrorizing the criminal element in New Orleans? Thought you'd play the good guy for a change?"

"The district attorney is the good guy, Miss Jones. Most of the time. My prosecution arguments weren't personal. I did my job."

"Something happened. You look like hell. Though not in a bad way." Her gaze moved from his profile down his body. Her mouth slightly curved. "I like the look, in fact.

Smile and you might even make it to human."

She continued to study him with eyes as sharp and savvy as his own. Too sharp for such a pretty face. Too full of life's hard knocks. "Careful," he said. "I charge extra for insults."

"You're very bitter, aren't you? Let's see." She tipped her head and narrowed her eyes. "Maybe you didn't actually walk away from the D.A.'s office. Maybe you were fired. You rolled over on a case you shouldn't have. Maybe took a bribe. It happens. Frequently. Instead of disbarment, they gave you the option of resignation. You were married, right? Of course. You and your wife were showing up in the society section of the paper all the time.

"This fall from grace ultimately ruined your marriage. You're not wearing a wedding band. And your wife would never allow her husband out the door wearing clothes that look like they've been left in a dryer too long. She left you in search of greener pockets when you lost the job. And she took the kids. You're rarely allowed to see them. Breaks your heart, especially when you're forced to pay out the wazoo in child support."

J.D. pulled his car to the curb and slammed on the brakes, throwing Holly half out of the passenger seat. "My life is none of your damn business," he said. "I don't have the time and I am not inclined to listen to your smart-ass conjectures. Get out."

Holly stared at him. Her lips parted and her blue eyes wide.

"Get out," he said. "Walk your pretty butt out of here."

She glanced down the line of warehouses toward the river beyond them. The street was narrow and shadowed.

Derelicts were sprawled against the buildings, drinking from bottles in dirty paper bags. "Fine. Sure. Whatever you say, Damascus." She swallowed. "Who needs you anyway."

Grabbing up her purse, she exited the car, slamming the door as hard as she could. She didn't look back, just started walking, her tumble of black hair swirling around her back, her long legs eating up the pavement.

The car idling, J.D. watched her make a wide arc around a leering bum, zigzag her way through street garbage from an overflowing Dumpster, then round a corner, disappearing.

The woman had brass, no doubt about it. Too damn much of it for her own good. He suspected spite and stubbornness made up a big part of her psyche. Holly no doubt was convinced it was pride, but her pride could too easily get her throat cut if she wasn't careful.

Christ, he didn't need this. He checked his watch, again. Twelve sharp. Beverly would be waiting, having ordered herself an iced tea and him a cola.

"Dammit," he said through his teeth, then let his foot off the brake.

J.D. eased his Mustang down the street, took a right at the corner, and slowly moved the car behind Holly's beautiful body.

Holly walked with hands fisted in either stress or anger. Probably both. If he was smart, he'd let her go. She wasn't his responsibility. The last thing he needed right now was more responsibility. Especially one with an attitude who looked like Miss October in *Penthouse* magazine.

Pulling up beside her, he let the window down and yelled, "Get in."

"Take a hike." She didn't so much as glance at him.

"I don't have time for this, Miss Jones. Get in."

A gang of tattooed skinheads stepped out from an alley in front of her. Their faces broke out in lascivious smiles. Her confident step hesitated. She clutched her purse, glanced around at the Mustang.

He lifted one eyebrow at her and smirked.

Wisely, she reentered his car and slammed and locked the door, ignoring the crude shouts and whistles from the delinquents who clutched their crotches and made lewd comments. "Freaks," she said.

J.D. turned a corner onto Esplanade Avenue, then reached for his cell phone and called Beverly.

She answered before the phone rang twice. "Where are you?" she said. "I've been waiting for fifteen minutes."

No point in reminding her their meeting wasn't until noon. Beverly was obsessively early to any engagement, especially with him. He glanced at Holly who continued to ignore him. "Sorry, sweetheart. A problem dropped into my life and I'm running late. Order me my usual. Be there in twenty minutes at the latest."

"This is important, John. I've got to talk to you about Patrick."

"I'll be there."

"I found him with a pornographic magazine last night."

"Twenty minutes. I swear it."

"What would I do without you?"

"Don't worry, honey. It'll be okay. Twenty minutes."

As he disconnected, Holly looked around, again with the slow curving of her lips. "Girlfriend?"

He didn't respond, just tossed the phone onto the backseat, on top of the file labeled DAMASCUS, LAURA.

The car was gone. J.D. wasn't surprised. Leaving a car parked in the river warehouse district was asking for trouble. As he leaned back against the Mustang, arms crossed over his chest, the heat of the sun-baked street seeping up through his Nikes, he watched Holly pace, growing more frantic by the second, and though she was trying hard not to cry, her voice quavered dangerously.

"Oh my God. What am I going to do? All my clothes, my makeup, my money—"

"What the hell were you doing leaving your money in the car?"

"In my suitcase. You don't think I was going to walk around this place at two in the morning with my purse stuffed full of money, do you?"

He looked up and down the street—mostly vacant since it was Sunday. Even the too-often-stupid tourists knew better than to leave a vehicle in the area. "You're sure this is where you parked it?"

She glared at him, her face flushed by heat and anxiety.

He shrugged. "So I drop you off at the station and you file a report."

"You don't understand." She sank against the car beside him and stared at the curb as if she could will her car to suddenly materialize. "I have exactly ten dollars on my person. Every last dime I owned, which wasn't much—five hundred dollars—was in my suitcase."

"Family in the area?"

She shook her head.

"Friends?"

She hesitated, and her dark brows drew together as if she were considering possible alternatives. "Just Melissa," she finally said, though not fully convincing J.D. as he watched her avoid, once again, looking into his eyes.

"Anyone back in Branson you can call?"

Looking away, she shook her head. "Not really."

"Not even a boyfriend."

"No one."

"You gay or what?" He grinned.

"Excuse me?"

"You don't look like the kind of woman who wouldn't have some guy on the hook."

"God, my car has been stolen and you're being sexist."

She dug into her purse and extracted a crumpled box of cigarettes. She tried to light one with a disposable lighter, but her hand was shaking too badly. J.D. took the lighter and lit it for her, watched her soft red lips form to the filter.

"Thanks." She blew out a stream of smoke and sighed. "I'm keeping you from your girlfriend, I take it."

He glanced at his watch. Late again. By now, Beverly's angst would have risen another notch. Sure, he could make a sweep by the department and drop Holly off, drive away, and not look back. But he was a sucker for women in distress, and he knew she would find little sympathy among the overworked vice cops. Besides, what was she supposed to do now with no money? Knowing the slop she was probably fed for breakfast, she would be looking at the very real possibility of wandering the streets unable to eat if Melissa didn't show. Besides, whether he wanted to admit it to himself or not, he wasn't ready to walk away from Holly Jones. She intrigued him, made him second-guess his first impression that she was a hooker. Too clean. Too refined. Too damn vulnerable.

Besides, he couldn't shake that niggling feeling that he had seen her before.

"Hungry?"

"Famished."

No doubt he was going to regret this, but what choice did he have? "Get in."

"I wouldn't think of it. Wouldn't want to cramp your style or anything."

"Fine. Stay here and starve."

As he walked around the Mustang, Holly's blue gaze followed him. As he turned the ignition, she opened the door and dropped into the seat, crossed her legs, and refused to look at him. Pride again. If they had all day he might expound on the detriments too much pride could have on a person's life.

J.D. was a prime example. If he hadn't given two hoots about proving his father was right about his marrying Laura, she wouldn't be dead now . . . and neither would his children.

On the way to the restaurant, J.D. made a call to vice and reported the theft of Holly's car, description and plates. Detective Chris Wallace told him they would look into it but promised nothing. New Orleans was a haven for auto thefts thanks to tourists who too often left their cars unlocked. J.D. didn't relay this bit of information to Holly at the moment. She was on the verge of hysteria.

Desire Oyster Bar was packed with the lunch crowd, many of whom were already immersed in the French Quarter mentality of boozing themselves into oblivion by two in the afternoon. College punks and tourists who would sleep off their drunkenness through the afternoon and start again when the sun went down and the jazz bands moved onto the streets to contribute to the celebratory atmosphere. As J.D. and Holly stood at the crowded entrance, he spotted Beverly in a booth near the back. Her smile froze as she noted Holly.

"Oops," Holly offered, flashing him a knowing look. "Looks like your friend isn't pleased to see me. Maybe I'll just take a seat at the bar."

"Right."

As Holly headed for the bar, J.D. wove his way through the tables, noting Beverly's attention was focused on Holly. She might have the patience of Job, but there was no denying her twinge of jealousy over women he occasionally dated.

"Sorry I'm late." He slid into the booth.

Beverly forced her gaze across the table. "Who is she, John?"

"A client."

She smiled tightly and reached for her tea. "Very pretty."

"Really? I hadn't noticed." He reached for his cola.

"Every head in the place turned to watch her cross the room. Unless you've been stricken blind, you noticed."

"Not my type." He grinned. He wasn't in the mood to

have his patience rubbed any rawer than it had already been.

"I know you better, John. You needn't lie to me."

"What do you want me to say, sweetheart? That her fabulous ass turns me on and I fantasize about fucking her? Is that what you want to hear?"

"Do you?"

Sitting back in the seat, he stared at her as his stomach began to burn.

Her face blushing, Beverly lowered her gaze.

J.D. reached across the table and took her hand in his. "Sorry. It's been a tough twenty-four hours. I'm on edge. I didn't mean to take it out on you."

"What you do with your life is no business of mine." She swallowed. "I just don't want to see you hurt again. Call me protective."

He squeezed her hand, her fingertips cold as chips of ice against his own. "Okay, Protective, what's up with Patrick?"

As she poured out the latest news about her son, J.D. picked at his gumbo and did his best to focus on her voice amidst the din of conversing diners. His attention continued to drift to Holly, who sat at the bar, her long legs crossed, her dark hair lying in loose spirals down her back.

Beverly had been right. It seemed every man in the place watched her. Why not? She was every man's wet dream. Pouty lips, sleepy bedroom eyes, hinting of unbridled sexcapades. Though she wore nothing more figure enhancing than a tight pair of faded jeans and white midriff cotton blouse, she had the kind of body to stop traffic.

Some niggling memory continued to bother him, and as he watched her chat with some beer-gutted man in a cheap suit, flashes of faces and names zipped through his mind, but none of them fit.

"John, are you listening to me?"

"You found him with a porno mag." He shrugged. "He's sixteen."

"Hormones. Curiosity. Experimentation. I know. John, he suggested I divorce his father."

The man in the cheap suit sidled closer to Holly. He was sweating now, his mouth stretched in a jackass grin. J.D. felt like driving his fist into the guy's teeth.

"He wants to live with you, John. That's how miserable he is at home. He said as much to Eric this morning. They got into a fight. I mean a real fight. Patrick actually took a swing at him." Her voice grew tight. "Eric threatened to send him to military school. I'm at a loss as to how to deal with this."

"I can recommend some decent counselors."

"Eric would never stand for it. God forbid anyone get wind his family life is anything but perfect. All he can think about is his damned political career."

The creep reached out and touched Holly's hair.

"I think Eric is going to run for the Senate."

J.D. frowned. "You knew it was going to happen as soon as Strong announced his bid for the presidency. Eric would be the logical candidate to take his seat."

"Like I'm going to divorce Eric now."

"It would sure as hell shoot the wheels off his image."

Holly gently shoved the man's hand away.

"John, maybe it would be good for Patrick to come stay with you awhile."

He blinked. "You're joking, right?"

"Maybe if he had some time away from whatever pressures he's going through right now."

"Beverly, I can hardly take care of myself, much less a sixteen-year-old."

"Just for a couple of weeks."

Holly slid off the stool, her fixed smile more furious than friendly.

"Are you listening to me? For God's sake, John."

The man made a grab for her.

J.D. slid from the booth, plowing into a waitress and sending her tray full of drinks flying. He crossed the floor in five strides, twisted his fist into the back of the man's suit, and wrenched him off his feet, slinging him aside so he landed ass-first into a horrified woman's bowl of scalding jambalaya.

As the place erupted into a cacophony of screams and scrambling bodies, J.D. clenched one hand onto the stunned man's shirt collar and drew back his fist.

"Enough," Holly said as calmly as possible. Cautiously, she moved closer, putting her hand lightly on his arm. "No problem here, Damascus. The guy's drunk and stupid. Let him go."

J.D. looked into her eyes.

"Such chivalrous machismo turns me on, Damascus. But unless you want me to rip off my clothes right here, you'll back off. Besides, I don't have the money to bail your cute butt out of jail." He looked at her mouth, curving now in a genuine smile.

J.D. took a deep breath and released the drunk who scrambled toward the door. His rush of adrenaline subsided so swiftly he felt as if every muscle in him had turned to rubber.

"Who the hell is going to pay for this mess?" the manager shouted.

Only then did J.D. remember Beverly. He looked toward the booth. She was gone.

The apartment where Damascus lived wasn't impressive by any means. A scattering of empty cola and beer cans dotted the furnishings, and half-folded newspapers were strewn at the base of the futon.

Holly suspected, sparse as it was, this apartment hadn't known a woman's touch in a long time. But it was a place to crash until Damascus returned from his appointments, and until she could figure a way out of this mess.

Her car, her clothes, all the money she had saved— everything was gone. She'd spent many years of her life in New Orleans and knew the chances of finding her belongings were slim to none. The chop shops would find little to interest them in the car, but she knew that whatever gang member had hot-wired the Taurus wasn't interested in the tires or pitiful radio. Money and jewelry was what would interest them—anything they could hock to buy drugs.

She might have made a few phone calls in the years past. Put out the word they had hit the wrong cache and her car would materialize where it had disappeared. Everything would be returned, including a few hundred dollars extra to repay her for her inconvenience. Back then, she could have used the same scenario with Melissa. One phone call would tell her everything she wanted to know about her missing friend. She might have found out who the john was with the slasher fantasy, if it was a fantasy.

Now she had the time to consider the situation and suspected whoever had come jumping out of the door draped in black and wielding a knife was someone the police department would want to keep anonymous, which would explain why they dismissed her case.

When Melissa had called Branson, she was terrified. The murders had started again. There was mammoth fear among all the New Orleans prostitutes. Angel Gonzalez had not been the serial killer who butchered his way through the girls over a period of months.

Knowing Holly would be arriving, why did Melissa disappear? It didn't make sense. They had been like sisters . . . closer than most sisters, Holly thought. They had known one another since they were thirteen and placed with the same foster family.

Family. What a lie. Ruth and Conrad Jacobson abused both Holly and Melissa. Conrad enjoyed sex with little girls, and Ruth got off on physical abuse. The two girls made a pact to stick with one another no matter what nightmare besieged them.

Just one phone call and her questions and mounting worry over Melissa would be assuaged, but she couldn't take the risk. If word leaked on the streets that Holly was back in town, she'd be dead before sunrise.

Feeling the muscles in the back of her neck tense, Holly

opened the fridge. It was devoid of staples, stocked only with bottles of beer, a chunk of moldy cheese on a plastic plate, half-eaten cold pizza in a box, and a bag of chicory coffee with the logo of the Cafe du Monde.

Holly reached for a beer, unscrewed the top, and turned back to the living area. She didn't care for beer, but she needed something to relax her nerves. Otherwise, Damascus would return to find her hanging from the ceiling by her fingernails.

What had happened to Damascus in these last years? Before her exit from New Orleans, the prominent A.D.A. had lived in a renovated, plantation-style home in the Garden District. He'd looked and dressed like a model for *Gentleman's Quarterly*. The papers had lauded him and Jerry Costos as future political candidates who would clean up crime and corruption and bring respect to the state.

Something had happened to turn Damascus inside out. Divorce? Maybe. This was certainly no home sweet home. But she doubted that even the ugliest of divorces could bring this sort of destruction to a man's career. Still . . .

Pictures of children were scattered around the living room, on walls behind his unmade bed, in stand-up frames on the thrift-store coffee table, and plastered to the fridge by Mardi Gras magnets. Freeze-frame images of a boy and girl, smiling, beaming, some including J.D. in his better days. None, she noted, including his wife.

The phone rang. The message machine picked up.

"John? It's Beverly." Pause. "I trust you're okay. You've really got to get a handle on your temper, you know." Pause. "Or your jealousy. I sensed your mind wasn't exactly on our conversation, what with that woman being there . . ." Pause. "It's simply not like you to be so . . . distracted when it comes to Patrick. I'm really disappointed in you. Call me."

Girlfriend?

Holly watched the red light of the machine flicker.

Maybe. She had watched them from the bar—before the drunk had intruded with his bourbon-scented breath and his fresh hands. Watched the woman's face as she looked for any sign in Damascus's body language that indicated Holly was more than an acquaintance. For a second, her pretty eyes had locked with Holly's. There had been a nervousness in her gaze. A flash of anger, perhaps. Certainly annoyance. The look had said, "Back off."

Holly was well acquainted with those types of looks, anytime she came within flirting distance of a woman's husband. Damascus's reaching across the table and holding her hand had helped.

Recalling the image, Holly felt a twinge of envy in her chest. She tried to recall when a man's touch had been proffered by compassion instead of lust. Long ago, she had been naive enough to actually believe a man's gentle touch meant comfort and caring. But for her, such kindness had always come with strings attached. Kindness preceded abuse. As a hooker in New Orleans, she had lost the ability to trust long ago.

J.D. finished his two afternoon court appointments, met his after-hours clients, and assured May she would get paid for her overtime—just as soon as his clients paid him. Then, he stopped by Fang Fang Chinese Take-Out and returned home to find Holly already asleep in his bed.

Obviously, she had found plenty to occupy her time. His clothes had been separated into clean and dirty. The clean were folded and stacked on the bureau, and the soiled were in a pile near the bathroom door. Newspapers and empty cans had been discarded, the trash removed from the apartment. She had washed the food-encrusted dishes he had left in the sink, dried them, and put them away.

He dug a cigarette out of her pack and stood by the bed, smoking and watching her. Her dark hair formed a spray like shadows over the white pillowcase. Her breasts rose and fell in deep sleep. Her midriff shirt had ridden up, her jeans down, exposing a sapphire nestled in her navel. It winked like blue fire at him. She had bathed recently. The air felt warm and humid and smelled like soap. Damp tendrils clung to her high cheekbones and he felt the irritating stir of a need to reach down and finger the curl away.

Hell, admit it. He wanted to lay his body down beside her. The times he had taken a woman to bed over the last years had been infrequent—never here. Not in this bed. This hole-in-the-wall had been his escape from the real world.

Yet, he had opened his door for a stranger. Why? Because he hoped to fuck her? Maybe. Because she was lost? And he was lost? Because in her desperate eyes he had seen a reflection of himself? Or maybe it was nothing more than him feeling uncomfortable over the prospect of her wandering these streets when a serial killer was out there feeding his sick fantasies on helpless women. Yes, on all counts.

He returned to the kitchen and quietly, so as not to disturb her, extracted the hot boxes of lo mein and steamed rice from the sack, his gaze drifting again and again to Holly's purse. He couldn't shake the feeling there was more to Holly Jones than met the eye. Her face had continued to nag him through the afternoon.

He'd made a call to the records department at the force and wrangled a favor from Melanie Shultz, an old girl-friend. She had scoured the computer files for any infor-mation on Holly Jones and turned up nothing, no previous Louisiana driver's license or car tags. Melanie had snooped through the three main credit bureaus using the social security number Holly had supplied the department when taken into custody, finding not so much as a credit card. He might have coerced her into checking with the IRS, but he would be pushing it.

He took a cautionary glance into the bedroom—she was soundly sleeping—then he opened her purse, a big straw bag accommodating the registered-with-permit .38 with which she had shot the chief of police, a collection of lip-sticks, bottle of perfume, breath spray, key ring of several keys, and a small leather wallet. He flipped it open, searched the empty pockets, and withdrew her driver's license.

"Isn't there a law against snooping through people's personal belongings without a search warrant?"

He looked around.

Her thick hair a tangle around her face, her full mouth pressed in irritation, she stared at him with a look of dis-gust. She grabbed the purse from his hand and turned it over, spilling the contents onto the kitchen counter, her hard, sleepy gaze never leaving his.

"Why not do a strip search as well, J.D.? You never know. I might be hiding crack in my panties."

He leaned back against the counter and crossed his arms as she scattered the purse contents for his perusal.

"Please, help yourself." She lifted the tube of breath spray and fired a stream into the air. It smelled like mint toothpaste. "No anthrax here, Damascus. No small nuclear devices, fake passports or visas. Would you care to see a copy of my birth certificate as well?"

"Maybe."

She rolled her eyes and proceeded to snatch up her belongings and shove them back into the purse. "Just when I thought there was an inkling of a nice guy in you, you go and blow it."

He reached for the carton of lo mein and extended it to her. "Truce."

"I'm not hungry."

She turned away, hauling her purse with her, and flopped onto the futon in the living room. "I work my butt off cleaning up this pigsty and this is the thanks I get."

"Maybe if you were a little more forthcoming, I wouldn't be inclined to snoop."

"I'm none of your business. Right or wrong?"

Right. She was none of his business. After retrieving a fork from the kitchen drawer, he began to eat as he joined her on the futon, stretched his legs out, and propped his feet on the coffee table.

"So what now? You have no money or car, no family, or so you say. You came to New Orleans to see your friend, whom you can't locate at the moment."

Folding her arms around her purse, she hugged it to her stomach. "I have to find Melissa."

"Still not answering her phone?"

"No." She looked at him, then the carton of lo mein.

"So we take a drive over to her place. Check it out."

She frowned, hugged the purse tighter. "Melissa wouldn't ignore my phone calls, especially when she knew I would be arriving in town last night. She was thrilled I was coming. We haven't seen one another in . . . four years."

Sighing, she ran one hand through her dark hair. "God, I've missed her. We were so close for so long. We were family—sisters. Twins. We knew each other's thoughts before we spoke them."

He watched the sharp flint in her eyes soften into fondness. Her lips curved slightly as her thoughts appeared to drift. When she spoke again, her voice dropped to a sultry tone that made heat coil in his stomach—no ulcer pang, this, but pure, unadulterated lust.

"You ever meet someone you just clicked with, Damascus? Like they were brought into your life for a reason, to save you in some way? To give you a buoy to hold on to when your entire life appears to be sinking in quicksand?"

Turning her blue eyes to his, she watched and waited. A boat on the river let out a blast from its horn, the deep sound muffled by the fog rolling over the city. Something stirred inside him.

She drew away, slightly turning one shoulder to him. "You wouldn't understand. You had family, didn't you?

A powerful father, a socialite mother. Someone there for
you at night when you turned out the lights. You needn't
be afraid of shadows."

Holly left the futon. "God, I hate this town," she said,
more to herself than to him. "I hate the smell of it. The
heat and humidity. The crawling tourists and the freaks. I
tried to talk Melissa into coming to Branson. It was safe
there. Little crime. She could start over, but she was
afraid. She'd been turning tricks since she was fifteen. She
didn't know how to deal with the real world. She simply
couldn't see herself as anything but a hooker."

A hardness returned to her eyes. " 'Once a whore always a whore,' she used to say. It's like a stench that
becomes so embedded in your soul it can't ever be
scrubbed away. Like butchers. You ever smelled a
butcher, Damascus? No matter how often they bathe, they
still smell like fresh blood. Or mechanics with oil under
their fingernails and the stink of gasoline seeping from
their pores when they sweat.

"Melissa isn't any different than any other woman, really. She dreams of a husband and kids. Santa Claus and
birthday parties. But what decent man wants an ex-hooker
for a wife? What if the kids were to learn of her past?
Who's to say someday she doesn't come face-to-face with
an old john and suddenly all her nasty little secrets are
spewed out for the entire world to witness?

"Those are the things you don't consider when making
the choice to become a prostitute. You think only of the
moment, of surviving. When you're fifteen and homeless,
have nothing to eat, and some smooth-talking dude in a
nice suit and driving a BMW offers to help and promises

you'll never be hungry again, you grab it. Turn a couple of tricks. You've got money in your pocket to buy a Big Mac and maybe a new pair of sneakers with enough change left to hold you over until you figure a way out of the situation.

"Except, there is no way out. Because once you sell your body, Damascus, you also sell your soul . . . your self-esteem, if you had a decent esteem to begin with. Most don't. It's already been ripped out of you by some drunken pervert who smells like fresh blood."

J.D. put aside the lo mein and left the futon, moved toward Holly as she stared at her feet, her body visibly shaking, her hands fisted. Her head slowly rose and the pain in her eyes slugged him.

"C'meer," he said gently, reaching out to her.

"Don't." She backed away, her gaze avoiding his, her body appearing so brittle she might fracture if he touched her. As she turned away, he grabbed her arm, drawing her back, though she struggled, futilely, as he wrapped both arms around her and held her against his chest.

There was no doubt in his mind now that Holly Jones was, or had been, a hooker. She hadn't been speaking so much about Melissa as she had been about herself. In one swift but heart-punching glance, those eyes had reflected her nightmares and shame. She had escaped New Orleans, put the life behind her. Settled into Branson where life was clean and offered no memories of her past. Now she was back and the memories were crushing her.

"It's okay." His lips brushed her temple, the resistance in her body melting little by little as she sank against him, her slender fingers twisting into his shirt as if to keep herself from collapsing. "Wanna talk about it?"

She shook her head. "No."

"Might help, honey. Get it all out. Hey, I'm a terrific listener."

"Why should you care?"

Right. Why the hell should he care?

He backed toward the futon, tugging her with him. They settled on the futon, and though she attempted to squirm away, to put distance between them, he held on, locking his arms around her so she nestled partially across his lap, her face buried against his throat.

"Who did you work for?" he asked.

No response.

He shifted away, placed one finger beneath her chin, and tipped up her face. "Look at me, Holly."

Slowly, her lashes lifted and she looked into his eyes. "Was it Tyron?"

"Yes."

A moment of silence passed between them as the old spear of white-hot hate for the bastard cut through his belly. In a flash, he imagined the woman in his arms as a young girl, alone and frightened on the New Orleans streets. Helpless and desperate enough to trust the smooth-talking pimp in his flashy car and Armani suit—his convincing them he was some guardian angel sent to rescue them.

"He can't know I'm back." Her voice quivered with desperation. "Please understand. If he was to discover I'd returned to New Orleans—"

"I'm well aware of how he deals with women who walk out on him, Holly."

He touched her cheek and felt a shiver run through her.

She pulled away. Withdrew to the far end of the futon, her fingers lightly brushing her cheek where he had touched her. J.D. knew that she would not trust a man's touch. He wasn't even certain himself why he had reached out to her. Held her. Looked into her eyes and felt slammed by a desire to kiss her. Not simply kiss her. But protect her.

He dug into his pocket for his cigarettes. Lit one, never taking his gaze from Holly, her pale face, her tense body. He could almost hear her reerecting her wall against him, brick by brick, each second her old attitude forming a barrier between them.

"Was Melissa on drugs?"

Her head snapped around and her eyes flashed. "Of course not."

"How do you know?"

"She wasn't into that sort of thing."

"You said yourself that you hadn't seen her in four years. People change, Holly."

"I know Melissa. No drugs."

"Then maybe Tyron got wind of her contacting you. Found out that she was about to take a hike from his stable."

She bit her lip and sank back against the futon. "Tyron is stupid and mean as a snake, but he's not into murder."

His eyes narrowed as he smoked. He wanted to argue the fact, but no point in upsetting her more than she already was.

"Hey," he said, waiting until she forced herself to look at him again. "Let's go find Melissa."

6

Sunset in New Orleans brought little respite from the miserable heat and humidity. The frequent fog felt like steam against the skin and made breathing difficult. As J.D. eased the Mustang to a stop, the beams of the headlights formed a hazy pool of diffused illumination on the damp, brick street.

Bodies moved like wraiths through the condensation, formless, genderless. A man's drunken shout, a woman's tense laughter, distant music from a lone street musician filling the air with soulful saxophone blues—all lent a haunting loneliness to the night. There was a reason Anne Rice set her vampire novels in New Orleans. It was, indeed, a city of lost souls.

Killing the engine, J.D. looked around at Holly as she gazed out the passenger window, her body tense. "Sure you want to do this?" He sure as hell wasn't, not with the image of Cherry Brown's body still seared into his mem-

ory. Not that he was particularly concerned for himself—
he would be out here regardless, searching, as he had in
the past.

She didn't respond.

He checked the gun in his shoulder holster. Mugging
and murders in the district were the norm. Besides the
hookers who worked the streets, the area seethed with
junkies who, if they weren't wired on drugs already, were
desperate to find a way to purchase what they needed to
get them through the night. During the many frantic nights
he had roamed these sidewalks and back alleys searching
for his family's killer, it had been a miracle that he had
not caught a bullet or a knife in his heart. Thinking back,
he suspected that he had been looking for such an end to
his misery—wanting it as desperately as he wanted to put
a bullet between the freak's eyes.

Holly took a breath, pulled on the handle, and opened
her door.

"Wait." J.D. locked his door, then walked around, and
stood by Holly as she exited the passenger side, nearest
the sidewalk. J.D. noted the total absence of hookers nor-
mally loitering in the area, perhaps turning a trick in the
alley. The girls would be frightened, of course. Cautious.

He took her elbow. "You okay?"

She nodded and together they moved down a narrow
alley exactly one block due east from Cherry Brown's
apartment. The alley led to a courtyard—not the pretty,
atmospheric patios where some of the nicer restaurants
and clubs had set up business, but a weed-infested, cob-
blestone area with a crumbling fountain of scum-covered
water. Here, the hot fog settled into the creases of his skin

and crawled along his scalp. Mosquitos hummed like buzzing fans.

Holly paused, her eyes narrowing as her gaze swept the crowded apartments, two stories of dilapidated structures that appeared to be held together only by the filigreed railings along the balconies. Dim light of low wattage bulbs shone behind the glut of dingy half-sheeted windows. Muted television chatter rolled through the fog from somewhere to their right.

Footsteps behind them. He looked back over his shoulder, left hand easing beneath his sport coat. No one there.

Finally, as if she had acquainted herself with her surroundings, Holly moved to a staircase and climbed. J.D. followed. The ancient iron steps protested against their weight, grating rustily in the quiet, causing curious faces to peer out from behind curtains.

A light shone from Melissa's window. Holly knocked on the door. Nothing. She dug into her purse, extracted the ring of keys, held it up to the light until she located the key she needed.

J.D. took it from her. No way was he going to let her walk into that room and find her friend laid out like an autopsy cadaver. She started to argue, then shut her mouth and stepped aside. Her face looked brittle enough to crack.

He removed the gun from the holster, pointed it up, turned the key in the lock, and nudged the door open. His breath caught in his lungs as he cautiously stepped into the room, his gaze locking on the bed against the far wall. Empty, thank God.

Holly stepped in behind him, her arm brushing his, her

body close. "Melissa?" she called softly. "Are you here? It's Holly." As she moved toward the dark kitchen, he caught her arm, felt her trembling.

"Stay here." He eased toward the unlit room, the intense heat in the unair-conditioned apartment making sweat rise. The stench of something rotten washed over him so he couldn't find a breath in the thick air. His heart began crashing in his ears and the butt of the gun became slippery in his hands. Feet braced apart, his eyes throbbing in their attempt to see through the shadows, he hit the light.

Scattered across the table was food swarming with flies and roaches, a solitary TV dinner, partially eaten, a pan with dried-up macaroni and cheese, an open container of milk that had grown thick as cottage cheese.

Behind him, Holly caught her breath. He glanced back at her, shook his head, nodding toward the closed bathroom door. He eased toward the door, toed it open, hit the light.

A tabby cat, frightened by the sudden burst of light, leapt from the tank top of the toilet and exploded toward the door, a flash of movement that made J.D. recoil and anchor the gun in preparation for firing. Yowling pitifully, the cat ducked between his legs and made a frantic escape toward the living room. From the corner of his eye, J.D. saw Holly make a grab for the terrified feline before it slid beneath a chair against the wall.

The room was empty. Only the scattering of cat feces and puddles of rank urine gave any hint that something was amiss. Obviously the cat had been locked up for as long as the food had been wasting in the kitchen.

Lowering the gun, relaxing his tense shoulders, J.D. returned to the living area before allowing himself to take a much-needed breath.

Holly, on her hands and knees, was softly coaxing the cat from beneath the chair. "Here, Puddin'. Kitty, kitty. It's okay, sweetie. Pretty kitty. That's a good girl. Poor baby." She tugged the trembling tabby from under the chair and cradled it in her arms like a baby. Only then did she turn back to J.D. She looked on the verge of shattering.

"Will you believe me *now*?" she said, her tone razor sharp with fear and anger.

He holstered the gun and studied the surroundings. Neatly made bed where several pillows had been arranged against the wrought iron headboard. Numerous candles cluttered the sofa table, most partially melted from use. Not normal candles, but those used in the local voodoo community, Santa Barbara and Black Devil candles, both of which were used to turn away evil. There were bottles of oils and containers of incense. Rosary beads hung from crucifixes on the wall, as did Mardi Gras beads and voodoo dolls. Melissa was obviously afraid that some sort of evil would come knocking at her door.

Hugging the cat to her, Holly said, "We have to go to the police. Now."

"With what?" He picked up a gris-gris satchel and opened it, fingered the locks of hair, bits of chicken feathers, and splinters of bone. "There's no evidence of foul play here, Holly."

She glared at him in disbelief, her anger mounting.

"There isn't a cop in homicide who would find a reason

to think that something had happened to Melissa. She might have simply taken off."

"And left her cat behind to starve?"

"It happens." Stooping, he studied the floor for any evidence of blood. None that he could see. If the cops decided Melissa's disappearance warranted an investigation, they would utilize luminal to locate blood stains that couldn't be seen otherwise. "If, like you say, she was frightened, she might have simply decided to take a hike."

"You're unbelievable. After everything I've told you—"

"I'm just coming at you with what you're going to face if you report this." He stood. "Look around for her purse—anything that might be a clue that she left the apartment against her will."

"But the food—"

"She wouldn't be the first to leave her kitchen in a mess. Hey, you saw mine, right?" He grinned.

She didn't.

"Don't touch anything in case they check for prints." He moved toward the front door. "I'll knock on a few doors, see if anyone saw or heard anything suspicious."

J.D. stepped from the apartment. He took a deep breath. What had happened to his ability to remain emotionally detached in the face of someone else's misfortune?

Oh, yeah, there had been misfortune here, despite the fact that the apartment, aside from the spoiled food and hungry cat, showed no evidence of mischief. While he wouldn't admit as much to Holly, he was acquainted with Melissa's adoration of her cat. Every time she had dropped into his office on business, she'd had the purring feline with her. Her only family, she'd admitted, scratching the tabby between its ears. Her baby.

No way in hell would she have deserted the cat.

Yet, there was no indication that Melissa had fallen prey to the same fate as Tyra and Cherry, or any of the other hookers who had been killed. In all cases, the M.O. had been identical. Murdered in their beds.

That very reason had been why he would never accept that his family had been slaughtered by the same serial killer who butchered hookers. Laura's body had been found in Woldenberg Park. The kids in his wife's SUV, laid out peacefully in the backseat as if their throats had been cut while they were sleeping.

She was losing it. The panic that had shadowed her for the last few years was coiling in her chest like a snake prepared to strike. Stay calm, she told herself as she gripped the trembling cat in her arms and moved woodenly through the small apartment.

Something had happened here, despite what Damascus had said. Something. She could almost feel Melissa's terror. Perhaps she had been eating her miserly dinner when someone arrived at her apartment. Perhaps she had been thinking about her appointment with the warehouse john—worried, as was the norm. Even in less stressful times, a hooker always wondered if this would be the trick that would go bad. A sadist who got off on pain. A freak fried on heroine. It all came crashing in on her, the memories, the cold, bone-chilling fear, the sense of self-disgust. Helplessness. No way out. Her knees felt weak, her leg muscles burned as if she had just sprinted a hundred-yard dash.

Holding her breath, she tiptoed through the kitchen, avoiding looking toward the fly-infested food. Everything seemed in place. What was she looking for exactly? No open kitchen drawers where some maniac might have rummaged for a butcher knife. No upset chairs. No broken dishes.

She moved into the bathroom, careful not to step in the cat's leavings. Puddin' suddenly squirmed in her arms as if terrified of being trapped again. Holly hugged her and whispered comfortingly until the animal quieted.

Makeup and perfume bottles lined up neatly on the counter near the sink. The towels were in place, no sign that they had been used since washing.

Again into the living room, a cautious glance under the bed where Melissa usually hid her purse. It wasn't there.

Her stomach cramping with a magnifying sense of dread and loss, Holly sat on the floor and looked around. There were many framed photographs placed amid the crowd of candles, incense, and oils. Images of friends and family, past and present. Shots of Melissa's parents before they had been killed in a car accident, cradling their youthful, innocent baby in their arms. Melissa's fifth birthday party, a juggling clown and presents stacked high on a picnic table. Another of a Christmas tree and Melissa sitting among stores of opened presents.

Then there were those including Holly. Gangly teenage girls with their arms hooked around each other's shoulders taken at Jackson Square, their first day in New Orleans. More of Holly alone, each one a caricature of the previous

one, the hardship of their existences carving her face into
a maturity that belied her young years.

Holly closed her eyes. "Oh God, Melissa. Where are
you?"

*He stands in the dark and fog, the nearest vapor light one
block away, casting not a solitary shadow on the parked
Mustang. He's not at all surprised to find the car here.
He expected as much. The brilliant ex-prosecutor would
again be haunting the streets and alleys, looking for his
family's killer. What does surprise him is J.D.'s coming
here, to Melissa's apartment. How had he known about
the missing girl?*

*He laughs softly. Coincidence perhaps. Perhaps one of
the whore's friends has reported her missing. Yes, perhaps. But there have been no cops snooping around.
Nothing on the police scanner to indicate that Melissa
Carmichael has disappeared. As if the department cares.
As if they want this nasty trouble to escalate. Not again.
That's what will make this newest foray so much fun. Before it's all over, again, he will have them dancing on a
wire.*

*Ah, blessed power. The aphrodisiac of complete con-
trol.*

*He moves through the fog to the Mustang. The humidity
has settled over the windows in a thick, wet haze. He is
tempted to write some cryptic note with his finger on the
condensation, feed J.D. some clue that will foster anger
and suspicion. Not yet. Too early in the game. This time
he will be more careful. He'd acted too quickly those*

years before, murdered a hooker too soon after she had serviced her last john.

But watching Angel Gonzalez tried for the slayings had been entertaining, if nothing else. In some twisted way, he had been in control even then. Because of him an innocent man was tried and convicted and put to death. A rose by any other name would smell as sweet.

Moving down the cracked and buckled sidewalks, he stays close to the buildings, avoiding the diffused light from the overhead streetlamps. It is a long walk to his destination, but he enjoys this time. Enjoys the vibrations of anxiety he feels in the air. The night is unusually quiet, the area vacant. That, too, pleases him. The district fears him. Even now, the whores are trembling behind their locked doors. He needn't kill again for a while. The terror that he has brought to this community is enough, for the moment, to instill him with the sweet, sweet feeling of domination and authority. It fills him with euphoria as he almost glides down the backstreets to the river, pausing to drink in the scent of the muddy water before continuing down the stretch of old warehouses that have not yet been converted into art galleries and such nonsense.

He hums as he walks, invigorated by what is to come.

The building is ancient, with crumbling bricks that had been lain by sweating slaves' hands a hundred and fifty years ago, the timbers deteriorating, eaten away by age and mildew, crumbling into fine dust that makes his footsteps all but silent.

He has researched the history of the cavernous building, which juts out over the river on pilings. Once food was brought here to await its trip up the river on boats, to the plantations between New Orleans and Baton Rouge. Hooks for slabs of beef still dangle from the overhead beams, bones of the past. Early in the century, when electricity had become the norm, giant lockers had been installed to keep the raw meat cool. It is here that he stops. Presses his ear against the massive door, and listens, his breath coming in short, audible pants of excitement. He heaves open the door and enters.

She is there, just as he left her. Huddled in the corner of the locker, the kerosene lamp on the floor filling her wide, pretty eyes with flames of fear. Her wrists and ankles are linked together with wire, her arms upstretched above her head and anchored to the wall. She's smarter than most, knowing that if she struggles, the thin hobbles will slice into her flesh and cause her pain. Still, as she stares up into his eyes, her body trembles enough so the wires cut into her skin, causing fresh threads of blood to dribble. She makes a mumbled sound behind the black tape over her lips.

He smiles. "Hello, Melissa. Miss me?"

Just as J.D. expected, the bleary-eyed cop on the night shift wasn't particularly concerned about Melissa Carmichael's mysterious disappearance. He typed out a report and tossed it into the stack of a dozen others he had received since coming on duty. No doubt he was pissed because he was stuck behind a desk and not out prowling the streets in hopes of making a collar that would get his name in the paper and a commendation from the mayor.

Throughout the interview, Holly had managed to keep a tight rein on her irritation. The cat struggling in her arms had helped, refocusing her short-wired patience each time J.D. suspected she was on the verge of climbing across the cop's cluttered desk to slap him.

J.D. had answered most of the questions and offered comments of his own. No indication of violence. Yes, he had knocked on a few doors, but the neighbors had not seen or heard anything suspicious. No, they had not seen Melissa, but that wasn't unusual, considering she came and went mostly during the early hours of the morning. Hookers didn't exactly work the nine-to-five shift.

By the time he pulled the Mustang to the curb in front of his apartment, Holly had fallen asleep with the cat curled up in her lap. He didn't notice the patrol car parked across the street until he had shaken Holly awake and exited the Mustang.

The uniformed officer moved toward him through the fog and shadows, one hand locked on Patrick's arm, tugging his reluctant nephew along.

Shit.

"What the hell is this about, Patrick?" J.D. stared at Patrick, who attempted to yank his arm from the cop, avoiding J.D.'s eyes.

"Found him wandering the warehouse district. Said he belonged to you."

"Did he?"

"Does he?"

"In a manner of speaking."

As Holly exited the car, Patrick pinned her with his angry eyes, his expression growing sulky. "Who the fuck is that?"

Holly moved up beside J.D., gently stroking the cat.

Her expression looked sleepy and amused by his nephew's belligerence.

J.D. took Patrick by the scruff of his shirt collar. "Thanks."

"Keep him off the streets. Next time, I'll take him in."

"Right." He was tempted to tell the cop to take the kid in anyway. Give him a taste of what was in store for him if he didn't get his act together.

Patrick jerked away from J.D. and shuffled toward the apartment, hands jammed into his baggy jeans pockets. Mounting the steps, he stood, shoulders hunched, head down, and kicked the door.

The cop smirked. "Enjoy your evening." Then he returned to the patrol car.

J.D. glanced at Holly, who was scratching the tabby between its ears, her drowsy gaze still assessing his nephew. "Bev isn't going to be pleased," he said, glancing again at Holly, who narrowed her eyes as she appraised Patrick more closely.

He didn't bother looking at Patrick as he unlocked the door, then waited for the seething teenager to enter. His mind was ticking over just how he was going to deal with this sorry turn of events. The only experience he'd had with delinquent teenagers was with those who had found their way into the justice system. By that time they were already up to their ears in rap sheets and on their way to juvenile lockdown.

Patrick flopped onto the futon, hands still jammed in his pockets, his sharp gray eyes focused on Holly as she moved to the kitchen to rummage through the cupboards for a water bowl for the cat. "New girlfriend?" he sneered.

KATHERINE SUTCLIFFE

"None of your business."

Patrick rolled his eyes and slumped deeper into the futon.

"What the hell are you doing out at this time of night?"

"None of your business."

"Drinking?"

"Not yet."

"Drugs?"

He smirked. "Not yet."

"Maybe I'll just haul your smart-aleck ass down to the lab and have you drug tested."

"Fine. I don't give a fuck."

"You ganging it, Patrick?"

"What if I am?"

"I'll kick your ass."

"Nice one, Mr. Prosecutor," Holly whispered behind him. "Judge Judy would be very proud of your technique. Rip out his throat and let him bleed all over the floor, why don't you?"

Stepping around him, carrying the box of cold pizza, she moved to the futon and dropped down beside Patrick. "I don't know about you guys, but I'm starving, and I happen to love cold pizza." She peeled a slice from the box and proceeded to eat, offering a slice to Patrick. He ignored her.

His hands on his hips, J.D. stared at his nephew and tried to control his rising frustration. "What am I supposed to do with you now? Your mom is freaked over your behavior. I'm gonna call her up at two in the morning and tell her you were picked up wandering around the damn warehouse district?"

Patrick shrugged and glanced at the pizza.

"What were you doing there, Patrick?"

"Nothin'."

Raking one hand through his hair, J.D. searched the ceiling for patience. It was one thing to remain cool when there was no emotional involvement, but it was another when the kid was his own flesh and blood, a semigrown image of his son. Perhaps that had been part of his recent problem, his resistance to get involved more deeply in Patrick's life. Although Billy had only been seven when he died, the boys were uncannily similar. He couldn't look into Patrick's eyes anymore without thinking of what he had lost.

"Christ." He sighed. "Eric is gonna be pissed."

"Who's Eric?" Holly asked, chewing her pizza.

"My dad," Patrick snapped at the same moment that J.D. replied, "My brother."

Her eyebrows shot up, and she shifted her gaze back to J.D. "So Beverly is your sister-in-law. Interesting."

J.D. narrowed his eyes at her before focusing again on Patrick, who had apparently noted the look that had passed between him and Holly. A new kind of anger flushed his nephew's face.

"I'll have to call your mom. If she's already discovered you're gone, she'll be beside herself with panic."

"If she *had* discovered him gone," Holly said, "I suspect she would have already called you."

Patrick gave her a nasty look. "Why don't you mind your own business? Who are you, anyway? My uncle's newest piece of ass?"

She smiled. "I was only going to suggest that J.D. take

you home. You could crawl back through whatever hole you crawled out of, slither beneath your bedcovers, and she would never need to know you were ever gone, and no one would need to get freaked over this incident."

"Maybe I don't wanna go home. Maybe I want to live here."

"Maybe you don't have a choice." She tossed the pizza crust back into the box. "You're a minor and therefore your parents are obligated by law to remain responsible for your welfare. They're also responsible for any mischief you commit while wandering the streets in the dead of night. Aside from that, you've put your uncle in an uncomfortable situation. He obviously loves you very much, but he also has a responsibility to your parents, especially his brother. By involving your uncle in whatever emotional flux you're experiencing toward your parents, you risk alienating him from your mother and father. What happens then?"

She tapped her temple with her index finger. "Think consequences, Patrick. I realize that at your age, consequences have a way of becoming diluted by swarming hormones. Been there and done that, so I can tell you from experience that your actions risk ruining any hope you might have of your uncle helping you through this difficult time. If you drive a wedge between J.D. and his brother, you can bet your father will nip any future visitation with J.D. in the bud. I don't think that's what you really want, is it?"

He stared at the toes of his sneakers, face red and miserable.

"Is it?" she asked softly.

Shrugging, he shook his head.

"Hey." She laid one hand on his shoulder, drawing his angry eyes back to hers. "I know it's tough. Sometimes adults don't understand what's going on in a teenager's mind. They forget what it's like to be young and confused. Trust me, if you hang in there and keep it together, it'll get better. It just takes time."

He opened and closed his mouth, then turned away, swallowed hard.

J.D. allowed Holly a faint smile of gratitude, then moved toward the door. "Come on, pal. Let's get you home before our goose is cooked with your dad."

Reluctantly, Patrick got to his feet, heels scraping the floor. At the threshold, he stopped and looked back, skewering Holly with his eyes. "I don't give a fuck what my dad thinks. And I don't like you and your been-there-and-done-that shit. You don't know nothin', okay? You think you know me and what I'm feelin', but you don't and you never will."

Patrick stood in the deep shadows inside of his house, watching through the window as his uncle's car silently, and without headlights, backed from the driveway then eased off down the street, the red taillights swallowed up by the fog.

J.D. had hardly spoken during their short drive. He was pissed for sure. But so was Patrick. The anger made him want to puke.

He pressed his sweating fists to his forehead and squeezed his eyes closed.

It had happened again. J.D. had called him Billy. In the short space of minutes, with so few words shared between them, he had slipped and called him by his dead son's name.

Dammit! When would J.D. ever look at him and not wish that he was Billy? Billy was dead, and Patrick Damascus was alive. He could make J.D. forget the past if he would only give him a chance. J.D. needed him as much as he needed his uncle. They were both . . . alone. There were soccer games and concerts and movies to see. J.D. wouldn't stand him up at father-son picnics. No way. Not like his dad, who was constantly making his mom cry. God, that's all she did anymore. She couldn't do anything to please his dad. He was always picking, picking, picking at her, do this and do that and reminding her—all of them—that he had a reputation to live up to and if they screwed up then his career, his stupid career, would be ruined. He had a mind to—

Banging his knuckles against his forehead. Bastard. Fucking hypocrite. He had a mind to—

But his mother needed him to be strong. J.D. had said so on the drive over. His parents' marriage was screwed up and his mother was very unhappy and surely Patrick didn't want to add to her misery and stress.

Now J.D. was driving home, to be with that woman. He wouldn't think about him, Patrick, because he was surrounded by photographs of his kids who were dead and no longer here to love him and need him. What if he married her? That would be the end of everything. Of them. They would go on to have more children and there would be no time at all for Patrick.

Pressing his fists into his eyes, thinking of the magazine, that catalogue of smut, knowing that J.D. would be doing to that woman what those women blazed across those glossy pages had been doing. He couldn't look at a woman anymore without thinking about it, without feeling those urges racing through his groin. Disgusting. Sick. Those kinds of women should be exterminated. Like her. The bitch with her long black hair and her full lips and big tits. He had actually gotten hard sitting beside her, smelling her. He couldn't control it any longer. Sick.

The room flooded with light. He spun around and glared into his father's eyes.

"What the hell are you doing up and dressed at this hour?" Eric demanded. "You've got school tomorrow."

He moved toward the door, his gaze still locked with his father's. Soon he would be as big as his father. Bigger. Taller, like J.D. And stronger, like J.D. Give it another year and the good legislative director would think twice about bullying him and his mother. He was going to make the son of a bitch regret he was ever born. Oh, yeah. Soon, his father was going to suffer.

7

Exhaustion poured through her, yet she couldn't sleep. Too wired. Her mind kept rehashing every detail of Melissa's apartment. The fact that she had simply walked away from Puddin' was the key.

Perhaps what had transpired had not taken place at Melissa's apartment at all. Perhaps something had happened as she was on her way to meet her john. Yes, that would make sense.

Was it too much to hope that Damascus was right? That Melissa had, at last, simply walked away from the life, from the fear, from the threat? Too much to hope for, surely. She would call her answering machine in Branson again, just to make certain that Melissa hadn't phoned.

As she paced, Puddin' lay curled up on the futon, purring contently now that her stomach had been filled by cold pizza and a bowl of warm milk. Holly glanced at her watch.

Damascus had been gone an hour.

Perhaps Beverly had been waiting for him when he took her son home. Beverly, with her genteel disposition and timid smile, sly flirtation from beneath the shadows of her long lashes, perhaps a tremulous word to coax a tender touch out of the man she so obviously desired.

Odd that Holly could find empathy to share with a woman of such obvious class. They weren't so unalike, really. Holly might never have known a childhood of being cherished by parents, as Beverly most certainly had, and Holly had never known a typical teenage existence of high school homecoming games and senior proms. But their mutual desire for the unattainable put them on an equal level. They both yearned for something they could not have.

Beverly wanted J.D. Damascus.

And Holly wanted a man who would love her regardless of her past, and for what she could offer for the future: a home and children, a wife who would never take for granted the treasures that such gifts could offer. Someone who would count her blessings every day and worship every moment of happiness as if it were her last. She didn't care about money. Didn't care about flashy cars or impressive houses or designer clothes. Materialism could never compare to permanence, to a man who would hold her in his arms at night and kiss away her nightmares. Or a child's unconditional love and trust that shines in his eyes when his mother tucks him into bed.

Holly's man was out there, somewhere. Waiting. Perhaps he had suffered, too. Then he would need her all the more. Cherish her. And she could fill up his emptiness as he filled up hers.

She picked up a framed photograph of J.D.'s kids. Beautiful children. The boy looked just like his father, gray eyes and a mop of thick, dark brown hair. The girl was probably more like her mother, blond, sparkling green eyes, and a scattering of freckles over her pug nose. Ribbons on pigtails.

Holly smiled and lightly touched the cherubic face with her fingertip, unfamiliar images of Damascus toying with her imagination.

Her gaze moved to another photograph, then another, then another. She wandered to the kitchen and studied the snapshots on the fridge, turned them over and noted they were dated years ago.

Odd. There didn't seem to be any recent photographs. No school photos. Could the divorce have been so ugly that the ex wouldn't so much as provide current pictures? Doubtful. Even if his wife didn't supply them, Damascus would take his own. Unless, possibly, the ex had moved away. How very sad for him. He obviously loved his kids very much.

She returned the photograph to the lamp table and wandered into the bedroom. Sleepiness had begun to tug on her eyelids at last. She regarded the bed somewhat wistfully. No. She wasn't so callous as to take his bed. She would fold out the futon, catch a few winks, then decide just how she was going to go about finding Melissa without blowing her cover.

A small, dim lamp burned on a desk in the corner. There were papers scattered haphazardly. Law books

stacked high. More photographs. She moved to the desk
and allowed her gaze to wander. It caught on a folder
labeled DAMASCUS, LAURA.

She picked it up. Flipped it open.

The breath left her. Shock punched her in the stomach
as she focused on the grotesque images of a slaughtered
woman laid out on the coroner's slab.

Throwing the file down, she backed away, her body
shivering and burning at once. She backed into a wall,
one hand covering her mouth, her wide eyes still fixed on
the file that shimmered slightly under the amber light.

> DAMASCUS, LAURA.
> LAURA DAMASCUS.
> MURDERED.
> DECAPITATED.
> EVISCERATED.
> August, 1999.

Oh God, oh God, oh God.

Her gaze flew to the children's photographs, her shock
equaled by a swelling sense of fear that escalated the
pounding of her heart as her eyes burned into those of
Damascus's son. Her hands curled into fists, the nails cutting painfully into her palms.

Where were the children? The beautiful, smiling children?

No recent photographs.

Oh, no. Surely not.

She approached the desk again, cautious, as if the file
would fly open on its own and reveal Laura's body in

colored detail. Her hands fumbled for the desk drawers, opening one, rummaging wildly. What was she looking for? Anything to prove that her instincts were wrong. His children, his beloved, beautiful children were not dead as well. Not possible. Not his entire family! Why? No, no, they were, perhaps, living with J.D.'s parents. Laura's parents.

Another drawer, digging, searching. A small box of Matchbox cars—a collection of Indy racers, red and blue and green. An envelope of fine, blond hair and a pair of pink ribbons. A scrap of yellow newspaper, neatly folded. Her trembling fingers opened it.

She closed her eyes.

The engine idling, J.D. sat in the Mustang outside his apartment, Emile Pandolfi music drifting from the CD player into the hot August night. He considered turning the car around and returning to Eric's house, apologizing to Patrick for his annoyance and preoccupation. He'd slipped and called the kid Billy again. Stupid.

He looked toward his apartment. Holly Jones had crawled under his skin and he couldn't shake it. The fear and shame in her eyes had obliterated his initial disappointment over her past. Instead, he had been flooded by fresh fury. Yet another woman destroyed by Tyron Johnson. The mounting anger gnawed at his belly even as Pandolfi's piano drifted sweetly into the humid night air. So did his suspicion that Johnson might have had something to do with Melissa's disappearance. Especially if she had indicated that she intended to get out of the business.

"Son of a bitch."

At three in the morning the Lucky Lady Casino was shoulder to shoulder with gamblers who, earlier in the night, had lost their paychecks or their winnings and were desperate to win them back. As the slot machines pinged and sang, crowds pressing against the craps tables shouted out their encouragement as a pair of dice danced across the green cloth.

At the Caribbean Stud table, J.D., a drink at his elbow and a cigarette in an ashtray, studied his hand. Three kings.

"Make it good, Charlie."

The dealer, with a sympathetic smile, gave a shrug and a nod toward the black box on the edge of the table. "It's up to the machine, J.D."

He looked toward the box that dealt out the cards, five to a hand. An emotionally detached machine that didn't give a damn if a man's entire livelihood rested on the fall of the cards.

J.D. tossed his kings facedown on the table. "Just qualify, for God's sake."

Charlie laughed, then flipped over the dealer's cards. Grimaced. "Dealer doesn't qualify."

The man sitting beside J.D. threw down his cards. "I'm outta here." He drunkenly stumbled off his stool, then wobbled his way toward the craps table.

As Charlie raked in the bets from the remaining six

men at the table, he gave J.D. a sympathetic look. "Cards suck tonight, buddy. Blackjack is hot."

J.D. glanced up at the progressive jackpot total. Five hundred thousand, the highest in the casino's history. All he needed was a royal flush. Hell, a straight flush would do. Ten percent of the progressive jackpot would be fifty thousand bucks.

He placed a dollar chip in the jackpot slot, followed by another ten dollar ante.

Charlie shook his head. "You're a glutton for punishment, Damascus."

"Begging for it apparently."

He looked toward a blond waitress wearing a form-fitting black dress and winked. Carla flashed him a smile and sidled up close, her perfume washing over him in a wave.

"We don't see you around here much these days, J.D. Don't break my heart and tell me you've got a girlfriend."

He grinned.

She moved closer, lowered her voice. "So why are you really here, Damascus? Tell me you're not harrassing Tyron again."

He shrugged. "I'm looking for Melissa Carmichael. Have you seen her?"

"Not in a couple of weeks."

"She mention anything to you about leaving New Orleans?"

"Melissa was always talking about getting out of the life. Then again, they all do."

"She mention it to Tyron? Maybe one of the other girls mentioned it to him?"

"Haven't heard any whispers about it. Why?"

"Can't find her."

She raised one eyebrow and smiled. "Honey, if you're after a little friendly companionship, you don't need to look up a hooker. I gave you my phone number already."

He grinned and placed his empty glass on her tray. "If you hear anything about Melissa, give me a call."

"Sure. On one condition. I dig up anything, you take me to dinner."

"You got it."

Carla smiled. "Another drink?"

"A double, and this time don't water it down."

She looked at his mouth, her lips curving. "Would we do something like that?"

He grinned and watched Carla walk away. The indecently short skirt nicely showed off her long, slender legs.

He thought about Holly.

As he smoked, his gaze searched the room, his mind still sifting through the events of the last couple of days. Tyra. Cherry. Now Melissa. All Tyron Johnson's girls—just like before.

He won the next eight hands. Nearly three thousand dollars worth of chips stacked neatly before him as his companion gamblers shouted him on and the pit boss began to make phone calls and security was forced to deliver more chips. Gamblers wandered from the nearby craps and blackjack tables and began to wager among themselves on how much longer J.D.'s streak of luck would continue. The waitresses swarmed around him like bees near a hive, plying him with doubles, brushing their bodies against him while their eyes danced in anticipation of healthy tips.

Just as J.D. had expected, Tyron made his entrance, followed by his entourage of beautiful women and body-guards. As usual, he looked like a Wall Street broker: Armani suit, dark tan that set off his sun-streaked blond hair, and ice blue eyes that skewered J.D. immediately.

J.D. was well aware that his presence in the Lucky Lady would eventually reach the sleazebag pimp. No way J.D. would ever have made it up to Johnson's penthouse—not with the goons who prowled the hallways to keep trouble from his door. It had only been a matter of time before J.D.'s sniffing around the casino asking questions would lure the creep out of his apartment.

Tyron's mouth curved even as his jaw muscles worked in anger as he moved toward J.D.

Charlie glanced toward Tyron, then cleared his throat. "Place your bet, Damascus."

"I'll sit this one out."

The waitresses scattered, as did the other gamblers, returning to their games at the craps and blackjack tables.

Tyron smiled, showing capped teeth that had cost him a small fortune. "I see you're still blowing your money, J.D."

"I see you're still cutting people's throats, Tyron."

Tyron took the chair next to his and reached into his suit coat pocket for a thin cigar. He used J.D.'s Bic to light it, eyes hard as he grinned. "You got me all wrong, J.D. I don't decapitate men's wives. I only fuck 'em."

"Are you saying you fucked my wife before you killed her?"

"Now wouldn't that just be icin' on the cake. How sweet would that be? Me makin' your pretty little wife pant and moan."

"I think she had more class than that."

"I doubt it. She married you, didn't she?"

J.D. reached for his drink. "Where is Melissa?"

Tyron looked away as he smoked, his jaw working again in anger. "I'd like to know that myself. Just like I'd like to know who the hell showed up for Melissa's john and shot the son of a bitch. Bad for business, know what I'm saying, J.D.? Melissa and I are going to have ourselves a talk when I find her."

"I've seen your kind of talk, Tyron. She's much too pretty to have her face cut up."

"Girls answer to the man. You know that." He put out his cigar in J.D.'s drink. "Now I'm gonna save you a lot of time, my friend. You stay away from my girls. I hear you've been knockin' on their doors and snoopin' round my business. I'm tellin' you one last time, and unless you've gone deaf, as well as dumb, you'll disappear. I find out you been walkin' my streets again thinking on diggin' up some shit on me, we're gonna have ourselves a chat. Up close and personal." He tossed a hundred dollar bill on the table. "Buy some flowers for your kids' graves, why don't you? From their Uncle Tyron. With love."

Holly awoke, startled, and sat up in bed. Sunlight flooded the room through the sliding glass doors as the rotating buzz fan on the nearby table did little more than disrupt the air immediately around it. Heat penetrated the apartment so her T-shirt and jeans clung to her with perspiration. The clock showed eleven-thirty. No sign of Damascus, no indication that he had come home after she had fallen into a fitful sleep.

Again, a banging on the door, then a rattle of a key in the lock.

The door opened suddenly and an immense, angry African American woman barged in, her hair in gray corn rows and massive silver hoop earrings dangling from her lobes. She stopped short upon seeing Holly.

"Where the hell is J.D.?" she said so loudly the startled cat scrambled under the coffee table and arched its back.

Groggy, Holly shook her head. "I don't know."

The woman stormed through the apartment, her weight shaking the floor as she moved into the bedroom, stopped, planted her hands on her hips, and muttered to herself.

"Who are you?" Holly asked. When the woman didn't respond, she raised her voice and repeated, "Excuse me? Who are you?"

She turned and speared Holly with a look. "I might ask you the same thing."

"A friend."

"Um hmm. I know your kinda friend."

"What's that supposed to mean?"

"You got no idea where that man is?"

"He never came home last night."

Shaking her head. "That ain't good. Not good at all. Lord, Lord, what am I gonna do with that man? He done missed two court appointments this mornin'."

"Once again, who are you?"

"May. I work for him."

Holly rose from the futon, rubbing her eyes.

May dropped into a chair that creaked with her weight. "He gone and done it now. Judge gonna have his butt on a plate." She watched as Holly scooped up Puddin' and moved to the kitchen, poured milk into the cat's bowl, then a glass for herself. "When did you last see him?"

"Two this morning."

"What? What did you say?"

The obvious occurred to Holly. May was deaf as a doorknob, or close to it. She returned to the living room and sat the glass on the coffee table. "Two this morning," she said more loudly, looking at the woman directly. "He left to . . . take care of some family issues."

"Beverly again?"

"Sort of."

May gave a disapproving grunt and shook her head.

Holly moved to the bedroom, to the desk, and picked up the DAMASCUS folder. The images within had roused memories and nightmares throughout the night. She carried it to May, watched the woman's face as she opened the folder.

"What happened?" Holly asked.

May shut the folder and stared at the wall. "This ain't good."

"Who killed his wife?"

"Same one who killed them hookers. Gonzalez. So the D.A. say, anyhow. J.D. don't believe it. Been eatin' him up these last four years. Chewed the heart right out of him."

Holly braced herself. "And the children?"

May's chin quivered. "Done killed them as well. Cut

their sweet throats. Lord, he loved them babies. They was his world."

Holly sank onto the futon. "Why? It doesn't make sense."

"Cops said Laura was just a victim of circumstance. At the wrong place at the wrong time. Found her body in Woldenberg Park. Said she was killed sometime after midnight."

"What was she doing at the park after midnight?"

May at last met Holly's eyes. "Don't know. J.D. was out of town. He speculates that she was taken there for the killing. You know, someplace public. He thinks that Tyron Johnson killed her and copycatted the murders." She watched Puddin' pad across the floor and jump into Holly's lap.

"May . . . are you aware that the killings have started again?"

Her brow furrowed. "Girl, what are you sayin'?"

Standing, the cat cradled in her arms, Holly walked to the front door and opened it. Heat radiated off the old brick street where tourists ambled along the sidewalks, sweating. "Figures that you wouldn't have heard about it," she said. "The cops will keep it quiet, considering the wrong man was executed for the previous murders. Two women have been killed recently. Same M.O. Slaughtered in their apartments. Another woman is missing. A friend of mine. Melissa Carmichael."

"Melissa? Ain't she one of J.D.'s clients?"

Holly nodded.

With a huff of exertion, May left the chair. The phone rang. May didn't wait for the answering machine, but lumbered across the room and snatched up the receiver. Holly watched her, hoping the caller was J.D. May met her eyes and shook her head, frowning as she spoke to the caller, then looked at Holly and mouthed: "You Holly Jones?"

Holly nodded.

May replied into the phone. "She's here. I'll tell her." She hung up the phone. "That was a Detective Chase. Said your suitcase was found. Got it down at the station."

"I need a ride."

May nodded. "Come on."

According to the testy, coffee-logged officer, Holly's luggage had been found near a Dumpster on Canal Street by a foot patrol cop. Her clothes were all there, but the money was gone. Figured. No sign of her car, of course. Figured.

As Holly took care of the necessary paperwork to retrieve her belongings, May waited in the car, continuing to call J.D.'s apartment—no answer—then the office—no answer. By the time Holly returned to the car, May's concern was mounting. Stuck in traffic, horns blaring and a rap station crashing from a boom box perched on the shoulder of a Hispanic teenage boy wearing a Grateful Dead T-shirt, she drummed her big fingers on the steering wheel and shook her head.

"This ain't good. He don't miss his court and client appointments unless he's on another one of his tears."

"Which are?"

"Self-destruction." She pursed her lips. "Catches up to

him now and again. Stands to reason if the killin's have
started again. Man got a lot of anger and grief bottled up
inside him. I swear he gonna explode one of these days.
I told him so, too. If his temper don't kill him, the damn
ulcers will." Her eyes widened and she pointed at the day-
timer on the dashboard. "Hospital. Get the number."

Holly located the number and read it off to May as she
punched the cell phone, then inquired if Damascus had
been admitted into emergency. Another dead end. No
sooner had she disconnected than the phone rang. May
answered and listened, her eyes rolling in exasperation.
She glanced at Holly and nodded.

"When did you pick him up? I been lookin' for that
man for the last four hours. Um hmm. Assault? On who?
Tyron Johnson. Lord have mercy. All right. I'm on my
way."

Damascus, smoking, sat on a bench beneath a
No Smoking sign as May stood between a pair of detectives, one of whom was talking with the D.A. on the
phone. Holly sat beside him, occasionally risking a
glimpse at his profile. Eyes bloodshot, face pale beneath
his dark beard stubble, he stared straight ahead. The cigarette between his fingers shook each time he took a drag.
Sweat rolled down his temples.

He had refused to speak to her so far. Aside from his
initial glance, which had spoken volumes, he had ignored
her.

Finally, May joined them. "They ain't gonna press

charges but Tyron intends to file a restrainin' order against you."

In response, he blew a thin stream of smoke through his lips.

May and Holly exchanged glances.

"Can you walk outta here," May asked, "or do I need to roll you out?"

He tossed the cigarette butt to the floor and crushed it beneath his shoe. "Anybody ever told you you've got a smart mouth?"

"You, every chance you get."

As he attempted to stand, Holly caught his arm. He yanked it away and moved toward the door, one hand pressed against his stomach. May's look of exasperation turned to concern, and she shook her head, then followed, Holly trailing behind, wondering just how she was going to face this man now that she knew the entire truth about his life.

Now what? If she was smart, she would take her suitcase from May's car, walk off down the street, and not look back. She hadn't come here to get involved with a man who, as May described, was bent on self-destruction.

She had returned to New Orleans to find her friend, to remove her, once and for all, from the life. Before she ended up like Tyra and Cherry, slaughtered by a soulless monster who, like a bad dream come to life, had roused from hibernation to feed again on the helpless. Holly wanted to help Melissa get out before Tyron's power and control could destroy what little hope and spirit Melissa had left.

May paused and looked back. "You comin'?"

She ran her hot palms up and down the butt of her jeans. "Sure," she finally said. "Sure."

She sat in the backseat behind J.D. during the ride back to his apartment. He continued to say nothing, head rested back against the seat, his eyes closed as May expounded on the consequences of his behavior.

"Judge is pissed at you. I do mean pissed. Said he was gonna report your breach of ethics to the court and your clients to the Committee of Professional Conduct and get your ass disbarred. Then what you gonna do? What am I gonna do, for that matter? You go gettin' disbarred and I'm outta damn job. Just who the hell is gonna hire a sixty-year-old black woman who's deaf? And what you think you're doin' goin' up against Tyron? That man is mean as a snake and you go threatenin' to kill him? That ain't good, J.D. You look like shit. Do you need a doctor? You bleedin' again?"

Raking one hand through his disheveled hair, he groaned and sank more deeply into the car seat. "Christ," he finally said, his voice a hoarse whisper. "You're shouting again, May."

"Obviously I ain't shoutin' loud enough 'cause I don't think you're hearin' me real good."

"I hear you, for God's sake. People in Montana can probably hear you."

"When's the last time you put anything in your stomach?"

He sighed. "I don't remember."

"You got food in your pantry or am I gonna have to go shoppin' for you again?"

"Somebody just shoot me and put me out of my misery."

"Tyron is gonna shoot you if you ain't careful."

"Not if I shoot him first."

"And end up in prison? What good is that gonna do you?"

"Enormous good, I assure you."

"Um hmm. In prison with all them drug dealers and murderers you put away. Wouldn't they just smack their lips to see you comin'? You wouldn't last a week 'fore somebody take you out with a shank."

"You think too much, May."

"One of us got to think, and lately I ain't seen you doin' much of it."

She pulled the car over to the curb outside J.D.'s apartment. "You gonna talk to the judge and try to calm him down or do I need to?"

"Be my guest. He likes you."

As J.D. left the car, May looked around at Holly. "Keep an eye on him. He's sick. If he starts throwin' up blood, get him to the hospital and call me."

Holly grimaced. "Blood?"

"Got him a bad, bad ulcer. I'd be surprised if he got any linin' left in his stomach at all. Put him to bed and feed him some Cream of Wheat. I bought him some last week. And ice cream. Puts the fire out."

Holly nodded and exited the car, dragging her suitcase after her.

May rolled down her window and shouted at J.D. as he mounted the steps to his apartment. "Go to bed, do you hear me? I'm cancelin' your appointments for the next two days. Make him go to bed," she directed Holly, who nodded and lugged the suitcase onto the sidewalk.

As May merged her car into the traffic, Holly hauled her suitcase up the steps and into the apartment where she hesitated on the threshold, watching J.D. pick the Damascus folder up from the coffee table and stare at it before turning his red-rimmed eyes on her. Again, he said nothing. Just turned away and entered the bedroom. She heard him slap the folder onto the desk.

Taking a deep breath, she stepped into the apartment and closed the door. As she sat the suitcase down, Puddin' slinked from under a chair and made a mad dash across the floor and began to weave around her legs.

Every instinct in her warned that she should get the hell out while the getting was good. Whatever philanthropy Damascus had earlier shown her had changed into a barely contained disgust. What had changed since he'd left her at two that morning with a smile of gratitude over her treatment of his nephew? Granted, hangovers had a way of corrupting personality. But there was more going on here than that. There was a mammoth-sized difference between a fuzzy brain and the anger she could feel vibrating the stuffy, hot air.

Holly cleared her throat, then shouted, "Do you want Cream of Wheat first or ice cream?"

Nothing.

Cautious, she moved to the bedroom door. Damascus stood at his desk, the file open. His shirt was soaked with sweat.

"I'm sorry about your family," she offered softly. "It's . . . horrible. You have every right to be angry."

Finally, he turned. His eyes were hard and glassy. "I wonder," he sneered, "how a woman like you could fuck for a man like Tyron Johnson."

Slammed by the viciousness of his words, by the look in his eyes, she took a step back. Her face burned.

He moved toward her, his hands fisted.

She backed into the living room, her gaze locked on his. She wanted to run, but she had never been one to back down easily from an unsettling situation. Only twice in her life had she ever fled—once from a butcher who always smelled like blood, the next time from New Orleans. She had run both times in fear for her life.

She was in no danger now. As furious as he was, Damascus wouldn't hurt her. Not physically. But still, in that moment, she wanted to escape from the pain in his eyes that unnerved her as much as his insults. The unsettling hurt squeezed her heart, while his look of disgust invited all her old self-loathing. Watching the revulsion glittering in his red eyes, Holly was suddenly a hooker again. All the shame and humiliation she had attempted to sweat out of her system these last few years boiled up inside her.

She set her heels and stopped retreating. Damascus moved close and ran one finger along the curve of her cheek, his mouth forming a smile that made her ache to claw his face.

"So tell me, Miss Jones, what do you charge for a blow job?"

"More than you can afford, Damascus," she replied, hating the trembling of her voice and the sting of tears rising to her eyes.

"You owe me three hundred bucks. If you get down on your knees right now, we'll call it even."

She slapped him hard enough to drive him backward. Enough to make fire explode on her palm. Enough to cause a small red bud of blood to bloom at the corner of his lips. Shock flashed across his face, then fury. Still, she didn't back down. She advanced on him, her hands in shaking knots, preparing to strike him again with fresh ferocity.

"There isn't enough money in this world to make me go down on you. You want the sordid details? Okay. I walked the streets for a while until Tyron set me up in an apartment for his special clients who had more money than brains. Clients who demanded a higher class of whore. The irony was the big shots with their million-dollar bank accounts were just as pitifully appalling as a crack head derelict who simply needed someone to comfort him through his shakes."

Holly turned away, swept the cat off the futon, and moved to the door. She stopped, looked back into his dark eyes, and drew in a shallow breath. "I'm sorry for you. Not just for what happened to your family, but your lack of humanity. For a while, I actually believed you had a spark of caring for someone other than yourself."

sore. In and out of sleep, he was bombarded with images: the autopsy photos of his wife; the detailed report of her murderer's meticulous evisceration; the identically mutilated bodies of Tyra Smith and Cherry Brown.

When the images of his wife's autopsy photos weren't crashing in upon him, causing him to awake suddenly with his body shaking uncontrollably, Holly Jones wormed her way into his thoughts, gnawing at his conscience.

Why the hell should he give a damn that she had worked for Tyron? Not simply give a damn, but be infuriated enough to verbally assault her, to smear her past into her face and gloat over her look of embarrassment and pain?

Why should this particular woman be any different from the others he came face-to-face with every day? So what that she was beautiful enough to stop traffic. Sure, he wouldn't have minded spending a few hours indulging his more base machismo fantasies between her long legs. It was the idea that Tyron Johnson had had her that had set something off in him. As if the son of a bitch had, once again, trespassed into J.D.'s personal and private life. Stupid. Holly Jones was nothing to him. A stranger with pretty eyes and an attitude that set his teeth on edge.

There were twenty calls on his message machine. Six from Beverly and three from a very surly Patrick wanting to know why J.D. had missed his soccer game the night before. Two from his irate landlord threatening to evict him from his office space. One call from his mother, something about a family dinner party she would like him to attend. A few messages from angry clients he had left high and dry in court. Nothing from Holly. What did he expect? She had every right to hate his guts.

After another force-feeding of Cream of Wheat, followed by a generous portion of Rocky Road ice cream
and three Tums, Damascus showered, shaved, and rummaged through the clothes Holly had neatly folded. He
dressed himself in jeans and a chambray shirt, rolling the
sleeves up his forearms. Leaving the apartment, he
glanced back at the bowl of water Holly had put down
for the cat.

After a twenty-minute walk in the suffocating humidity,
Damascus found his car where he had parked it in the
casino's remote lot and headed for the police station. The
deejay on the local radio station warned his listeners of a
brewing hurricane that was barreling its way up the Gulf,
straight for New Orleans. Hurricane Holly, the storm had
been named. The irony of it might have made J.D. laugh
had it not made his stomach hurt.

Travis Killroy, the chief of police, was a lean, sinewy
man with hard, deep-set eyes the color of slate, and a
complexion riddled by old acne scars. One arm in a sling,
he slouched at his desk, which was crowded with untidy
stacks of files, reports, and a scattering of plastic foam
cups partially filled with cold black coffee. A cigarette
dangled from the corner of his mouth, which clamped
with irritation as J.D. entered his office without knocking.

"What the fuck do you want?" he snarled at J.D. behind
a stream of cigarette smoke.

J.D. kicked the door closed. "What do you think I
want?"

Killroy sank back in the chair, his eyes narrowed. "I
got nothing to say to you, Damascus."

Bracing both hands on the desk, J.D. leaned toward the chief, who was once his friend, back when they shared the desire to protect the city from the scumbags of the world. "Think again, Travis. Unless you want me to go public with your recent sick forays into perversion, you'll spill your guts over what you know about the murders of Tyra Smith and Cherry Brown."

"You into blackmail now?"

"Why not?"

Killroy thumped cigarette ashes into a coffee cup. "We got ourselves a copycat."

"If you really believed that, this department wouldn't be burying these cases from the public."

"I don't intend on setting off hysteria again in this city."

"You and Jerry Costos know your asses are in a crack, Travis. Gonzalez didn't kill those hookers or my family, and now you know it. You've always known it, but you cared more for your own fucking job than you did for taking the time to find out the truth."

Killroy rose from his chair, planted one hand on the desk, and thrust his face into J.D.'s. "Then tell me why the killings suddenly stopped after we arrested Gonzalez."

"Maybe he hotfooted it out of state. Or maybe he's playing a game with you. Don't you find it a touch ironic that Tyra was murdered around the same time that Gonzalez was executed? The sick son of a bitch is thumbing his nose at you."

Killroy slammed his fist against the desk hard enough to cause a cup to tip over, spilling coffee to the floor. The dents in his face turned deep purple. "We had DNA evidence to link Gonzalez to that hooker."

"One hooker."

"He was seen with two other victims before they were killed."

"Circumstantial."

"His semen in her wasn't circumstantial."

"You tell me why he would have left that kind of evidence inside her when he was so damn meticulous with the others. It doesn't fit, Travis. He didn't have intercourse with the other victims before he killed them."

"Well, maybe this particular piece of ass turned him on."

"Christ. You've turned into a dick."

Killroy kicked his desk, then dropped again into his chair. He took a deep, steadying breath, and averted his eyes. "He had a sheet of priors as long as my leg. Solicitation. Battery. Shit, the creep was on probation for child molestation."

"And he was convenient."

Raking one hand through his thinning, ginger-colored hair, Killroy sighed. His gaze, less angry and more sympathetic, swung back to J.D.'s. "I know what you're thinking. Hell, we all know what you're thinking. But Tyron Johnson had an alibi during the times of the murders. Specifically your family's murders."

"Marcus DiAngelo." J.D. gave a dry laugh. "As if anyone with intelligence would believe that bastard."

"Look. You got every right to hate that scumbag. He's trash. Bad news. But for a minute, just for a minute, think with your head and not with your heart. You once had the best damn instincts of any prosecutor in this state. Hell, in the entire country. But you've allowed your perspective to become clouded by your grief and hate for Johnson."

Killroy tapped his temple with one finger. "Think like the brilliant attorney you once were and less like a man who was forced to bury his wife and kids. If you can do that, you'll understand why Costos did what he did."

More quietly, he added, "Pull it together, pal. You're losing it. This shit is gonna kill you if you don't."

Shoving away from the desk, his gaze still locked on Killroy's, J.D. shook his head. "I recall a time when our families got together for Sunday picnics. While Laura and Mary Ann pushed the kids on swings, you and I would share our ideals of justice and bringing the criminal element in this city to its knees. So what the hell happened to you? You're consorting with hookers and turning a blind eye to the truth."

J.D. turned for the door.

"As a friend I'm advising you, Damascus. Stay out of this. And stay the hell away from Johnson."

J.D. looked back, into the eyes of a man he once would have trusted with his life. "You're no friend of mine, Killroy. Not anymore."

The approaching hurricane has turned the night air dense, the clouds scuttling over the moon straight above. It peeks out at him occasionally, a pale, pockmarked face that appears to wink and smile. He likes the moon. It fills him with power. Someday, if ever NASA allows a civilian to buy a place on a rocket ship, he is going to go there. He imagines himself standing on the barren landscape, waving back at Mother Earth. He will feel like God. More than he already does.

Thanks to the impending storm—three days out, according to the storm trackers—the tourists have vacated the city in droves. Bumper-to-bumper, horns blowing as they move north up Interstate 10. Running like cowards. Unlike him, they can't appreciate the dynamics of such intense and incredible power as the storm will provide. Already he can feel it on his skin, the ozone titillating his nerve endings like an aphrodisiac. He becomes one with the electricity, floating along, through the shadows, humming to himself.

He had not planned to kill again for a while. But the tall blonde intrigues him. He has followed her since midnight, from street to street, watching her pause only briefly to speak with other whores. They don't know her. He can tell by the way they greet her, then watch her as she walks away. She's new to the district.

He lets her round a corner, disappearing from the streetlight, then counts to twenty. Slowly. Holding his breath as he does so, his eyes closed. He can hold his breath for as long as two minutes. He has trained himself to do so. Control over a person's own body is imperative. One never knows when the body will be called upon to do something miraculous. Godlike.

Twenty. Releasing his breath, he shifts the pack on his back and pushes his bike away from the curb. He glides through the shadows like a hawk, the wind in his face. The whores on the street corner call to him, but he ignores them. They aren't the kind of prey that interests him at that moment. Hunkering low over the handlebars, he *streaks around the corner, his mental wings outstretched, soaring. The tires hum upon the brick pavement.*

As he passes beneath a streetlight, his shadow looms beside him, monstrous. Back into the dark, he slows down until he sees the blonde ahead. He drifts into an alley and parks behind a Dumpster, watching as she lights a cigarette.

A car creeps toward her. The window rolls down. She takes a step back and shakes her head. The driver pushes and she turns away and continues walking. The car follows and he can hear the man's voice in an insulting tone as he waves money at her. She says something back, then tosses her cigarette through the open window, into his lap. The car tires squeal on the pavement as the driver takes off, shouting something foul at her. She shoots him the finger.

His heart pounds. His scalp sweats. This one isn't easily intimidated. It might take special measures to frighten her. She might even fight him. Ah, but the ultimate outcome would be all the sweeter. The satisfaction of breaking her mentally all the more exhilarating. She might prove to be more gratifying than Melissa, who is beginning to bore him. At first, her fear had exhilarated him, but over the past few days she has become as emotionless as a storefront dummy, staring at him with lifeless—fearless—eyes. She didn't so much as flinch when he waved a knife beneath her nose and told her in detail what he would eventually do to her.

He waits as the blonde disappears through the darkness, then pushes off on the bike, turning his face into the sudden blast of electric wind that barrels down the street, kicking up litter so it swirls like dancing aberrations in the air.

The unexpected current of hot wind tunneling down the narrow street brought Holly to a stop. She ducked her head against the sting of driving grit and the swirl of paper scraps. The wind felt hot and smelled rank with the stink of river mud.

She waited until the gust had passed, then moved on along the route that she remembered too well. She would never forget it. It had all come rushing back to her like a bad dream, infusing her with a filth that would later send her to the shower to attempt to scrub away the sordid memories. To no avail, of course. She could scour her flesh down to the bone, but there would never be a way to cleanse the past from her brain. Branson, and the few places she had settled in those years after she had escaped New Orleans, had only brought her brief emotional respite. A shrink might call it denial. And he would be right.

There was no way of denying her past now. Funny how all the old instincts came rushing back. The way of walking and talking. It all came disconcertingly naturally, which was a good thing at the moment, she supposed. If she was going to find out any information about Melissa from the girls, she would have to become one of them again. They wouldn't trust her otherwise.

Still, the charade had gotten her nowhere—yet. She had been fortunate so far that she had avoided running into anyone who might have recognized her from the past. All new girls. Most of them very young. All hardened. And fearful. She had recognized it in their eyes when speaking of Melissa. No, no one had seen her in days. Holly had known better than to question whether Melissa might have mentioned leaving town. A hooker working for Tyron Johnson didn't advertise to others her plans to ditch Tyron. Too many of his girls, looking for a way to win points with him and a few extra dollars, would gladly snitch on their best friend.

Holly lit a fresh cigarette and stood for a moment, looking up at the sky where clouds raced across the moon's face, white light briefly dappling the brick street, glistening phosphorescently upon the hoods of parked cars.

Due to the approaching storms, the streets were virtually empty. Tyron would be pissed. Ninety percent of his take was due to tourists, and without the tourist trade, the girls would be hard-pressed to meet their nightly quotas of johns. If the hurricane did slam New Orleans, he would force them to move into cities farther north for a while. Baton Rouge and Shreveport, where business was getting better since the influx of casinos such as the Horseshoe and Harrah's enticed high rollers away from Vegas.

Silence pressed down on her, all the more intense because it lacked the presence of the usual traffic hum or the distant wail of music from Bourbon Street. It was as suffocating as the humidity, which made her feel as if each breath was inhaled through a damp, wool blanket.

A sound came from behind her, and she turned, catching a glimpse of movement at the end of the street. No car. The brief flash of moonlight somehow contorted the shape of the image in the distance so she was forced to squint to make out that it was a biker, his feet planted on the street as he straddled the ten-speed and watched her.

A college brat, no doubt. His old man's money burning a hole in his pocket. As she watched, he turned the bike away, sailed down the street in the opposite direction, took a right at the corner, and disappeared.

Releasing her breath, Holly flipped the butt of her cigarette into a drain and continued walking. Her feet hurt like hell and she looked forward to peeling herself out of the skintight, indecently short dress she had taken from Melissa's closet. She no longer felt comfortable in the revealing clothes. Not that she ever had, but she could hardly pass as one of the girls dressed in her own garb, which made her look more like a schoolteacher.

Another clue that Melissa hadn't simply walked away from the life: Her clothes were still in the apartment. Then again, had she chosen to escape Tyron Johnson, she could have left behind any and all reminders of the life, as well as leaving behind her personal items to throw him off for a few days. It was a trick the girls often used when they wanted to buy enough time to get clear of his far-reaching tentacles. God, she prayed that was the case this time, but the fear that continued to squirm in her stomach refuted that hope.

Too quickly, the moon disappeared behind a bank of clouds that bathed the street in shadows. She was forced to carefully watch her footing, her spike heels catching on the occasional crack in the sidewalk. She glanced up briefly as, engine purring, tires whispering, a car crept by her, the indistinguishable features of a man peering out at her. She looked away quickly, averting her eyes and keeping her head down, an indication to the potential john that she wasn't looking for business. The car moved on, taillights like red demon eyes winking back at her.

When she looked up again, the biker was back, ahead of her, just far enough from the intersection that the streetlight only backlit his form, one foot braced on the street, the other still resting on the bike pedal. A sluice of uneasiness flashed through her. It was almost as if the creep was stalking her, playing games. Thank God she was nearly home.

Reaching the alley leading to the courtyard of Melissa's apartment, Holly slipped her shoes off and picked up her pace. The bricks felt cool and damp and she made a wide arc around a scattering of broken glass.

She knew without looking that he was behind her. She felt him. Glancing over her shoulder, she saw him parked at the end of the alley. A cat toying with a mouse. Instinctively, her hand went to her purse. The weight and feel of the gun there reassured her, yet when she reached the wrought iron steps, she took them two at a time, the squeak of the rusty iron sounding extremely loud in the quiet. By the time she reached the door, she had the keys in her hand and fumbled them into the lock as she continued to glance down at the shadowed courtyard, expecting to see the biker appear at any time.

Slamming the door behind her, she slid the bolt into place, lay her head against the door, and tried to breathe evenly, her heart exploding in her ears and her body shaking. Puddin' ran to greet her and slinked round and round her ankles while she continued to listen, eyes closed, for the sound of the grating steps outside the apartment.

Eternal minutes ticked by. Nothing.

At long last, she managed to breathe evenly. She was

being paranoid. The biker was nothing more than some Tulane student trying to work up his courage to approach her.

She had every right to feel paranoid, of course. Not only was there a killer at large, but she had been forced, when leaving Damascus's apartment, to resort to moving into Melissa's place. What else was she to do? With no money, she couldn't check into a hotel. She was risking Tyron showing up, or one of his goons, to check on Melissa. But again, what choice did she have? She wasn't about to go back to Damascus. Not after he'd rubbed her past in her face with such blatant disgust.

At the memory of his verbal assault, anger sluiced through her. She scooped up the cat, tossed her shoes to the floor, and turned for the kitchen. She heard it then, the squeak of the flimsy steps, and she froze, cold dread working up her spine. Slowly, allowing the cat to slide from her arms, she turned back to the door and withdrew the gun from her purse. Staring at the doorknob, barely breathing, her senses expanding to the point of pain, she waited.

A knock.

She swallowed and whispered, "Go away."

Louder, more insistent this time, the knock reverberated through the room. She lifted the gun and pointed it at the door. "Go away," she said more loudly, the tone surprisingly strong and steady.

"Holly? It's Damascus. Open the damn door."

She closed her eyes, relief flooding her. Not just relief, she realized as she lowered the gun that felt as heavy as an elephant in that moment. A thrill sang inside her as she moved unsteadily to unbolt the door. Stepping back, allowing the door to swing open, she stared up into J.D.'s eyes.

He looked down at the gun. "Women with guns turn me on, FYI."

"I'm not amused, Damascus. You scared the hell out of me."

As he stepped into the room, she risked a look down into the dark courtyard.

He glanced at her. "Looking for someone?"

She closed the door and relocked it before shooting him an annoyed look. He was dressed in faded jeans and a gold and black Saints T-shirt. No shoulder-holstered gun tonight unless he'd somehow stuffed it into his jeans, which was doubtful considering how tightly they fit him, showing off every hint of his masculinity. "I was followed, for your information."

The condescending smirk returned to his lips as he assessed her. "I'm not surprised. I like the blond wig, but I prefer your own."

The wig. She had totally forgotten about it. As she yanked it off, her own dark hair fell in a wave over her shoulder. She tossed the blond mop onto the bed.

"So where did you get that?" Damascus grinned. "Frederick's of Hollywood?"

"Right. Along with my crotchless, edible panties, thank you very much."

"Hey, I didn't come here to fight with you again."

"Just insult me."

"I wasn't aware that old Frederick was insulting."

"He's not. It's your tone I find insulting."

She returned the gun to her purse, shoved it under the bed, then sat in a chair and crossed her legs. The short dress barely covered her crotch. She smiled at him spitefully. "If you came for that blow job, you're out of luck, J.D. I'm off-duty."

He sat on the bed. Puddin' jumped in his lap. As Damascus proceeded to scratch the purring cat between the ears, he looked Holly up and down, his expression dark, his eyes slightly narrowed.

"What are you doing here, Holly?"

"What does it look like I'm doing?"

"You look like a tramp."

"FYI, I am a tramp, or so you so blatantly reminded me three nights ago."

"I'm sorry."

She looked away from his eyes.

"What you did with or for Tyron is no business of mine. I don't want what I said to—"

"Undermine my resolution to put the life behind me?" She flashed him an incinerating glance, refusing to acknowledge the emotion crawling up her throat. "You must really value your opinion, Damascus. I don't care what you think about me. Now what are you doing here, really?"

He dragged one hand back through his hair and looked around the room. "Hell, I don't know. I told myself that I was going to run to the store and somehow I ended up here. Figured this is where I would find you. I take it you haven't found Melissa."

"What do you think?"

"I think your being here is stupid. I think your walking

those streets looking for her is even dumber. There's a murderer out there, Holly—"

"Just what am I supposed to do, Damascus? Forget my best friend is missing and go back to Branson?" She laughed. "I couldn't do that even if I wanted to. I've barely got enough cash in my wallet to buy a hamburger, much less the gas to get me home."

She pushed up from the chair and began to pace. "God, I had almost forgotten what it's like to be so damn desperate. Walking those streets, it all came rushing back to me, how easy it would be to earn a quick fifty bucks. Sell out for a little security."

She turned on Damascus and narrowed her eyes. "It's a sorry thing when the greatest achievement of your life is just how good an orgasm you can supply a john."

He looked away, color staining his face.

"What's wrong? Don't tell me you haven't come across one of your hooker clients that you wouldn't mind spending a little quality time with. Don't tell me you haven't looked at me since figuring out my past and not toyed with the idea of laying me. Maybe that's why you're really here. You're less concerned about my welfare than you are curious about whether I'm a good lay or not."

"The thought has crossed my mind, but that's not why I'm here."

"No? Maybe you're just fooling yourself."

She approached him, her gaze holding his, and moved between his spread knees, her thighs nestled between his, the rough material of his jeans brushing her flesh.

Running one finger along the line of his jaw, she whispered, "Maybe you told yourself that you were lonely in that hot, cramped apartment. Feeling sorry for yourself over the loss of your family. Maybe you were thinking about Beverly, tempted to invite her over to discuss Patrick, in the back of your mind thinking this might be the one time you conveniently let your resistance slip. Or maybe you needed a diversion from your hatred for Tyron."

She forced herself to smile, to ignore the sensation of pleasure she experienced over the touch of her finger on his stubbled jaw. "There are a great many reasons why a man searches out the company of a hooker, Damascus. Mostly self-denial. They want to take a walk on the dark side and need to justify their behavior to themselves."

She teased his ear with her fingertip, and he grinned. "You're toying with me, Holly. Besides . . ."—he eased his hand up the inside of her thigh—"that pin knife you have strapped to your leg could do a lot of damage." His fingers brushed the thin scabbard on her leg as his grin widened. "Then again, maybe you're more in the mood to get laid than you are to cut off my privates."

He cupped her in his palm, the touch ricocheting through her so fiercely she caught her breath. She felt like warm butter melting into his hand. She couldn't move, or breathe, as she looked down into his eyes, which were as hypnotizing as they were taunting.

"I thought so." His finger nudged aside the crotch of her panties and slid between her moist flesh, stroking gently, until her eyes fluttered closed. The heat brought a rise of sweat to her brow. "When is the last time a man gave *you* pleasure, Holly? Has a man ever given you pleasure? I doubt it. You faked it. That was part of your job, wasn't it? To make your john feel as if he was the best stud to walk the earth."

He swirled his finger inside her and she felt her body clench in response. She felt her breath catch and a groan work up her throat. The pressure between her legs mounted, the heat unbearably painful. She hated him for it, yet she could no more pull away from his hand and what it was doing to her than she could look away from his eyes, which were now a mixture of grief and anger and desire. They burned with it, and she realized in that instant just how badly she wanted him—had wanted him since his gaze had raked her up and down in her jail cell, filling her with a vulnerability that was as foreign to her as what he was doing to her body.

He moved so quickly she had no time to react. His hands grabbed her shoulders and he spun her down onto the bed, his body sliding over hers as his knees shoved apart her legs, forcing her dress up around her hips as he pressed the hard ridge of his penis against her. With his hands pinning her wrists to the bed, his weight sinking her into the mattress, he stared at her through strands of hair that had fallen over his brow.

"Tell me you want it, Holly," he said through his teeth. "Admit it and let's get this game-playing bullshit out of the way."

She turned her face away and closed her eyes.

His lips brushed her cheek. His tongue flirted with her ear, warm breath assaulting her gloriously, sending shivers throughout her. She arched her body against his, the rough zipper of his taut jeans against her as exciting as his warm tongue toying with her ear, enticing her to turn her head and part her lips, inviting him in.

Their tongues danced together before he smothered her mouth with his, an ungentle invasion as his lower body rocked and rubbed her, the friction as sensually erotic as what his tongue was doing inside her, deep thrusts, in and out, hot and wet, driving to oblivion whatever resistance she clung to.

His hands riveted her wrists to the bed, the dull ache of his grip as tantalizing as the pressure of his erection against her. A sense of helplessness sluiced through her—shockingly intoxicating, overwhelmingly intense. Her legs spread wider, curled over his buttocks. Then one hand released her, slid between their bodies, and plunged roughly into her panties, his fingers sliding between her slick cleft and entering with a forcefulness that made her whimper, not with pain but with a need so immense she buried her hand in his thick hair so she could kiss him with equal abandon.

Suddenly, he froze. Slowly lifted his head. Something in his eyes gave a warning that made her forget to breathe.

"Quiet," he whispered, his breathing heavy as he eased his hand from her body and shifted his weight from hers.

She heard it then, the creak of the stairs outside the door, a scraping of keys in the lock. Her eyes widened. "Melissa?" she whispered.

"Maybe," he replied softly as he slid from the bed, dragging her up with him. "I doubt it." He shoved her toward the kitchen. "Hide."

"But—"

"I said to hide, dammit."

She ran to the kitchen, nearly tripping over Puddin',
swung open the pantry door, then shoved aside a latch
hidden behind a two-pound can of string beans. The ob-
scured portal popped open and she slid into the black,
musty space, which was hardly big enough for her to fit
in, and pulled the door closed after her. All the girls had
a "panic room," a place to escape to if things turned bad
with a john. She and Melissa had used this one more than
she cared to remember. Now, however, as she listened to
the muffled voices, she felt locked in a coffin, unable to
find a breath in the darkness.

There were men. Several of them. Voices ugly. Dear
God. Tyron. No, no, it wasn't Tyron. She would recognize
his voice anywhere. His goons, perhaps. And they were
angry. They would be, finding Damascus there. They
would wonder why—

A crash. Scuffling.

Sudden silence. Her eyes closed, she listened to the
frantic pounding of her heart, her sense of suffocation
growing. The footsteps advanced, pausing at the kitchen
threshold. She waited for Damascus to call out. He didn't.
The footsteps came closer, hesitating, the soles of shoes
scraping slightly on the linoleum. As they retreated,
Holly's knees became weak. Where was Damascus?

Voices again. "No one here."

Slowly, her back against the wall, she slid to the floor,
her knees pressed against her breasts. She thought she
heard the front door close. But it might be a trick. An
attempt to lure her out. Where was Damascus?

She eased open the door. It creaked and her breath
caught, her senses excruciatingly expanded so even the

rush of fresh air felt like an assault. Cautious, she stepped from the pantry, her clothes soaked by sweat, her ears straining for any sound amid the odd, disquieting silence.

Carefully, on tiptoes, she moved toward the living room, stopping short at the sight: the chair and coffee table had been tipped over, and candles and picture frames were scattered and shattered on the floor. No Damascus. Oh God.

She went to the window and peered through the curtains to the courtyard below. Nothing. Her hands shaking badly, she flung open the door and ran out onto the landing. Faces looked out at her from the surrounding apartment windows, then disappeared just as quickly, unwilling to get involved in whatever crime had transpired. Swiftly, she descended the old stairs, feeling them tremble beneath her hurried footsteps. She ran in bare feet over the weed-infested courtyard to the alley leading to the street and froze.

Damascus sat on his heels in the dark, his back against the wall, his hands gripping his belly and his face bloodied. As she fell to her knees beside him, taking his face in her hands, she heard herself cry, "Please . . . someone call nine-one-one!"

9

Even if she hadn't recognized Damascus's mother from the society pages of the paper, Holly would have known her immediately.

A distinguished lady in her seventies, Helen Damascus had the look of a woman years younger, thanks to bone structure that had once made her one of the most beautiful women in New Orleans. She carried herself with a regalness that would rival royalty. Even at three in the morning, she was perfectly dressed, hair and makeup in place, her entire demeanor impeccable. The only chink in her composure was the slight trembling of her diamond-laden fingers as she shook Holly's hand, her gaze locked on J.D.'s face.

"The investigators tell me you can't identify the men who did this," she said softly, moving to her son's side and taking his hand.

"I'm sorry. No."

Her gray eyes looked into Holly's and regarded her
with an intensity that made her face burn. Of course, Helen was well aware of the circumstances of her son's beating. Where he had been and why. No doubt she suspected
Holly was a hooker, but still, she didn't show it.

"The doctors say he hasn't regained consciousness.
That he has a concussion." She gripped his hand more
tightly as she regarded her son's beaten face. There were
stitches over his eyebrow and beneath his chin. One eye
was black and swollen. "My precious boy," she whispered, her voice shaking. "He's gone through so much.
Now this. It just isn't fair."

Holly slipped one arm around Helen's shoulders. "He's
going to be fine. We have to believe that."

"Yes. Of course we do. I just worry. . . . He has to want
to pull out of this, doesn't he? Sometimes I believe . . ."
She shook her head and took a deep breath. "Since he lost
his family there have been times when I've feared he simply didn't want to go on."

"But he did, and he will. You mustn't give up hope,
Mrs. Damascus. The doctors have assured me this is not
life threatening."

"Helen!"

Beverly Damascus rushed into the room, followed by
Patrick, who immediately skewered Holly with a look that
fully reflected his thoughts over finding her there. As Beverly took her mother-in-law into her arms, holding her
tightly, she focused on Holly so fiercely that Holly backed
away into the small cubicle's corner, shut out of the family unit so suddenly a door might as well have been
slammed in her face.

Beverly then turned to J.D., tears rising. "He's not dying. Tell me he's not dying."

Holly moved toward the door.

"Miss Jones," Helen said. "Please. Don't go."

"I should leave. Really." She forced a smile. "You're family, and—"

"I'd like you to stay," Helen said, her eyes meeting Beverly's annoyed gaze. "She's a friend of John's. She should be here."

"A client, unless that's changed in the last few days."

"Friend or client," Helen declared with a tone of authority, "she's been very kind and supportive. I want her here."

"I won't be far." Holly offered Helen a grateful smile, then moved into the hall where she watched through the plateglass window as Beverly took J.D.'s hand and gripped it to her breast. Threads of conversation drifted to her.

"Is his father coming?" Beverly asked.

"I'm afraid not. What about Eric?"

"He's with the senator. A late night meeting. I put in a call. He'll be here momentarily. What is that woman doing here, Helen?"

Holly moved away, down the hall to the refreshment room where she poured a cup of coffee. Closing her eyes, she listened to the nurses chatter and the occasional bark of an agitated doctor. Sirens screamed in the distance. Somewhere a Detective Mallory was lurking, waiting for Damascus to regain consciousness. He had grilled her for an hour over the particulars of the beating, not fully believing that she had no clue as to who might have beaten

Damascus and why, though she had been frank enough to give him her opinion.

The adrenaline that had pumped through her the last couple of hours left in a rush. She shook with exhaustion and fresh fear. Not just fear, but remorse. John had been at the wrong place at the wrong time because of her. While Tyron had not been among the bullies who had beat him, she suspected that he had had something to do with it. Tyron was always tied to trouble in the district, one way or another. Perhaps he believed that J.D. knew something about Melissa's whereabouts. Or perhaps they had simply beat the hell out of him for sport. Regardless, if she wasn't such a coward she would do the world a favor and march over to his penthouse and put a bullet between his eyes.

"Why don't you leave my uncle alone?"

She jumped and turned at the sound of Patrick's voice. He stood in the doorway, face smoldering and hands jammed into the pockets of his baggy jeans.

"Just go away or I'll make you regret it."

"Enough, Patrick." Helen moved up beside her grandson, putting a firm hand on his shoulder. "While your parents tolerate such disrespect, I don't. Now apologize to Miss Jones."

He ducked his head and shuffled his feet.

"Now, Patrick. I'm not too old or you too big to put you across my knee and blister your butt."

"Sorry," he mumbled, then turned on his sneaker heels and stalked away.

Helen watched him go, her lips pressed, then turned back to Holly. "I apologize for my grandson. My only excuse is his parents have spoiled him rotten."

"He cares for his uncle very much."

"He's desperate for a father figure, I'm afraid. Alas, Eric's obsession with his job has left his son feeling neglected. Not to mention his wife," she added with a lift of one eyebrow. "I fear they've both become too dependent on John." She poured herself a coffee. "The companionship was good for John, for a while. It kept his mind occupied. I was grateful for it. But it's time that he get on with his life, and the fewer complications the better."

Holly sipped her coffee, then asked, "Do you consider me a complication, Mrs. Damascus?"

"Quite the contrary, my dear. I care only for John's happiness and well-being. If you are . . . involved with him, and he's content in your relationship, why shouldn't I be thrilled?" She tipped her head and smiled. "*Are* you involved with my son, Miss Jones?"

She put down her coffee. "That would depend on your definition of *involved,* Mrs. Damascus."

"Please, call me Helen."

"John's been very supportive since I came to New Orleans. As far as our being *involved. . . .*" She averted her eyes. Twenty-four hours ago she could have unequivocally answered no. Considering what had almost happened between them in Melissa's apartment, what was she supposed to think now? More importantly, what was she supposed to feel? Complications? If anyone had stirred up complications here, it had been Damascus, with his grief-stricken eyes and his hands that had made her ache and burn as no man had ever done. She had come back to the city to rescue Melissa, and now she was the one who needed rescuing. If she wasn't careful, she was going to become more than simply *involved* with J.D. Damascus. A woman with a past like hers had no business even contemplating romance with a man like him.

A nurse appeared, gently taking Helen's arm. "Your son has regained consciousness, Mrs. Damascus." She smiled and looked at Holly. "Are you Holly?"

She nodded.

"He's asking for you."

A grin touched Helen's mouth. "I guess that answers my question, Miss Jones . . ."

By the time they reached J.D.'s room, a doctor was in the process of examining him. Detective Mallory had appeared from nowhere, his hulk positioned in the corner of the cubicle, arms crossed over his chest, his gun peeking out from under his rumpled suit coat. Beverly remained as close to the bed as she could, face pale, eyes teary. She might as well have worn a flaming sign around her neck that declared I'M IN LOVE WITH JOHN DAMASCUS!

As the doctor turned away to speak with Helen, J.D. looked groggily toward Holly. She approached, hesitant, and took the hand that he weakly lifted to her.

"You're okay?" he asked.

She nodded and smiled, glanced toward Helen and the physician, who had been joined by Beverly and Detective Mallory. Bending closer, she whispered, "Was it Tyron?"

"His goons." He took a breath and grimaced. "Tyron's way of reminding me to butt out of his business."

"Could you identify the men who did this?"

"Maybe. It all happened too fast." He closed his eyes. "I'm usually quicker on my feet than that. Guess I had

my mind on other things." He closed his hand more firmly
on hers.

Holly spent the remainder of the night curled
up in a chair in the waiting room, too wired on caffeine
and worry to sleep. The television chattered, a local news
channel focused on the advancing hurricane, scenes of
businesses barricading storefront windows, endless traffic
bumper-to-bumper on the freeways, images of the French
Quarter streets dark and empty and the bar owners grum-
bling about the money they would lose without the tourist
trade. She suspected it was all much ado about nothing.
No doubt by the time Hurricane Holly reached the Louisiana coast it would have blown itself out to tropical storm
status, or veered away completely to slam Texas or Flor-
ida.

She didn't believe for a moment that the police would
find the men who assaulted Damascus. Tyron wasn't that
stupid. When he had "business" to take care of, he brought
in men from other areas. By now they were probably back
in Shreveport, or possibly Dallas, having given Damascus
a vicious warning to stop snooping into Tyron's business.
Tyron would be gloating, high off other people's pain—
especially when he had administered it in one way or
another.

If anything positive had come out of this event, it had
been the opportunity to plead her growing concern over
Melissa to Detective Mallory. When informed that she
had filed a missing person's report days before, and noth-

ing had apparently been done about it, he had assured her that he would look into it.

Voices interrupted her thoughts, and Holly looked around. Beverly stood by a man who must have been John's brother. Yes. No doubt about it. The hair was the same, a dark brown disheveled mass that looked haphazardly combed. He wore jeans and jogging shoes and a T-shirt. He didn't look happy. And neither did Beverly.

Beverly glared into her husband's face. "Where the hell were you, Eric?"

"I told you. Jack and I—"

"Jack? Really?"

"What the hell are you insinuating now?"

"That maybe you were with another one of your girlfriends. Who is it this time, Eric? Your secretary? Maybe some cheap little coed you picked up at O'Brien's?"

"Get off it, Bev." He reached into his jeans pocket and withdrew his cell phone. "Call him if you want."

"Like I would believe a word that bastard says. The senator has the morals of a tomcat. For God's sake, your brother is lying in that bed nearly dead and you don't show up for two hours?"

"Like my being here is going to do J.D. any good. Besides, *you're* here, *honey*. What the hell does he need me for when you're crying all over him like some lovesick teenager?"

As Eric turned on his heel and stormed away, Beverly touched her temple with one hand, her attention swinging toward Holly, who averted her gaze to the magazine on her lap.

"Miss Jones, may I have a word with you?"

Holly wasn't surprised that Beverly would eventually approach her. As Beverly sat down next to her, Holly unfolded her legs from beneath her and crossed them, instincts roused as if she had just come face-to-face with a pissed cobra. On the surface, Beverly Damascus might appear to be docile as a mouse, but Holly hadn't survived the streets without developing an uncanny ability to detect a potential threat when she saw one. Beverly Damascus wasn't happy about Holly's intrusion into J.D.'s life.

Beverly gave her a tight smile. "The doctor just informed us that they're keeping John a couple of days for observation. He took a hard crack to the head, it seems. There's really no point in you remaining here. The morphine they gave him for pain has pretty well knocked him out."

"Why don't you simply say what you mean, Beverly? You want me out of here."

"I wouldn't be so crass as to put it that way, but, yes. I think it's best that you leave."

"Why?"

"John has his family with him. Besides . . . it's obvious that he wouldn't be in this situation had it not been for you."

Holly looked away. "You don't beat around the bush, do you?"

"Not when it comes to John's welfare . . . and happiness. He simply doesn't need more complications in his life."

Holly looked away. Beverly was right, of course. The same thoughts had drummed through her head these last few hours.

Beverly sat up straight, her fingers clutching her purse and her eyes sharp as chips of green glass. "Look . . . Miss Jones. Let me point something out, just in case you're getting the wrong idea about John's interest in you. He's a sucker for losers. Since his family was murdered, he's taken on the role of savior for any down-on-her-luck woman who stumbles into his office with a sob story."

Her gaze raked Holly and the short, tight dress she was wearing. "It's quite obvious what you are, Miss Jones, so I wouldn't take John's interest in you for more than what it is."

She turned and walked away, and Holly stared after her. Beverly's parting shot disturbed her more than she wanted to admit to herself. She was right, of course. With John's kiss and touch, she had wanted, briefly, to believe otherwise. With one brush of his lips on hers, her wall of restraint had crumbled. Why?

She hadn't allowed herself to get close to a man emotionally and physically since she had put the life behind her. Not that there had been many men. A date here and there. A potential relationship when she had lived briefly in Dallas. But always, when recognizing so much as a hint of emotional charge, she had bolted, convincing herself that no man would accept her past—all of it—and forgive her for it. But the fear had gone even deeper than her fear of rejection. She simply wasn't—and never would be—willing to put the life of a man she loved in jeopardy.

"Miss Jones?"

Holly blinked and looked up into Helen's eyes.

"Are you all right, dear?" Helen sat down beside her. "You're quite pale. Should I get a nurse? Perhaps you need something to relax you. You've been through a terrible ordeal."

She shook her head. "I'm fine. Really."

Helen extended her hand, a key in her palm. "John's apartment. He wants you to go there. In fact, he ordered you to."

Holly looked at the key, wanting to refuse it. But what choice did she have? It was that or return to Melissa's apartment. While she had to return to retrieve her things and Puddin', the idea of staying there after what had happened unnerved her more than she wanted to admit to herself. Hesitantly, she accepted the key, curling her fingers firmly around it.

Helen smiled. "Go home and get some rest. John will be out for some time."

"Right." She nodded and smiled, relief easing the tension in her spine.

Helen dug into her purse, extracting a wallet, and money from it. "Knowing my son, his refrigerator is stocked with little more than cold pizza and beer. If you wouldn't mind, perhaps you can pick up a few things for when he comes home. Something healthy. Meat that isn't out of a can and some fruit and vegetables." She chuckled. "You know how mothers are. I'll rest easier knowing that when he gets home he'll have something decent to eat."

Holly accepted the money—five one-hundred-dollar bills. "This will buy a lot of fruit and veggies, Mrs. Damascus."

"Buy something for yourself. Fix the place up a bit. Just, please . . ." She cleared her throat. "Don't tell him I gave you this money. His stubborn pride, you see. He never allows me to help him. Says he's a grown man and can stand on his own two feet."

Holly laid her hand on Helen's. "You love your son very much."

"John is my pride and joy. While Eric may have been born with steely ambition and will no doubt excel in politics, John was gifted with intelligence, and most importantly, a conscience. For a man who has prided himself on his ethics and kindness, he's seen more than his share of sorrow."

"I'm sorry."

"So am I, dear." She stood. "I'll have my driver take you to John's."

Tyron Johnson, aka Dr. Yah Yah, was an Armani-suited hoodlum and practitioner of all things voodoo, partly because he feared the hex himself, but mostly because he enjoyed the surge of power he experienced believing that every time he poked a pin in a doll he was delivering excruciating pain to the enemy of the day.

He had never snuffed a man personally, although in his younger days, he had come close to it. Somehow beatings were more pleasurable. It was the pain he enjoyed inflicting. A dead man couldn't suffer.

Tyron had turned thirty-five the day before, and he was still feeling the effects of celebrating. His head hurt like hell and his stomach churned, as if he was on a boat in choppy water. He had called his mother and father in California the night before and enjoyed hearing their pleasure over the news that he had been promoted to vice president of the DiAngelo Investment Corporation.

It was bullshit, of course, but what they didn't know wouldn't hurt them. As if they could be proud as a peacock over their son being a pimp.

What mattered to them was that he sent enough money home every month to keep them well fed, clothed, and sheltered, not to mention the occasional vacation to Palm Springs to rub elbows with movie stars. The only downside to the conversations were the references they made to his past and how proud they were that he had managed to pull his life out of the gutter and become a success.

As a juvenile delinquent, he had spent most of his teenage years in lockup. He had nearly driven his old lady to suicide with despair, as had his younger brother, Spencer. Now, it went without saying that they never mentioned Spencer when they spoke. As far as they were concerned, Spencer was dead.

Luck had played a big part in Tyron's life. Had he not taken on the part-time job of running drugs for Marcus DiAngelo, he wouldn't be in the prestigious position he was now. Marcus had recognized his potential. Took him off the streets and out of the ghetto-gang threads, dressed him in style, and gave him a taste of the good life. Classy whores and clean coke. Parties with movie stars and politicians, pockets stuffed with five-hundred-dollar bills, and gold-trimmed automobiles that made the babes drool when he drove by.

All thanks to Marcus DiAngelo, who owned Tyron's body and soul and half the politicians in five states. The man had clout. Lots of it. And because of that, Tyron carefully watched his P's and Q's. DiAngelo wasn't a man to cross. If he played his cards right, Tyron suspected that he would be in line to take over DiAngelo's territory should he decide to retire. So what that he had to kiss DiAngelo's ass and put up with his peculiarities. Everyone had their little quirks.

DiAngelo's happened to be his adoration and obsession with Elvis Presley. He had five million dollars tied up in authentic Elvis memorabilia. Autographed photos. Cars and motorcycles that had belonged to the King. Sweat-stained jumpsuits he wore in Vegas. A house in the Caribbean that had once belonged to Elvis. The damn toilet seat that Elvis had been sitting on when he croaked.

Elvis, Elvis, Elvis.

He'd decorated his house outside of New Orleans identically to Graceland, right down to the tacky Jungle Room. "Blue Suede Shoes" had become his national anthem. He played or sang it constantly, even owned a pair of blue suede shoes that had reportedly been worn by the King during a concert at the White House.

Whatever flipped the wop's switch. It was no skin off Tyron's nose.

Yes, life was definitely good. Most of the time. Today, however, was an exception.

As he relaxed in his art deco chair, he closed his eyes in bliss as Honey performed oral sex on him. Blow jobs were her specialty. She could suck a man's entire soul out through his penis. Send him to la-la land with a twist of her tongue.

God knows he needed a bit of relaxation after reading the letter from his brother, Spencer. Spence, doing life in prison, had been gang-raped twice in the last week and the prison officials still refused to offer him refuge from the tormenters. Spence was considering suicide. Something needed to be done about the problem and quick.

As if Tyron didn't have enough on his plate, what with his girls getting murdered, opening up that old kettle of rotten fish again.

Cops were sniffing around him like a dog on a scent and J.D. Damascus wasn't helping any. No doubt about it, he was going to have to call in the big guns, so to speak. Not that he liked asking DiAngelo for favors. DiAngelo's favors came with strings attached. But since it was more than apparent that the wrong man had been executed for the French Quarter murders, things were going to get ugly again and the last thing he needed was the police snooping too deeply into his business. The idea of sharing the same fate as Spence freaked him out.

Honey lifted her eyes and stared at him. "You got a problem or what?"

Apparently, he did. He had gone limp as a noodle— what with his mind being bothered by thoughts of his brother and Damascus. His face began to burn as she smirked at him, as if the problem was his fault. It was, of course, but he didn't appreciate her pointing it out.

"Maybe I just don't like looking at your ugly face, bitch."

He punched her in the eye so hard she sprawled on her back on the floor, making a mewling sound as she grabbed her face. Standing, he stuffed himself into his trousers and zipped up his pants, giving her a kick in her ribs for good measure.

"Just for that, you ain't gettin' a fix. See how you like that, bitch."

She rolled to her hands and knees, her stringy blond hair over her already swelling face. "I'm sorry," she whimpered. "Please—I gotta have it, Tyron. I'm hurting."

"Should have thought about that before you got smart. Now get the hell out of here."

The door opened and Marcus DiAngelo walked in, five feet three inches and pushing two hundred pounds. He stepped aside as Honey, one hand plastered to her eye, ran from the room.

"Problems?"

"Bitch is gettin' sloppy is all."

"She's getting expensive. She's costing us six hundred a day. Is she worth it?"

Tyron shrugged.

"I don't think so." Marcus dropped onto the sofa and crossed his legs as he lit a cigar. "From my understanding, she hasn't turned a trick in days. Too damn strung out to do her job."

Tyron knew what that meant, and Marcus was right. It was a shame to lose a bitch with Honey's talent, but the bottom line was, when one of the girls couldn't meet her quota because she was home shooting up and so damn stoned a john wouldn't touch her, she had outlived her usefulness.

"I'll take care of it," Marcus said. "I'll have Vince deliver a cocktail that will blow her mind, literally." He chuckled.

Well, if she had to go there wasn't a nicer way to do it, Tyron supposed. She'd be dead before she hit the floor.

"So what's up?" Marcus asked. "Your message sounded urgent."

Tyron poured himself a glass of V8 juice. "I got a big favor to ask."

Marcus smiled.

"It's Spence." He gulped his juice. "He's having some problems."

"So you mentioned."

"Damn warden won't do nothin' about it. Got it in his mind that Spence deserves this kind of brutality."

"You're asking me to shake him up a little. Right?"

"You know, put the fear of God into him."

"That might take some doing. Lot of strings to pull, know what I mean?" He scratched his head. "I could speak to Mr. Carrelli. He isn't known for being subtle, however. It might get messy."

"I don't fuckin' care how messy it gets, Mr. DiAngelo. Splatter his brains for all I care. My brother doesn't deserve this kind of treatment."

"Spence screwed up big-time, Tyron. We both know that."

"Spence would never have gotten caught if it hadn't been for that bitch." He slammed his glass down and clenched his fists. "I'm gonna kill that whore when I find her."

"Any progress there?"

He shook his head and paced to the plateglass window where he looked down at the river. A pair of barges crept by, along with the *Delta Queen,* radiantly white in the overcast day.

"Somebody's got to know somethin'. Melissa knows.

Bitch. I got this gut feeling that's why she lit out. Maybe
Shana contacted her—"

"Shana's a bright girl. I doubt she would put her friend
in that kind of position."

"Those bitches were joined at the hip. Eventually, when
Shana felt the dust had settled, I'm sure she would contact
her." He turned back to Marcus. "You got to know somebody who could help me find her."

"I can't afford to get my contacts in deep shit, Tyron.
You know that."

"What about Senator Strong?"

Tyron knew the minute he made the blunder that he
had crossed the line. And if there was any man alive who
you didn't want to piss off, it was DiAngelo. His dark
eyes bored into Tyron like a drill bit.

DiAngelo stood, shifted his silk suit on his shoulders,
and slid his hand into his breast pocket, causing Tyron to
take a step back and swallow hard.

"How many times have I told you about that, Tyron?"
Marcus withdrew a lighter and relit his cigar, his gaze still
drilling Tyron. "You are never to discuss my relationship
with the senator. Not with me . . . or anyone."

"Sorry. I forgot."

"That kind of brain fart will get you buried in the
bayou . . . what's not first eaten by the gators. Nasty business, that . . . getting eaten alive by gators."

Sweating, Tyron nodded. He'd attended such a hit once,
a drug dealer who thought pocketing a goodly portion of
DiAngelo's money was worth the risk of getting caught.
Tyron still awoke occasionally remembering the man's
screams, his thrashing about as two of Marcus's men

bound his arms and legs and tossed him onto the muddy shoal, laughing hysterically as the gator crept out of the water and snapped off the man's head with one quick chomp.

"Need I remind you that you've grown wealthy off the senator and his cohorts? Their appreciation of our girls and good coke, not to mention my financial backing, is paying for this apartment and that Viper you're driving. If I go putting the finger on Jack for favors, and he gets caught, me, you, and half the elected officials in Louisiana will go down the drain with him. Got it?"

He nodded. "Got it."

"You gonna have that kind of brain fart again?"

"No, sir."

A smile slid over Marcus's mouth. It wasn't friendly. A little like a snake charming a terrified rat before he swallowed it whole.

"Get over this Shana bitch. She's gone. Face the fact. Your brother got stupid. Even more stupid than you, Tyron. Besides . . ." He moved closer. "I do believe your obsession with Shana has more to do with your pride than it does concern over your brother. Then there's the matter of your unrequited love for her." He shrugged. "We both know it simply isn't smart for a pimp to go soft on one of his girls. Screws up his logic. Gets in the way of business."

His face growing hot, Tyron lowered his eyes. "She was special."

Marcus grunted a condescending laugh, then turned for the door, paused, and looked back. "By the way . . . I understand someone beat the hell out of Damascus."

That image brought the smile back to Tyron's face. "Just a friendly reminder to keep his nose out of my business."

"Just be sure you don't kill him. I don't want your stupidity to call attention to me. Besides . . . I'm enjoying his suffering. Good payback for all the hell he brought me during those racketeering trials."

Tyron laughed. "Enjoy it better than 'Blue Suede Shoes'?"

DiAngelo's face turned dark and his jaw knotted. "Ain't nothing better than 'Blue Suede Shoes,' you stupid fucker. Apologize to the King before I blow out your mash-for-brains."

Stepping back, Tyron threw up his hands and looked toward the ceiling, his voice raising an octave as he said, "I apologize. I didn't mean nothin', Mr. Presley."

DiAngelo left the apartment, slamming the door so hard the photograph of Elvis on the wall cocked to one side.

10

One hundred miles off the Louisiana coast, Hurricane Holly had lost some of her oomph. Still, as a tropical storm, she drove with tremendous force, slashing rains, and terrible thunder, submerging streets and whipping stop signs as if they were perched on flexible rubber.

Arriving at his apartment, stiff, sore, and semilucid from the morphine the doctors had pumped into his veins the last two days, J.D. stopped just inside the threshold. At first, he thought he had somehow walked into someone else's place.

The air smelled of floral room deodorizers and pine disinfectant. He could see his reflection in the polished wood floor. Instead of his old drapes, which reeked of smoke, there were frilly cafe curtains on the windows. Nothing fancy. But they lent a definite hint of homeyness to the usually stark place.

Beverly dashed around him, out of the rain, and

stopped, her gaze sweeping the room. Her surprise immediately turned into annoyance. "Seems Miss Jones has been busy."

"Apparently." He tossed his cigarette butt out the door just as Puddin' appeared from under a chair and began to circle his legs.

Beverly, her arms burdened with a grocery sack, moved to the kitchen where a colorful ceramic chicken had roosted on the countertop. A Crock-Pot sat near it. As she lifted the lid, the aroma of stew wafted through the apartment, causing J.D.'s stomach to growl. A diet of hospital Jell-O had left him feeling ravenous.

He hadn't seen Holly since his first night in the emergency room. Nor, according to Beverly, had anyone else. In his lucid moments, he had called his apartment, getting no answer, and his panic had mounted. The idea that she would be out on the streets looking for Melissa and putting her life in jeopardy had caused his blood pressure to soar, which had resulted in their pumping enough sedatives into his system to send him disembodied through a spiraling universe. Now, however, relief that Holly was apparently okay left him feeling bone weary from exhaustion.

He limped to the kitchen where Beverly was glaring into the fridge, stocked so heavily with food there was no room for the staples Beverly had bought. She slammed the door and turned to face him.

"Seems someone has set up housekeeping."

He opened the freezer door, inspected the frozen veggies, then reached into the array of different-flavored frozen confections, extracting a grape Popsicle.

"She's manipulating you, of course," Beverly said.

"I hardly think stocking my fridge with Popsicles is manipulation."

"Come on, John. Look at this place. It looks like something out of *Better Homes and Gardens*."

"What's wrong with that?"

He reentered the living room and eased down on the futon that was now festooned with colorful, plump pillows and a mulberry-colored chenille throw. A vase of sunflowers sat on the coffee table, beside an assortment of magazines—*Better Homes and Gardens* and *Southern Living*. A ceramic ashtray boasting a grinning gator sat beside them. No doubt about it, Miss Jones had been busy. She'd turned his apartment from shabby to . . . froufrou. Not exactly congruent with his mood and personality these days, but he had to admit to himself that the woman's touch not only amused him, but also pleased him.

He sucked on the Popsicle and watched Beverly simmer.

She moved to the bedroom door. "I thought Miss Jones was destitute. If that's the case, I wonder where she got the money for all this."

He frowned. "What's that supposed to mean?"

Turning, she glared at him with an expression that was unusually vindictive for the Beverly he knew. "What do you think I mean? How else does a hooker get her money?"

"That's not very nice. I'm surprised at you."

"I can't believe you would become involved with a woman like her, John."

"I'm not involved. Besides, what I do with my personal life is none of your business."

"Gee, that sounds familiar. Seems that was your pat excuse when I warned you that Laura was going to turn your life into a shambles."

"Don't bring my dead wife into this." He rubbed his throbbing temple. "Get a grip before you piss me off." Shooting her a warning look, he added, "If you paid as much attention to your own relationship with my brother as you do to my business, maybe you wouldn't be so miserable."

Color drained from her face. Her eyes widened and teared.

Regret slammed him. "Hey, I'm sorry. Come here, sweetheart."

She sat down beside him. He put his arm around her and pulled her close, so her head nestled on his shoulder. He kissed her brow. "I'm sorry. I shouldn't take out my frustrations on you. I know you only want the best for me."

"I love you, John."

"I know." He stroked her hair. "I love you, too."

Lifting her head, she gazed into his eyes, the subtle scent of her perfume making his body tense. "I mean, I really love you. I'm in love with you." She lightly touched his bruised cheek. "I'm sorry if that offends you."

"It doesn't offend me, Beverly. You're not confessing anything I don't already know."

"I would leave Eric in a minute if I thought—"

"It's not going to happen, honey."

"Patrick loves you so much—"

"I'm not in love with you, Bev."

He felt her stiffen and lurch with a sob. Holding her more tightly, he said, "You and the kids mean the world to me, sweetheart. I'm here for you when you need me. You know that. Hey, you wouldn't like being married to me anyway. I'm moody and sloppy and generally pissed off at the world. I couldn't keep you in the lifestyle that you've grown accustomed to. You're champagne and caviar and I'm warm beer and Vienna sausages. You enjoy garden parties and I hate 'em."

She gave him a watery smile. "I could learn to like Vienna sausages."

"No, you couldn't. It's one of the reasons we never hooked up in college. You were meant to be a socialite. You'll make the perfect senator's wife one of these days."

"I once thought those things could make me happy, John. But they don't. I'm only happy when I'm with you. Please . . ." She cupped his cheek with one hand. "Give us a chance."

She pressed her lips against his. They were trembling and soft. Warm and moist. As her hand slid around the back of his head, she pulled him closer, deeper into the kiss.

The front door opened.

Carrying a sack of Brahms's ice cream, Holly stood in the threshold, rain drizzling down her face. Her gaze collided with J.D.'s as he raised his head, shoving Beverly away out of reflex.

"Sorry," she said. "I didn't realize . . . I mean, I wasn't expecting you home for another couple of hours."

She moved to the kitchen as Beverly, her expression

smug and her eyes sparkling with rekindled hope, stood and straightened her blouse.

"I thought you might enjoy ice cream for dessert, what with your ulcer. . . . I'll just put it away and get out."

"Beverly was just leaving." He flashed Beverly a look that made her snap up her purse and tuck it under her arm.

Holly slammed the freezer door so hard the chicken on the countertop clattered. She turned and gave Beverly a look cold enough to chill boiling water. "Please, don't leave on my account."

"Wouldn't think of it." Beverly allowed her a tight smile. "I really must go. I have to pick up Patrick from school."

As she exited the apartment, slamming the door, J.D. winced. The Popsicle had begun to drip on his jeans, and he tossed the remainder into the gator ashtray as Holly leaned against the kitchen doorjamb and crossed her arms. Her pitch-black hair flowed over her shoulders. Her jeans were tight and faded, and she wore one of his Saints T-shirts, tucked into the jeans.

"It's not how it looks," he said.

"Oh?"

"There's nothing going on between us."

"Come on, Damascus. She had her tongue thrust so far down your throat your tonsils were gyrating in delight."

"So I had a weak moment."

She shrugged. "It's really none of my business, is it?"

He stood and moved toward her. "No, it's not."

She turned back to the kitchen, proceeded to stir the stew in the Crock-Pot as he joined her, pressing close to her back and sliding his arm around her waist. Her hair smelled like magnolias and her body felt damp from the rain. He felt her stiffen as steam rose off the stew in a hot, moist cloud.

"Miss me?"

"I'm glad you're okay."

"Why didn't you come back to the hospital?"

"Busy, as you can see."

"Place looks nice. Where did you get the money for all this?"

She lay down the wooden spoon, her back rigid. "Where do you think? What, no comment? You're imagining I went out and turned a few tricks, Damascus?"

"I like it better when you call me John."

"You haven't answered my question."

"You're a beautiful woman, Holly."

"Answer me."

"I really don't care where you got the money."

She tried to move away. He pinned her against the counter, his body pressed hard against hers. "I don't care," he repeated, nuzzling the warm skin behind her ear.

He felt the resistance that had turned her body tense slowly leave her. "I'm sorry I hurt you. But the thought of Tyron touching you . . . made me a little crazy, I guess. I got . . . confused, Holly. Hell, maybe I was jealous. I don't know."

Her head partially turned, her hair brushing his lips. "Jealous?" The word was whispered, tremulous. Disbelieving. He didn't blame her. He'd been driven crazy these last few days thinking about it, the pang of possessiveness that he felt over the woman whose soft body warmed his own in that moment.

She turned in his arms. Her wide blue eyes looked up into his, searching. Cautious. "Jealous?"

Pressing his lips lightly to her forehead, he closed his eyes. "Maybe. Yeah . . . maybe. I don't know. You drive me crazy. When you walked out on me . . . I don't know. Those few days were hell. I kept trying to convince myself that you were nothing to me but another charity case. Fine. Let you go. But somehow in a short space of time you filled up this place and it wasn't right without you."

Christ, he felt tired suddenly. As if the confession had drained what little reserve of strength he had. As if she sensed it, her arms slid around him, held him close, her body bracing him, holding him. Her lips brushed his cheek as she nestled against him.

"You're exhausted, John. You should lie down."

"No." He held her closer, his hands rubbing her back. "Not yet."

"You're trembling. Come on. I'm putting you to bed."

He suspected that his trembling had little to do with his weakness, but he followed her anyway as she took his hand and led him to the bedroom. As she sat him on the bed, she dropped to her knees and untied the laces of his joggers, her long hair sweeping over her shoulders as she removed his shoes. The scent of magnolia lifted from her and he felt a heat rush through him that had nothing to do with the dull aches in his body.

She tossed the shoes aside and looked up, her hands drifting along his thighs, warm through his jeans. Her eyes were liquid indigo pools in which he hungered to drown.

There was obliteration there—of his pain, his memories.

He touched her cheek. She pulled away.

"Holly."

"Lie down. Rest." She stood, placed her hands gently on his shoulders, and pressed him back, onto the bed.

He caught her hand—too tightly perhaps—and their gazes clashed. "Don't leave. Please. Lie here beside me."

"I can't." She shook her head. "Please, John. Don't ask me."

"What the hell are you afraid of?"

A spasm of emotion crossed her face. Her chin quivered. "You. I'm afraid of you. I'm afraid of how you make me feel. Damn you, Damascus, just let me go. Why did you have to come looking for me?"

As she drew away again, he closed his hand more tightly on hers, drawing her back, forcing her down beside him though she refused to look at him. He held her tense body against him and stroked her hair.

"Stay. Just for a little while. You feel so damn good."

She remained silent then. Motionless. The rain beat against the roof and slashed against the windows as lightning shot sporadic illumination through the dim room.

As they lay there, embraced by the drone of the storm and the collecting shadows of the late afternoon, a realization crept into J.D.'s thoughts as he continued to hold Holly. She believed he wanted her body, just like the others who had held her, whispered lies into her ear, games played by lonely johns who hungered only for sexual surcease.

Reluctantly, he released her and rolled to his back, watched the play of lightning flash in streaks over the

ceiling. A long moment passed before she moved, rolled
to her back as well, and looked over at him.

He grinned. "Anyone ever tell you that you look beautiful in shadows?"

Her lips curved. "No."

He slid his hand over hers, closed his fingers gently
around it, and looked back at the ceiling. She continued
to watch him, her cheek nestled in the down pillow.
Minutes ticked by, then she rolled to her side and moved
closer, rested her head on his pillow, so near he could feel
her breath brush his cheek.

"Feeling better?" she asked.

"Yes."

She touched the bruise on his brow, then her fingertips
drifted to the cut near his mouth, lingered there before
moving slowly to ease over his lower lip. His eyes drifted
closed as the touch warmed him and caused his heart to
beat faster.

Careful. Careful. The last thing he needed was to lose
control.

Closer. "You're very good to me, John."

He smiled, eyes still closed.

"I don't understand why."

"Not every man walking the face of the earth is a jerk,
honey."

Closer. Her body pressed against his. Her hand lay on
his chest. Surely she could feel the fast, strong beating of
his heart. Her words teased his ear.

"Would you like to kiss me?"

"Of course."

She cupped his cheek in her hand and turned his face

toward hers. No trepidation in her eyes now. Something else. "Then why don't you?"

Moving her body partially over his, she lowered her lips to his, a feather brush that sluiced through him. He cradled her head between his hands and tipped her face, lifting his mouth against hers firmly. He parted her lips, drawing in her breath, and setting fire to his stomach. His sweat began to rise and his breathing quickened.

Christ. One kiss and he was lost. Restraint crumbling.

She drew away from the kiss, slid down his chest, her hands sliding under his shirt and tugging it up so she could press her lips against his belly, tongue twirling around his navel. He groaned, twisted his hands into the sheets, and gritted his teeth. With one flick of her tongue he'd grown hard as a crowbar and there wasn't a damn thing he could do about it.

Her hand slid over the ridge in his jeans, then she cupped him in her palm, slid her face down to his crotch, and breathed against it. The heat made him tense. His hips rose and his legs spread to accommodate her. Every instinct collided in his brain, caution and testosterone a dangerous amalgamation that made his body shake.

What the hell was she doing?

"Holly." He groaned it, his hands reaching for her, fingertips sliding through her hair.

Her head lifted and her gaze speared him. "I know what you're doing, John." Her lips curved as her fingers tugged at the zipper of his jeans. "I know what you want. Really. Did you think I would believe your attempts to make me trust you? Compassion. Understanding. Patience. Been there and heard it all, Damascus."

Holly's tongue flicked along the straining rise beneath his underwear. Her breath felt warm and moist through his cotton jockeys, and he gritted his teeth.

"A man like you couldn't really give a damn about a woman like me."

Fingers parted the Y fronts of his underwear and her tongue licked his engorged head, sending a jolt of white-hot fire and pain through him. Blissful pain. Consuming heat.

"Stop." He moaned, eyes closed.

"Let's get it over with. It's inevitable. I owe you big-time for your *kindness*, so let's stop the game playing, why don't we?"

"Stop it." He grabbed for her and dumped her beside him on the bed, moving his body partially over hers to arrest her attempt to escape. "Look at me, dammit. Stop that and look at me."

He shook her. Her eyes flashed like the lightning erupting through the room as he pinned her arms to the mattress. "Hey, we both know men think with their dicks, Holly. Sorry about that. Can't help it. It's that testosterone thing that screws up our judgment. When a woman goes down on a man there isn't a whole lot we can do about it. You're right. There's nothing I would love more at this moment than to crawl between your legs, but I'm trying to prove something here and you're not making it easy for me. Get it through your head that that's *not* what I need from you right now."

Taking a deep breath to control his anger, J.D. closed his eyes, briefly, feeling Holly shake beneath him. "All I want . . ." He swallowed. "I want your arms around me.

So maybe I can sleep for the first time in years without nightmares and memories. I've got this gut feeling you can help me do that, Holly. *Please.* Just for a little while."

With a resigned sigh, he released her and rolled away, onto his back. "My head hurts. My body hurts. I don't want to fight with you again and end up saying something out of frustration that will make me feel guiltier than I already do. If you want to leave, get the hell away from me. I'm just too damn tired to deal with this right now." He zipped up his jeans and turned away from her, focused on the glass balcony doors where rain ran in runnels down the panes.

Thunder rumbled.

Minutes of silence ticked by.

The bed moved and Holly's body pressed against him. Her arm slid around his waist. Her face nestled against the back of his head. "I'm sorry," came her whisper.

The phone jarred him awake. The bed beside him was empty. Then Holly appeared at the bedroom door holding the cat in her arms.

He reached for the phone.

"Damascus, Mallory here."

Holly moved into the room as he listened to Mallory talk.

"Christ," he said, drawing Holly's gaze to his. She must have sensed the tension and dread that shot through him at Mallory's news. "Was she murdered like the others?"

Holly gasped and turned white. "Oh God."

He nodded. "Right. We'll be down in half an hour."

Gently, he hung up the phone.

"It's Melissa, isn't it? She's dead."

"They've recovered a body . . ."

Holly sank to the floor and the cat scrambled from her arms. She covered her face with her hands.

Sinking to one knee beside her, he took her in his arms, held her as she struggled to shove him away. "The body needs identifying, Holly. I'll go—"

"Bastard. That lousy bastard—"

"If it's Melissa—"

Her head snapped up, her face smeared with mascara. "They don't know for sure?"

"Not until I've IDed her."

"I'm going with you."

He touched her tear-streaked cheek. "I don't think that's a good idea. She's . . . been dead a while."

"I'm going with you," she repeated. "Melissa was my friend, dammit. Not yours."

By the time they reached the morgue, the rain was falling in sheets and rising fast on the streets, which were virtually empty. Thunder crashed as they stepped into the reception area where they were met by Mallory and his wife. They were surprised to see Holly with J.D. and shot him a concerned look before opening the double doors, allowing them access to the morgue.

"The young woman was found in someone's backyard at eight-twenty this morning. Brought up by flood waters from what we can ascertain." Mallory glanced again at Holly, whose face was as white as the clean smock Janice was wearing. Holly hadn't spoken since they had left J.D.'s apartment, hadn't so much as flinched at the lashing of wind-driven rain and the explosions of lightning. Her eyes appeared as glazed as blue glass.

J.D. understood the feeling, the cold shock and dread that was filling her up, the frantic holding on to a sliver of hope that the body would prove to be someone else's. He wanted to drag her back out into the rain, force her into his car, and lock the door until this was over. But, most of all, he wanted to protect her from the nightmares that would follow.

"Dead around three days, perhaps slightly longer," Janice said. "Slight putrefaction but not so severe as to hamper identification. Cause of death is strangulation. Obviously, this doesn't appear to be the same signature as the others, unless our serial killer is changing his normal routine to throw us off."

The diener, a tall, overly thin African American man wearing a green jumpsuit, stood as they entered the room, his long face expressionless. Janice nodded and he moved to the box and opened it, slid out the slab containing the sheet-covered body, then stepped back.

J.D. turned to Holly where she stood, frozen, her gaze locked on the covered form.

"Get the hell out of here," he said softly. "You don't need or want this kind of image to haunt you for the rest of your life, sweetheart. Trust me."

"I'm her only true friend. Her only family. I . . . have to do this."

He looked away, then nodded to Janice and braced himself.

Janice stepped forward and eased the cloth from the cadaver's face.

"Oh God," Holly sobbed. "It's not her."

He sits in the shadows of the locker, feeling the thrust of the storm throughout his body. He does so enjoy the power of it. The electricity tingles his nerve endings, fills him with a euphoria not unlike that which he experiences from the terror he can see in Melissa's eyes.

He has told her that he intends to kill her now. A lie, of course. He is enjoying the drawn-out torture. It is new to him, this putting off of death. It is unending arousal. When the orgasm comes, it will be the best of his life. As electrifying as the lightning plundering the earth and sky.

Closing his eyes, he feels the building shudder from the wind-driven waves against the pilings below. At any moment, the old building could cave. Yet it won't. He won't allow it. Not yet. He is one with the universe. He holds the power of the cyclone in his palm. It infuses him with Godlike control—domination over life and death.

At last, he stands, sways from side to side as the floor moves beneath him. With knife in hand, he approaches her, smiling as her eyes widen and her body writhes, wrists and ankles bleeding from the thin wires that he has bound her with these last few days. The red-gold hair that had felt smooth and soft as silk looks dull, the tangles like a rat's nest cushioning her head. A shame. It was her glorious hair that had first attracted him to her. Long and flowing, giving her a virginal look that he had found stimulating. A virginal whore. No doubt the perverts who bought her did so because they lusted for children.

Bending, he slowly peels the tape back from her raw lips. "Would you like to scream?" he asks. "Go ahead. I won't stop you."

She tries, but her voice is weak and drowned out by the rain pummeling the metal roof. He lightly places the knife against her throat, the keen blade biting just enough so blood trickles over her pale and bruised flesh. The flash of fear in her bloodshot eyes causes his blood to warm and sing in his veins. Fear is good. So very, very good. Fear invites respect. He has learned this from the others who did not respect him until he introduced them to fear. Oh yes, their smugness and contempt was soon transformed with the first flash of his knife.

"Beg," he whispers.

"Please."

"It won't hurt for long, Melissa. Pretty Melissa."

"Please . . . don't hurt me."

"You're the prettiest of them so far. Such wonderful breasts and lovely eyes. I think of them often, when I'm alone. Perhaps . . ." He ran the tip of the blade along her cheek, to the tender skin below her right eye. "Perhaps I'll cut out your eyes and keep them for a souvenir. Something to remember you by. It would be a shame for them to rot along with your head in the bottom of the bayou."

As the knife tip bit into her skin, her mouth flew open in a soundless wail. The beautiful sensation streaked through him—rousing his penis so intensely he thought he would burst.

"Pig," she sneers, her eyes suddenly wild with fury. "Worthless, stupid pig."

He freezes, stares at her mouth that has spat such vile and villainous words.

"Moron. Freaking imbecile, just kill me and get it over with. You're sick and disgusting. You can't even get it up like any normal man."

Stumbling back, as if from a blow, he trembles. Vomit rises in his throat. Control frays—pop, pop—like a splintering rubber band. The thunder centers in his head, mind splitting, and he drops the knife, covering his ears with his shaking hands to shield them from her accusations.

"Bitch," he groans, running at her, falling on her. He drives his fist into her mouth, her lips exploding beneath his knuckles. "Say my name, bitch. Say it." He slams her again so she bucks beneath him. Her throat gurgles. "Say it."

"God," she cries. "God!"

Arriving back at the apartment, J.D. coaxed Holly into bed. She was lost someplace between shock and relief that the murder victim had not been Melissa. Still shaking. Dazed. The bloated body of the Jane Doe she had viewed would continue to trouble her, regardless that it hadn't been Melissa. No one ever forgot their first cadaver. Not for their entire life.

At last, she drifted to sleep.

The doorbell rang.

He answered the door to find Jerry Costos, soaked, his hands jammed into his trouser pockets. J.D. hadn't had a face-to-face with his ex–best friend since the afternoon Jerry had asked for his resignation from the D.A.'s office. His first instinct was to slug him. That was fast eclipsed by a joy that surprised him. He had hated Costos with a force that had been equaled only by the extreme closeness they had shared during their college days, followed by the many grueling hours they had worked together in the D.A.'s office. He had hoped never to see him again. He hadn't wanted to be reminded of the loss he'd felt over Jerry's decision to prosecute Gonzalez as the French Quarter killer.

"What the hell do you want?"

"You going to let me in? I'm drowning out here."

"Why should I?"

"Come on, J.D. It's time we talked."

"You're four years too late."

He proceeded to close the door in Jerry's face. Costos braced his weight against it, gave it a hard shove so J.D. was forced to stumble back, allowing Jerry to enter the apartment. For an eternal moment, they stood nose-to-nose while thunder shook the walls around them.

"You look like hell," Jerry said.

"You can go to hell."

"I didn't come here to fight with you."

"Of course you did. You'd have to be stupid to think you could show up here and I wouldn't beat the shit out of you."

"Fine. You want to take a punch at me? Go ahead. I guess I deserve it. If it will make you feel better."

"Don't tell me you're only now feeling the bite of conscience."

Jerry turned away, ran one hand through his dark, wet hair. Jerry Costos was one of Louisiana's most eligible and sought-after bachelors. Tall, good-looking. The football stud type. He was still good-looking, but the last years had carved a hardness to his features that was undeniable.

"I heard from Mallory about your assault . . . among other things," Jerry said.

"The murders?"

He nodded.

"Figured that would bring you around. So how does it feel to know you had a hand in executing the wrong man for the French Quarter killings?"

J.D. closed the door and leaned back against it as Costos paced the room. "Then again, you've known it all along, haven't you, Jerry? Your resigning from the D.A.'s office was evidence enough. You son of a bitch, you rolled over for someone. Who was it?"

"I swear, J.D. The evidence proved—"

"That Gonzalez was at the wrong place at the wrong time. Hell, even Anna told you—"

"Profilers are not infallible, Damascus."

J.D. might have laughed had he not been simmering with anger. Anna Travelli was one of the FBI's sharpest agents—Hell on Wheels Travelli, the NOPD had nicknamed her during the first Quarter murders. Had Killroy actually listened to her, Gonzalez would still be alive, and the real serial killer on death row.

"So how is Anna?" J.D. asked.

Jerry dropped onto the futon. "Fine, I guess. You know Anna. She comes and goes. The job has always come first with her."

"Problems?"

"Yeah. She still refuses to marry me."

J.D. nodded, not surprised. Anna was FBI through and through. Quantico's highest-ranking female agent in the history of the force. "She's damn good at her job, Jerry."

Resting his head back against the wall, Costos stared at the ceiling. "Okay, I admit that I was pressured to put the case to bed."

"By whom?"

"Mayor Bixby. The governor—your father. And Senator Strong. He was running for reelection and was concerned that the negativity of the ongoing investigation was going to hurt him. Face it. The national publicity was decimating tourism. But I swear to you, J.D., I honestly believed at the time that we had the right man. Besides, there were no more murders after Gonzalez was arrested. And it wasn't as if Gonzalez put up much of a fight. He was going to prison, regardless, due to his attempted murder of Anna. The jackass actually got a hard-on over all the publicity. He was a nobody who suddenly found himself in the limelight."

J.D. limped to a chair and eased into it. His head throbbed like hell. He wanted to curl up beside Holly and sleep. The last thing he wanted was to debate Costos's screwup and open up more emotional wounds.

Jerry leaned forward, propping his elbows on his knees. His dark eyes looked deeply into J.D.'s own. "There hasn't been a day that I haven't thought about you and your family. Of how you've suffered."

"Thank God for small favors."

"You've got every right to hate my guts. But I wish you wouldn't. I've missed you, Damascus."

"Yeah? Well, I haven't given you a second thought,

Costos, other than occasionally wanting to kill you with my bare hands."

"We made one hell of a team. There wasn't a defense attorney out there who didn't piss his pants when going up against us. Had we been prosecuting O.J. Simpson, that creep would never have walked for those murders."

"Old news, Jerry. Why are you here?"

"Cut to the chase, right?" He nodded. "After leaving the D.A.'s office, I did some snooping of my own on Tyron Johnson. I still don't believe he was involved with the murders of your family, J.D. And whether you want to believe it or not, I still think Laura was killed by the same man who was butchering those women."

"Wrong place at the wrong time again."

Jerry nodded. "We're never going to know why she was at the park that night. But she was. Perhaps the killer mistook her for a hooker, then discovered the kids—"

"The M.O. is all wrong, Jerry. The killer always murdered the victims in their own apartments. There was a ritual he went through. Torture before death. He toyed with them sometimes for hours. Not in Laura's case. There were men who testified to jogging by that area shortly before the time of the killing. They hadn't seen or heard anything. Janice Mallory established that my wife was killed by a stab wound to her heart. No long, drawn-out bleeding to death before he butchered her."

"Johnson had an alibi for that night. Christ, give up this vigilante crusade against Tyron, J.D., before he puts you down. Let the department do its job."

"From what I see, they aren't doing a hell of a lot." He shook his head. "They would rather not find the killer at

all if it means the truth gets out to the public. The ramifications would end Strong's political career. Gonzalez's
family would sue the state for millions . . . and win. So
the department is going to stick its head up its ass and
play dead."

"What benefit is there in letting the public know about
this? It'll paralyze this city with panic and open a lot of
wounds that I'm afraid you aren't capable of dealing
with."

"I would run my arms and legs through a meat grinder
if it meant finding the man who killed my family, Costos.
You think I don't want it to end?" He gave a sharp laugh
and shook his head. "When I allow myself to believe, just
for a moment, that maybe it wasn't Johnson who killed
my family for revenge, I suspect every son of a bitch I
see. If it's not Johnson, then the bastard is living a normal
life, maybe with a wife and kids, enjoying Christmas and
birthdays, kissing his wife good night and playing football
with his son."

J.D. closed his eyes, tightly, and swallowed. "Why my
kids, Jerry? Even if they happened to see him killing
Laura, what were the chances they could ID him? They
were practically babies, for God's sake. It was pitch-black
out there. Christ, as prosecutors, we never made a case
on the testimony of young children. They aren't reliable."

"A panicked killer isn't going to stop long enough to
understand that." Jerry stood and walked to J.D. His face
looked tight with emotion. "I screwed up, John. We all
did. I may no longer be in a position of power, but I swear
to you, I'm going to move heaven and earth to help find
the man who slaughtered your family."

"Yeah? Then talk to the D.A. Convince him to get Anna back on this case."

"Christ. What makes you think I can convince the D.A. to pull Anna in on this case again?"

"C'mon, Jerry. Everyone in this town knows the D.A. doesn't fart without getting your advice first. You might have resigned from the office but everyone is aware that George Billings is little more than your shadow. Anna tried to tell you Gonzalez wasn't your man. Had she been allowed just a little more time—"

"I nearly lost her last time—"

"She stepped over the line last time . . . took too big a risk."

Jerry turned away.

"You owe me," J.D. said to his back. "You owe the women who've already died, and you owe it to the victim out there he's sharpening up his knife right now to kill. Take a trip to the morgue and check out the bodies of Cherry Brown and Tyra Smith and tell me you won't help to get Anna back on this case. Or better yet . . ."

He left the chair and entered the bedroom where Holly appeared to be sleeping deeply. He extracted Laura's coroner's file from the desk drawer and returned to Jerry, the file opened to display his wife's crime scene and autopsy photos.

"This is the memory I live with every second of my life, Jerry."

He flinched and looked away. "Jesus. What the hell are you doing with that?"

"Inspiration."

"You bastard." Jerry shook his head. "This is the kind

of crap that made you the best damn assistant prosecutor in this country. I was an ass to ask for your resignation, John. I'm sorry. Will you ever forgive me?"

"Yeah. Help me find my family's killer, and I'll forgive you."

Lying in the deep shadows of J.D.'s bedroom, the rain a constant drum on the roof, Holly had pretended sleep, her drowsy thoughts focused on the conversation between two old friends. She had tried hard to keep the coroner photos of J.D.'s wife from entering her mind. But she couldn't. Not when every word out of his mouth while discoursing with Costos bled with grief. They literally shook with it, the pain. The heartbreak. The nightmare.

Standing in the morgue, steeling herself to identify her friend, she had no doubt experienced only a small portion of the dread that he had had that night not so long ago. To look upon the bodies of his family—dear God, how could a human being survive such heartbreak and horror? To live with those dreadful images every minute of every day, branded into every waking and sleeping hour in his mind's eye and heart.

At last the voices faded. But for the rain, there was silence. No blaring traffic horns. No distant wailing of a saxophone from some street-corner musician.

Holly sat up, slid her legs from the bed, and rubbed her eyes. Every bone and muscle from her toes to her temples throbbed with tension. As if someone had bludgeoned her.

She swayed as she stood. Cautious, she moved to the bedroom door.

Damascus sat in a chair in a pool of lamplight, elbows on his knees, his face buried in his hands. His wife's folder was lying open on the floor.

He groaned and shook, fighting the emotions welling inside him.

Holly moved to him, eased to her knees before him, closed the file, and slid it away. Gently, tentatively, she touched his dark hair.

As if the touch had been the catalyst, the groan became a sob that tore up from the very heart of him. The words poured forth, a ragged, desperate sound of torment.

"Ah God, this is all my fault, Holly. All of it." He rocked, his fingers twisting into his hair. "I should have let her go. She wanted a divorce. I wouldn't give her one. I wanted it to work. I couldn't lose my kids. Christ, I loved them so much. Besides my job, they were the only thing that meant anything to me."

He raised his head and his streaming eyes looked at her with such mad desperation she felt her heart stop. "She would have taken them away—to Milwaukee, to live with her parents. I should have let her. They would all be alive now.

"I didn't want to fail, Holly. I didn't want to hear from my father 'I told you so.' The bastard didn't approve of us. Said it would never work. She wasn't from the right kind of family. Actually disowned me for doing the right thing and marrying her. Hasn't spoken to me in years because of it.

"It was the first time in my life I didn't bow to his demands. Hell, I didn't even want to be a lawyer. But he wanted us, me and Eric, to follow in his footsteps. He envisioned our stampeding our way through politics—all the way to the White House. The daughter of a used car salesman, who was forced to drop out of college because I knocked her up, wouldn't portray the proper image for a prospective First Lady."

He sank back in the chair, his shoulders sagging, his eyes staring off at nothing. "If I had only come home a day earlier. I could have, Holly. I needed time. I knew as soon as I came home that the arguing would start again. She wanted a divorce. I didn't want to deal with it."

"You didn't know," Holly said softly, her own eyes tearing and her heart hurting so badly for him she thought it would break.

"I gave her everything, except what she needed. I didn't love her. I mean . . . I wasn't in love with her. I cared for her. How can you not care for the mother of your children?"

J.D. closed his eyes and released a heavy breath. "I'm so damn tired of thinking. Of hurting. Regretting. I keep seeing their sweet faces, hearing their laughter. Sometimes at night . . . I swear to God I hear Lisa calling me. I feel her touch me. Butterfly kisses on my cheek. God, make it go away."

Covering his ears with his hands, his face ravaged by fury, he wept, "I want to kill that son of a bitch. Tyron did it. I don't care what the hell everyone else says."

He jumped from the chair, knocking Holly aside, and staggered to the bedroom. Sinking to the floor, Holly stared after him, his pain resonating through her, her own tears scalding her cheeks. How did one comfort a man in such pain? He needed someone to hold him, to kiss away his sorrow, to soothe the horrible raw wound in his soul.

Make it go away.

God, how she wished she could.

She looked up as he reentered the room, gun in hand as he moved toward the front door.

"What are you doing?" She scrambled to her feet.

"I'm going to do what I should have done four years ago."

Throwing open the door, he vanished into the gray sheet of driving rain.

Her legs felt leaden as she moved, stumbled to the door, sound lodged in her throat along with her heart. "Don't," she cried brokenly. "Oh God, John, don't. Please don't do it!"

She ran down the steps, whipping wind and driving rain punching the breath from her. Shielding her face from the deluge, she ran past him, stood between Damascus and his car door. "Don't do this. Please, give me the gun and listen to me."

He shook his head and shouted through the rain. "Get the hell out of here, Holly. I can't take it anymore. That son of a bitch has destroyed too many lives, including yours. He deserves to be exterminated, and if the cops won't do it, I will."

"Nothing is ever going to take away the pain of your loss. It was . . . horrible. So tragic. But killing Tyron won't bring them back. It won't rectify the injustice of it all. And what if you're wrong, John? Listen to me!"

She blinked the spray of rain from her eyes. "You have friends who will help you, John. Jerry Costos. Detective Mallory. Me. Please, let us help you. You're loved and needed by so many. Your mother who adores you. Beverly. Think of Patrick. Think about what this would do to them." She swallowed. "I need you, John. Desperately. God, you're the only friend I have in the world right now besides Melissa."

There came a sudden, ear-shattering explosion of thunder.

"I need you," she repeated more softly. "Please."

Little by little, as the rain drove down on him, J.D. relaxed. He stood with his head down, a man emotionally exhausted.

Holly moved to him, opening her arms to embrace him, hold him as he sank against her, gripping fiercely, one hand tangled in her hair as his body shook with sobs.

"It's okay," she whispered. "Cry all you want. Poor baby. Poor darling. Lean on me, John. Let me help you. I so want to help you."

They held one another, drenched by the deluge as lightning skirted across the sky.

11

They lay together on the bed, J.D. curled in Holly's arms, his head resting on her shoulder. She held him fiercely, her fingers gripping his wet shirt, her mouth pressed into his damp hair . . . aching to absorb the pain from his heart, assure him there would, someday, be sunlight after his storm.

Little by little his body had relaxed against her. His trembling had ceased. She needed desperately to drift away with him. Not yet. Not until she was certain that he had finally surrendered to sleep.

As she felt the easy rise and fall of his breathing, his heart beating against her, she tried to recall a time when she had lain so by a man, enjoyed the embrace of his arms around her.

Never.

The pleasure of it was boundless, the joy of it brought tears to her eyes. For that moment in time, she mattered to someone. She had made a difference. It was what she wanted most in her life, to make a difference to someone. She had come back to New Orleans to help Melissa. Pray, dear God, that she hadn't been too late. But if she was . . .

If she was, she would content herself in knowing that she had been John's port in a storm. The hand extended to him in a turbulent sea of despair.

A man with no hope.

She understood completely. The emptiness. The burden of guilt for mistakes. Broken spirits and dreams. She had been spiritually as low as a human being could get. But she was proof that beyond even the most cataclysmic storm, there is fair weather. She would make him see that. She wouldn't allow him to give up yet. Not ever.

Shutting her eyes, holding him closer, she felt a hot streak of awareness sluice through her. What was she thinking? She had no future with this man. Idiotic to even imagine it. She was a woman with a past that no one aside from a saint or God himself would forgive. The realization that she actually felt something for him other than pity staggered her.

Oh no. She wouldn't let herself go there. He might have nudged open that long closed and locked door to her heart, but she wouldn't allow him in. She wouldn't invite the kind of emotions that inspired the sort of daydreams normal women with normal lives confessed to friends over coffee.

If she was smart, she would get out now. Right now. Nip the fantasy in the bud. She had always been pragmatic regarding her future. Accepted it, for the most part. She was a realist, after all. Most mothers ingrained in their daughters' heads, "You can love a rich man as easily as a poor man." She, on the other hand, had long since acknowledged that she could a love a poor man as easily as a rich man. It wouldn't matter if he sold used shoes from street corners, as long as he loved her. No need in setting her standards too high, she told herself long ago.

Thinking that she stood any chance with a man like Damascus was ludicrous.

Once Holly assured herself that John was asleep, she slid from beneath him and moved to the living room. Puddin' lay curled on the futon, amid the pretty pillows and chenille throw. She glanced around the room, transformed from the dreary, unkempt apartment of a depressed, broke bachelor. The pride she had experienced from the makeover rushed through her again. Home sweet home. Pretty and comfortable. Nothing fancy. But . . . nice. The kind of place she wouldn't mind settling down in.

The idea that he had actually believed that she had turned a few tricks to get the money to do it sliced at her heart. But she wasn't surprised. Retired hookers were exactly that. Hookers. She may as well go through the rest of her life with a giant blazing *P* branded on her forehead. But that wasn't the worst of it. Not nearly the worst of it. A decent man, like Damascus, might, just might, forgive her prostitute transgressions.

But he would never forgive her for murder.

J.D. awoke, confused, with a splitting headache. Then he remembered the night before. Christ.

He hadn't come that close to killing Tyron since the

day he'd IDed his family at the morgue, since the obsession to find and kill his family's murderer had taken him over.

Not that it hadn't come rushing back over him occasionally. The shrinks who had counseled him had assured him that wasn't unusual. Antidepressants had helped for a while. But, eventually, he had weaned himself off of them because he didn't like their emotion-numbing qualities. He needed the piercing pain of his loss to keep him centered and focused.

But, he had to admit to himself, last night the pain and fury had crushed down on him more heavily than usual. Why? The beating he'd just taken hadn't helped. Lying there in bed for two days had given him too much time to think, to dwell on his hatred for Tyron Johnson—his manipulation, control, and abuse of women. The not-so-subtle threats the creep had made to J.D. each time J.D. found a reason to drag Tyron's sorry ass into court. The cruel notes of consolation the bastard had sent regarding his family's deaths.

Then Costos had shown up on his doorstep. Something had triggered inside J.D.

He couldn't explain it. He never could. It was there, the grief and fury. And it had overwhelmed him in that moment. The grief counselors had warned him about it and preached that if he didn't let them go—his family— the wounds would have no chance of healing. But he simply wasn't ready to let them go. He might never be ready.

Sitting up on the edge of the bed, he glanced at the clock. Seven-thirty.

"You okay?"

He looked up. Holly stood in the doorway, her expression concerned. "Yeah," he replied and nodded.

"May called to remind you that you have a court case at ten."

"Christ."

"To quote her, 'You best get your butt down there or Judge Patterson will find you in contempt . . . again.' "

"I'm not prepared."

She grinned. "Damascus, you could show up in court deaf, blind, and dumb and still win your case. Don't forget how brilliant you are."

"I was. Not anymore."

"Sure you are. Get dressed. I'm making you a decent breakfast. You're going to be at that courthouse by nine A.M. if I have to drive you there myself. Oh, and your mother called reminding you of dinner tomorrow at her place. She invited me as well."

He grinned. "She likes you."

"Nice lady. But I declined. I'm not the dinner party kind of gal."

"I want you to go."

She left the room and J.D. stood, took a deep breath to clear his head, and followed her.

Holly had prepared eggs, bacon, and grits with a side of buttered toast and a glass of milk. He tried to remember the last time he'd eaten a decent morning meal. He usually skipped it completely or made a quick stop at the local convenience store for coffee and a donut. The aroma of food made his stomach growl.

At the table, he flashed her a look as she poured him a cup of coffee. "You're spoiling me."

She smiled. "Enjoy it. We all deserve to be spoiled now and again."

He reached out and closed his fingers around her wrist. "Thanks. For last night. For this morning. For everything."

She shrugged as her cheeks flushed, and she avoided his gaze with a shy lowering of her lashes. "What are friends for?"

She pulled away and returned to the coffeepot, poured herself a cup before turning to face him again. "So tell me about your case. Something scandalous, I hope."

"A custody case. It's getting ugly. I really would like you to go with me tomorrow, Holly. To my mom's."

"Don't change the subject. Besides, to quote a gazillion women before me . . ." She giggled. "I haven't a thing to wear!"

"I'll buy you something pretty."

She buttered her toast, then put it down. "I can't. Please don't ask me again."

"Why?"

"I'm not . . . I'd feel uncomfortable. Besides . . . Beverly will be there—"

"I told you, there's nothing going on between us."

"She's in love with you, John."

"I'm not in love with her. And even if I was, Christ, she's my brother's wife. Eric and I might not particularly care for one another, but there's lines a man doesn't cross. My mom likes you. She told me so."

"She doesn't know me. How can she like me?"

"How can anyone not like you?" He grinned.

Averting her eyes, she focused on her toast. "I can think of a few reasons."

"Maybe you think too much."

They sat in silence as J.D. dove into the scrambled eggs and Holly nibbled on toast. The fog had begun to lift from his brain and he was beginning to feel human again. He glanced at Holly.

"I spoke with Mallory about Melissa. He's taking the CSI to her apartment. Not a great deal they can do but go over the place for any blood evidence. He'll speak again with the neighbors. Maybe they'll be more willing to talk to a cop than they were to me. A badge has a tendency to shake the truth out of people."

Her eyes lit up. "That's great."

"Don't get excited. Whatever happened to Melissa, if something has happened to her, it probably took place on her way to meet her john that night. At that point, about all they can do is circulate her photograph. Question any-one in the area who might have seen her. Any ideas in that regard? Places she hung out frequently?"

"She occasionally worked the River Rat Bar on Bour-bon Street. Not often. No need to, really. She had her regulars. An occasional tourist."

"Names, phone numbers of her regulars?"

She nodded. "But she kept it with her always."

"They'll question Tyron, of course."

Her face paled. "They won't tell him who reported her missing, will they? That's confidential, isn't it?"

"Of course," he replied softly.

There was something in the way the desperation had

widened her eyes that invited that niggling feeling of familiarity to tickle the back of his mind. At some point in his career, he and Holly Jones had crossed paths. He was certain of it.

Holly had been right. By eleven-thirty J.D. had wrapped up his case nicely. His client had attained full custody of her kids and her creep of a husband sat simmering in his chair, cursing his attorney for his incompetence. J.D. recognized trouble when he saw it, and Samuel Pierpoint was going to be trouble. He was a time bomb ready to explode. His defiance of the restraining order his wife had filed against him was evidence enough.

As his client shared tears and hugs with her parents, J.D. shut his briefcase and glanced up at Judge Patterson, whose eyes were narrowed and his mouth set in a grim line.

"Mr. Damascus, approach the bench, please."

Here we go, he thought.

"As I recall, the last time you stood before my bench I told you that if you didn't cut your hair and get rid of that stud in your ear, I would find you in contempt. Your appearance is blatantly disrespectful to this court and your client."

"No disrespect intended, Your Honor, but I don't see how my hair and stud have got anything to do with my capabilities to adequately represent my clients."

"I find it offensive."

"I don't."

The judge sat back in his chair. "One last warning. If

you appear before me in such a fashion again, I will hold you in contempt. Understood?"

"Understood, Your Honor."

"That being said, I congratulate you on your case. Fine job."

"I suspect we haven't heard the last of Mr. Pierpoint."

"Unfortunately, I feel you're right. Watch your back with that one. He's a nut."

"I suspect *nut* is putting it mildly, Your Honor."

They exchanged nods and grins, then J.D. left the courtroom to be greeted by Penny Pierpoint and her jubilant parents. Penny was a cute, petite, middle-aged woman whose crooked nose was evidence of her husband's abuse. The beating had hospitalized her for a week the year before. She hugged him and wept on his suit coat. Her body shook.

"How can I thank you enough, Mr. Damascus?"

"Be happy, Penny. Love your kids. Get the hell out of New Orleans and don't look back."

Her gray-haired mother laughed. "You needn't worry about that. Their bags are packed and first thing in the morning we're on a plane to California. She and the children will live with us until she can get on her feet and find a job."

He thought of telling them all that two thousand miles wouldn't make much difference to a man like Pierpoint. One way or another, he would insinuate himself into their lives again. But no point in stating the obvious. They knew Sam would be a bone in their throats until hell froze over. Let them enjoy this moment of victory for as long as it lasted.

"Well, well," came the voice behind him. "J.D. Damascus."

He turned and looked down into Anna Travelli's sparkling eyes. "I'll be damned."

"Nice job in there. There isn't an attorney alive who
can work the opposition like you, except for Jerry, of
course. Buy an old friend a cup of coffee?"

"I have a few things to tie up at the office. If you can
tolerate May's chicory, you've got a deal."

One couldn't appraise Anna Travelli and believe
for an instant that she had the biggest pair of brass balls
of any agent working for the FBI. Tall, slender, and fem-
inine, her face looked more worthy of a *Vogue* cover than
a cop's shield. She could have passed as Nicole Kidman's
twin. Glorious red hair and bone structure, skin as smooth
and pale as a magnolia petal with just a sprinkling of
freckles across her nose. She didn't so much as wince as
she sipped May's black, bitter coffee. Then again, having
spent the last ten years drinking the garbage served up in
police departments across the country, he was not surprised.

"You look like hell." She regarded him with those eyes
that were as unnerving as they were beautiful. "Fighting
again?"

J.D. touched the stitches on his chin. "Something like
that."

"Jerry filled me in on the situation. I refrained from
rubbing it in his face. I'm sure he's feeling shitty enough
as it is. Just spent the last couple of hours with the D.A.

and Chief Killroy. Obviously the department is keeping this as quiet as possible. One leak of these killings and heads are going to roll. Which probably wouldn't be a bad thing, considering. I just don't want Jerry's to be one of them."

"I can't see any way around it, Anna."

She nodded and shrugged. "He's a big boy. I think he can handle it. Truth is, it will be a relief for him. Whether you want to believe it or not, he's suffered these last few years from a bad case of conscience . . . not to mention missing you." She smiled. "So how's it going? Getting on with your life?"

"I'm still here. I guess so."

"Anyone special in your life?"

"A woman, you mean?"

She nodded.

He thought of Holly. In the past, when asked that question, he had readily responded, "No." But the denial now froze on his lips, and he felt stunned by it. Flustered. And he wasn't a man who was easily flustered. At least when it came to the women he had occasionally dated these last few years.

"Maybe," he replied.

"Anyone I know?"

"I doubt it."

"Potentially serious?"

He shrugged.

"Okay." She smiled. "Damascus the enigma. Always a man of few words, except in the courtroom."

"Loose lips sink ships . . . or something clichéd like that."

"So, we get down to business. The state executed the wrong man. Or did it? Can we be certain our perp isn't a copycat?"

"The signature is identical. He tortures first, then murders. Decapitation, evisceration. As you well know, there were certain aspects of the killer's signature that were never made public."

She nodded, her look becoming distant. She was headed for that place where few other people ever ventured. Or knew how to. Into the killer's mind and psyche. When Quantico had first dumped her in the NOPD's lap, she had been confronted by total resistance from the department. They considered profilers just one rung above psychics. Not that there wasn't a little of that going on as well in Anna's mind, but she was bright enough not to talk about it.

"We've established that our perp is a domineering killer. He gets his rocks off inspiring fear in his victim. It gives him a feeling of control and power that he otherwise lacks in his life. It's been established that our freak doesn't have sex with his victims. That doesn't mean he isn't experiencing orgasmic fulfillment. He probably masturbates during the torture. Uses a condom to avoid leaving semen that could be used to DNA him. Most likely, he undresses before he butchers her to avoid blood on his clothes—or he brings a change of clothes. But he's bright enough not to shower, knowing the CSI unit could pick up any pubic hair from the drain that could be later DNA-tested to nail him. He simply washes his hands of blood, redresses, and quietly leaves. Discards the clothes elsewhere and showers at home, or someplace else.

"He may or may not have had sex with these prostitutes in the past. He may choose them at random, but I doubt it. He watches her for a while. There is something about her that intrigues him. As I recall, most of the girls he killed four years ago were very young. Not hardened as badly by the life. Makes sense. A younger individual would be more intimidated by his threats. The greater her fear, the greater his pleasure.

"He's highly organized, obviously. Probably college-educated and highly intelligent. Holds a white-collar job. Socially competent. He probably was an only child, but if there were siblings, he was the favorite. But only because he kissed ass a lot. More than he cared to. Still does in his line of work. In short, he's a yes man. Possibly looked over for promotions he thought he deserved. Probably good-looking. Could charm the rattlers off a snake."

Anna set aside her cup of cold coffee, her dark green eyes unblinking as she looked at J.D. "Which brings me to Laura and my real reason for this visit."

He frowned.

"I've given this a lot of thought these past years. Toyed with it, really." She cleared her throat, unnaturally discomposed for a woman whose bluntness and getting to the point was renown. "I believe she knew him, J.D. They may have even been lovers."

The blood drained from his face as he sank back in his chair.

"I'm sorry," she said, briefly averting her eyes. "But nothing else makes sense. Why she was out that late, at the park. They had planned an assignation. She couldn't find a sitter and took the kids with her, leaving them asleep in the back of the car. Something happened to set him off. Maybe she told him she wanted to end it. This type of individual wouldn't take kindly to getting dumped. Remember, he must be in control of the situation at all times, and if not, he goes off."

She shifted in her chair. "Your marriage was in trouble. She wouldn't be the first woman to look for love in all the wrong places."

"Christ." He groaned as the onslaught of memories rushed over him. Anna's sympathetic voice drifted to him.

"Try to think back. For any clue that she had something going on on the side. Did she stay out late? Get phone calls from strangers? Behave nervously or guiltily?"

"No." He shook his head, heat returning to his face to make him sweat.

"Your son was in school during the day. What about Lisa?"

"Day care half a day three times a week." He took a deep drink of his cold coffee, shivering from the bitterness. "We argued about it. I thought she was too young. She was always picking up colds, and . . . Excuse me."

He left his chair and exited the office, made his way to the men's room down the hall. He closed the door and locked it, braced his hands on each side of the sink and tried his best not to vomit. Not possible. Not Laura. Not with another man. She wasn't the kind.

Right. Where was his head? He was a damn lawyer, for Christ's sake. There wasn't a woman out there whose head couldn't be turned by some smooth-talking son of a bitch, particularly when she was in a bad marriage. Feeling unloved and unappreciated. Her husband burying himself in his work instead of his home life. Three quarters of the divorces today were due to infidelity. What made him believe his was any different?

Could he have been that blind?

There came a knock on the door, and May called out, "You okay in there?"

"Yeah." He turned on the water and splashed his face.

"Ms. Travelli left. Said she'll contact you later. And you got a phone call from Chief Killroy. Says it's important."

J.D. dried his face and opened the door. May regarded him skeptically. "Damn. You white as a ghost. Should I call a doctor again?"

"Hell, no." As he returned to his office, May followed, droning on about case files, clients' unpaid balances, and the escalating eviction threats from their landlord.

"And your mother called. Said she wants you to bring Holly to dinner tomorrow. And Patrick has been suspended from school for a week. Call Beverly as soon as possible. Woman is hysterical."

He fell into the chair, reached for the phone, and called Travis Killroy. "Damascus here. What's up, Chief?"

"Then I take it you haven't heard."

J.D. didn't like the sound of that. "Heard what?"

"Sam Pierpoint just walked into his ex-wife's house and blew her away, as well as their kids, her parents, and himself. So much for restraining orders."

12

Jean Lancaster was pissed. Then again, she was always pissed. She never spoke below a level that didn't force J.D. to hold the phone away from his ear.

"The bastard has cleaned out my checking account. All of it. What the hell am I supposed to do now?"

He only half listened, still too numbed by the news about the Pierpoints. He kept seeing the joy in Penny's eyes, the relief in her parents'. And the kids. Two boys and a little girl. All gone. Just like that. Then there was the conversation with Anna. The stinking possibility that Laura had been unfaithful. That he might, just might, have been wrong these last four years believing Tyron had murdered his family.

"Are you listening to me, Damascus? Maybe you'll sit up and take notice over the fact that now I can't pay you."

"I'm listening, Jean. Did I not specifically tell you to close out that account—"

"I want him arrested."

"No can do. The account was joint."

"Whose side are you on, anyway?"

"It's the law. What's yours is his and his is yours. At least until the divorce papers have been filed. Are you going to divorce him now?"

"I'm going to kill the son of a bitch."

"As your attorney, I wouldn't advise that."

May appeared at the door. "Beverly is on line two."

"I'll call her back," he mouthed.

"Says it's an emergency."

He put Jean, still ranting, on hold. "What's up, Bev? I've got a client holding."

"Patrick has been suspended from school, that's what's up."

"For what?"

"He taped a pornographic photograph to his teacher's desk."

"Did you call Eric?"

"He drove up to Baton Rouge this morning. He won't be back until late this afternoon." She took an unsteady breath. "His principal wants to see me as soon as possible. I can't go down there and face those people alone, John."

"You want me to go along."

"Please."

He glanced at the pile of case files on his desk, then up at May, whose expression reflected her annoyance.

"Right. I'll meet you at the school in half an hour." Hanging up the phone, he fell back in his chair, rubbed his throbbing head. "Sometimes it just doesn't pay to get out of bed."

"Um hmm. Don't forget you got Jean holding on one."

"Tell her I'll call her back. On second thought, nicely suggest she find herself a new attorney. And call my mom. Tell her that Holly is coming."

May smiled. "I like the sounds of that."

"Yeah?" He stood and reached for the tie he had thrown on the desk. "Don't get excited. We're just friends."

"She's a mighty pretty lady. And nice. Real nice."

"She's hell on wheels, May."

"But she's nice."

"Right." He grinned. "She's nice."

Dan Peterson, the dean of St. Michael's School, sat behind his massive desk looking grim and flustered. He gingerly fingered the photograph as he glanced at Beverly, then J.D. Finally, he slid the color glossy across the desk to J.D.

"As you'll readily see, there is just cause for these actions, Mr. Damascus. The photograph is not only inappropriate, but also highly disturbing."

J.D. picked up the photograph, tilting it slightly so Beverly couldn't see it. He stared at the image, his mind refusing to fully register what he saw at first. It was a picture of a man sodomizing a woman's naked and mutilated corpse.

"I would say," he began softly, "that inappropriate and disturbing is putting it mildly."

Beverly, sitting on the edge of her chair, face chalk white, extended her hand. "Let me see it."

"No." He folded it in half and tucked it into his suit coat breast pocket.

"Of course we'll hold a hearing regarding this unacceptable behavior," Peterson said. "St. Michael's prides itself on the character of its students. This is a fine, well-respected establishment. We accept only the highest caliber of student here."

"What are you saying?" Beverly glared at Peterson, her eyes wide. "Are you permanently expelling my son?"

"That's exactly what he's saying." J.D. took her hand.

"You can't do that."

"Yes, they can, Bev."

"Just like that."

"Just like that."

"Mrs. Damascus, your son needs counseling. Desperately."

"My son is brilliant."

"Yes. He is. Which makes this apparent problem all the greater. Patrick has great intellectual potential. But emotionally, psychologically, he's a mess. I'm not sure I've ever witnessed an angrier young man. To be quite frank, I fear for the lives of the students as well as his instructors. With such tragedies as Columbine looming over us all, we simply can't be too careful."

"How dare you suggest that Patrick is capable of such a heinous act."

Peterson lowered his eyes. "I'm sorry, Mrs. Damascus. We'll contact you next week and let you know our decision."

Beverly paced the den, wringing her hands as tears streamed from her eyes. "Eric is going to be furious.

This is the last straw. He'll send him away, John. To military school. A scandal like this could hurt his political aspirations."

"This is hardly a scandal, Bev. Patrick wouldn't be the first politician's kid to get into trouble. Besides, a little time away in an institution where someone is willing to occasionally kick his butt might be good for him."

She turned on him, her eyes flashing. "I suppose this is all my fault. I'm not strict enough with him. Is that what you're saying?"

"He needs an authority figure, and with Eric so wrapped up in his career—"

"He has you. Or he did. You haven't given him the time of day since you became involved with that tramp."

"Keep Holly out of this."

He mentally counted to ten. His fuse was short and burning, his tolerance on the verge of incinerating completely. The doors Anna had opened regarding Laura had been bad enough. The news about the Pierpoints had driven him to the edge.

"I'm not Patrick's father. He's not my responsibility. Neither are you. I've got enough problems in my life for ten men, Bev. I just can't handle one more burden on my shoulders—"

"That's what we are to you?" she cried, her voice uncharacteristically shrill, verging on hysterical. "A burden? After the years I've stood by you during your rotten marriage and the nightmare of your family's murders and this is what I get in return? I'm a burden?"

He looked away. "I'm sorry. That's not what I meant at all."

"Of course it is." She gave a sharp laugh. "How embarrassing is that? And sobering. All these years I believed we actually meant something to you. You're no better than Eric. And your father. Wives are an unwanted but necessary responsibility—"

"You're not my wife, Beverly."

She glared at him, her face blotched and her eyes hard as stone. "And I never will be. Right?"

"Right."

He left the chair. "I'll speak to Patrick. But unless you're willing to get him into counseling—get him help—we can all talk until we're blue in the face, and it's not going to do a damn bit of good. I've seen enough boys like him paraded through the courts to know what I'm talking about. He's headed for big trouble, and if you don't do something now, the next call you make to me might very well be in an official capacity, to represent him during a trial."

"If my son needs a lawyer, it sure as hell wouldn't be a loser like you."

Narrowing his eyes, he rewarded her with a flat smile. "I'm going to forgive that nasty little jab because you're upset. And rightfully so. But if you don't get a grip, sweetheart, you'll have to take a number to speak to me on the phone."

Turning his back on her, he left the room, yanking the loose tie from his neck and shoving it into his pocket as he climbed the stairs, arriving at Patrick's door to find it locked. He beat it with his fist.

The door slowly opened, Patrick's eyes lit, and he smiled. "Hey."

"Don't hey me, punk. I'm not in the mood for your bullshit."

J.D. shoved open the door and moved into the room, which was a wreck of discarded clothes and scattered schoolbooks.

"Close the door," he snapped, facing his sullen nephew.

Patrick kicked the door closed and fell back against it, hands jammed into his jeans pockets. "What's up your ass?"

J.D. withdrew the photograph from his suit coat and flung it at him. It fell, open, at his feet. "Mind telling me where you got that garbage?"

"None of your business."

"You got any more?"

"None of your business. If that's all you came here for, you can get the hell out."

J.D. moved toward him, thrust one finger in his face. "Don't fuck with me, pal. I'm not your mother who's going to run from the room in tears and denial. I'll whip your ass if I have to."

Patrick's eyes widened and he shrank back against the door. "Hey, dude. Chill."

"Answer me."

"I found it. Okay?"

"Where?"

"Down by the river. There's crates and crates of 'em in an old warehouse."

"Okay. Let's go."

"Go where?"

"You show me this warehouse."

Lowering his eyes, his face flushing, Patrick shuffled his feet.

"You're lying, aren't you?"

He nodded. "Someone gave it to me. One of the guys at school."

"Who? Give me a name."

"I ain't rattin'. Give me a break. Like I would do that to one of my friends."

"Seems you care more about screwing over a friend than you do your family. Why is that?"

"Jeez, what's the big deal? It's just a photograph."

"That's not just a photograph. It's sick and perverted trash."

"It was just a joke, J.D. That stupid teacher pissed me off."

"Well, your sick joke has gotten you kicked out of St. Michael's and you've broken your mother's heart, not to mention humiliating her."

He shrugged and shoved away from the door, flopped onto his bed, and stared at the ceiling. "Big deal. I hated St. Michael's."

"You might appreciate St. Michael's a little more after you spend the next three years at military school."

"I ain't going to no military school. Maybe I'll just quit school. Maybe I'll just run away."

"Maybe you'll find your butt in prison after you're forced to steal or sell dope to survive. Maybe you'll get up close and personal to the creeps who participate in the kinds of perversion depicted in that photograph. They'd get off on a young, good-looking ass like yours. You'd spend half of your days and nights on your hands and knees accommodating those sickos, pal."

Patrick rolled to his side, his back to J.D. "At least I finally got your attention, huh?"

J.D. closed his eyes, the anger draining from him, leaving his head pounding and his stomach burning like hell's fire. He dropped onto the bed, stretched out on his back, and stared at the model planes overhead, rotating at the end of the string.

"Sorry. We love you, kid. We just don't want to see you screw up your life. You've got too much going for you."

Patrick shifted to his back, lay shoulder to shoulder with J.D. as they both watched the plane slowly turn. "I wish I was dead," he said.

"We'd miss you."

"Maybe my mom would. And you. But Dad wouldn't give a damn."

"Trust me." He swallowed. "His heart would be shattered."

"He's never loved me as much as you loved Billy. He doesn't love any of us."

"That's not true."

"Sure it is and we both know it. I hate him."

"We all go through those phases, Patrick. When parents are the enemy. We grow out of it."

"Yeah?" He rolled his head and stared at J.D. "Then how come you and Granddad hate one another?"

"I don't hate my father."

"Dad hates him. Calls him a bastard when Granddad's not around. Funny thing is, Dad's just like him. Only worse, I think."

J.D. could hardly argue that point. His brother had become as cold and manipulating as Charles Damascus. A chip off the old iceberg.

"I wish my mom would divorce him. We'd all be happier. I know I would. My mom deserves better."

"You're not helping her, Patrick. You're hurting her."

"I don't mean to. It's him I want to hurt. Dad. He's a liar and a fake. When I see him put on his false face and smile when he's in public, I wanna puke. He's a hypocrite and one of these days everyone is gonna know it."

J.D. grinned. "Look in the dictionary under politician and you'll find hypocrite, pal."

"That sucks."

The air conditioner kicked on, and the air blowing from the vent caused the model plane to spin wildly.

"I love you," Patrick said, his voice weary and sad. "I'll try to do better. For Mom. And you."

J.D. looked into his nephew's face. Patrick's eyes were closed, the anger that had earlier distorted his features was now gone, replaced by the youth who so reminded him of Billy—how his son might have looked had he lived to be sixteen. The pain and loss felt as sharp in that moment as it had four years ago. If only . . .

"I love you, too," he whispered.

J.D. eased from the bedroom, gently closing the door to avoid waking Patrick.

"What the hell are you doing here?"

He looked around into his brother's eyes, which were red-rimmed and furious. His suit looked rumpled and sweat stained, and it was obvious he hadn't shaved that morning. Jaw working and his hands in fists, Eric moved into J.D.'s face. "Answer me, you prick. What the hell do you think you're doing here?

J.D. shoved him back. "Back off, Eric. Patrick is asleep—"

"Who the hell gave you the right to butt into my family's business?"

"My family, too, Eric."

"My son, J.D. How many times do I need to remind you of that?"

"Maybe somebody needs to remind *you* of that." J.D. moved closer. "You want to fight me, Eric, then let's take it downstairs. Patrick is a wreck, mostly thanks to you. Seeing his dad and uncle bloody each other's noses isn't going to help him any."

J.D. moved down the stairs, Eric at his heels. Beverly stood at the bottom, wringing her hands, her eyes swollen and filled with tears. As she reached for Eric, he shoved her aside. "Stay the hell out of this. This is between me and J.D."

They entered Eric's office, and Eric slammed the door. His face red and sweating, Eric thrust one finger at J.D. "I've told you for the last time, you leave my wife and kid alone."

"Patrick is crying out for help. What the hell is wrong with you?"

"I don't need you breathing down my goddamn neck all the time. I've got enough to deal with with Dad and Jack, not to mention Beverly's constant whining and nagging."

"Maybe if you listened less to Dad and Jack and more to Beverly and Patrick, you might get a little less heat around here."

Eric smirked and moved closer, his face red. "What the hell do you know about being a father? Or a husband for that matter? Maybe if you'd spent more time at home, your wife and kids wouldn't be dead right now."

J.D. grabbed his brother's suit lapels and drove him against the wall. "You son of a bitch. If you weren't my brother . . ."

"Go ahead, John." Eric sneered. "Do everyone a favor and put me out of my misery."

"You're not worth going to prison over, Eric. But I'm gonna say this. You care so much for your damn career, you'd better stop and think about how all this is going to look to your future voters. Eventually, one of those bimbos you've been boffing on the side is going to crawl out of the woodwork and go to the tabloids. Or Beverly's going to get a stomach full of you and she's going to divorce you. Or Patrick's going to be pushed over the edge so he does something that will put his expulsion from St. Michael's in the shade. I wonder how Daddy will feel about you then, Eric? And Jack?" J.D. gave a short laugh. "He'll cut you loose. You'll be history. And I'll be on the sidelines laughing my ass off."

Releasing his grip on Eric, J.D. backed away. "Let's face it. You're nothing without Dad's and Jack's influence. If Dad hadn't bribed your professors, you would never have made it through college. If he hadn't bribed Jack Strong with financial backing, you wouldn't be legislative director right now. You're nothing but Charles Damascus's puppet and that's all you'll ever be."

As J.D. stepped around him for the door, Eric grabbed his arm, his shaking fist twisting into the sleeve of J.D.'s coat. "One last warning. Stay away from my son, J.D. Stay away from my wife. Or I'll hurt you. I swear to God . . . I'll hurt you."

13

Holly wasn't at the apartment when J.D. got home at six.

He tossed the gift-wrapped package on the coffee table, peeled out of his suit coat, flung it over the back of the chair, and headed to the kitchen for a cold beer.

He had never been one to care much for television, mostly due to his days working for the D.A.'s office. Watching himself interrogated by bloodthirsty reporters who slanted stories to boost the stations' ratings had set his teeth on edge and too often come close to damaging his case. But tonight he swept up the remote and turned on the set, dropped onto the futon, and focused on the news. The headline story was about the Pierpoint murders and suicide.

Chief Killroy spoke in his usual monotone about their turbulent divorce and custody case while the cameras zoomed in on the family's sheet-draped bodies as they were loaded into the ambulances that would transport them to the morgue. Photographs of Penny and her children were flashed on the screen, the three kids beaming with pleasure under a Christmas tree.

No point in second-guessing himself. He'd done his job. Won his case. No judge in his right mind would have allowed a man with a drug conviction and a history of physical abuse to have custody of his kids.

J.D. had drilled home to Penny there were agencies that could help her, which specialized in victim protection, but she hadn't been willing to go that far. It would have meant she would have had to change her name and disappear, cutting ties with her parents and friends.

If he had only pushed her a little harder . . .

Pressing the cold beer to his forehead, he closed his eyes and changed the channel. Senator Jack Strong's face filled up the screen, teeth flashing like a braying jackass as he expounded on how his opponent, Senator John Whitehorse from New Mexico, wouldn't stand a chance against him in the presidential primaries.

"Right." J.D grinned and swigged his beer. "Whitehorse will kick your ass, Jack."

The phone rang. Hitting the mute button, he left the futon and answered.

"Damascus. Killroy here. What the fuck are you doing to me?"

"I don't know. What am I doing, Travis?"

"Anna Travelli just left my office."

He drank his beer and waited.

"I told you to stay the hell away from this case. Now that freak has gotten involved. Fuckin' FBI, man. She's going to the goddamn media with this. Jesus!"

"Lady's got to do what the lady's got to do, Killroy. If you would have listened to her last time—"

"I'm supposed to listen to a goddamn psychic? Is that what you're suggesting?"

"Listen to me, you hardheaded prick. The son of a bitch who might have killed my family is at it again and this time you're going to catch him. I don't care if that means every official involved in this case loses their jobs and their asses."

Silence, but for Killroy's breathing in his ear.

Finally, "You don't know what the hell you're getting yourself into, Damascus. It's gonna get ugly. Real ugly."

"Are you threatening me, Killroy?"

"Fair warning. If you believed you had any friends still in this department, better think again. When this shit hits the fan and this department gets reamed up the yazoo, there won't be a badge out there who won't be after you."

"Careful, Chief. What you say can and will be used in a court of law."

"Take your goddamn Miranda and shove it."

The phone crashed in his ear. J.D. put down the receiver, smiling in smug satisfaction. At long last he had Killroy by the balls.

Holly arrived at J.D.'s apartment at just after two A.M. Her feet hurt like hell. She smelled like smoke and beer and craved a shower, desperately. Taking a job at one of the Bourbon Street bars had been a spur-of-the-moment decision. She needed money. They were short-handed and hired her on the spot. Probably not the wisest decision she had ever made. She was risking coming face-to-face with an old john or one of the girls, but she had never been dependent on anyone but herself to survive. And leaning on Damascus, especially when he was barely scraping by, had eaten at her.

As she stepped into the apartment, she froze. J.D. slouched on the futon, his feet propped on the coffee table, Puddin' sprawled across his lap. He wore nothing but his underwear, navy blue Y-fronts. One look at his face told her he was pissed.

"Where the hell have you been?" he said.

"Hi to you, too." She kicked off her shoes and headed for the kitchen to pour herself a glass of milk and contemplate how she was going to deal with Damascus, who was apparently in the mood for hell-raising.

She turned, jumping as he moved up against her, pinning her against the counter, his body so close she could feel his heat.

"I said, where the hell have you been, Holly?"

She swallowed. "Working."

His eyes narrowed and his mouth curled. "Anyone I know?"

As calmly as possible, she set down her drink. "Look, I'm too tired right now to go there with you."

He moved closer, slid one finger along her cheek, over her lips. "Aren't you going to ask me about my day, darling?"

"Okay. How was your day?"

"I won my case."

She forced a smile. "That's great. Congratulations."

"Of course, my client's ex topped off the celebration by blowing her and her entire family away before splattering his brains all over the house. Hip, hip, hooray. The great Damascus scores another one. Are you impressed?"

She stared up into his eyes, which were a tumult of emotion, pain, and anger. "I'm sorry," she whispered.

Closer. He nuzzled her ear with his lips, slid one hand over her breast, and gently squeezed. "Anna dropped in to see me. We discussed the case, and she pointed out that my wife was probably involved with the killer. Lovers. The spouse is always the last to know, as the old saying goes.

"Then there was my getting dragged down to Patrick's school. Kid's got himself expelled because he's into photographs of necrophilia. That was topped off by a call from Chief Killroy, who is, by the way, the pervert you nearly killed in that warehouse. Used to be a nice guy. Has a great wife and terrific kids, so you'd think he'd give a damn about what happened to my family, wouldn't you? But I digress. He's not very happy with me because Anna Travelli has gotten involved in the case. God forbid the FBI should throw open this can of smelly worms and actually force the department to fess up to their mistake.

"I dropped by Cherie's Boutique and picked you up a little something pretty to wear to my mom's tomorrow. Haven't been by there since Laura died. It was her favorite place to shop. Expensive, of course. But classy. She was one hell of a dresser. I'll grant you that. I'm sure she dressed up nicely to meet the dick who was screwing her.

"I come home needing a shoulder and you're not here. So I sit there for the next few hours and my mind is spinning a hundred miles an hour. I first worry that you're out there again looking for Melissa. Then I begin to imagine you in the clutches of a killer. That progresses to images of you on your knees for some john. Then I get pissed. And then I ask myself why I should give a damn and try to convince myself that you mean nothing to me. But some annoying voice in my head begs to differ.

"So for the last hour I sat on that futon arguing the case for and against my feelings for you. The prosecutor states that once a whore always a whore and the last thing I need in my life is another woman breaking my heart and screwing some dude behind my back. The defense attorney argues that people can change. Hell, I've made some pretty lousy life decisions myself. I can hardly cast stones. Why hold someone up to standards that even I haven't lived up to? Then you come in smelling like a cheap whore and confess you've been working and blow the defense's case to hell."

She turned her face away, the brutality of his words slugging her heart like a fist. "Obviously you haven't checked your messages, John. I called you and told you. I took a waitressing job. I invited you down for a drink on me."

Shoving him aside, she moved to the living room and snatched up her purse and shoes. "I'm outta here. Thanks for the charity these last few days, Damascus, but I made a vow four years ago that I wouldn't let myself be victimized any longer. If you need a shoulder while you wallow in self-pity, then give Bev a call."

As she reached the door, he grabbed her arm, spinning her around so fast her purse and shoes went flying. Her back flattened against the door, his hands planted on either side of her, she glared up into his sweating face, her anger evaporating at the desperation she saw in his eyes.

"Please." His voice quavered. "Don't leave. I'm sorry, Holly. I just . . . I'm sorry. It's been a rough day. I didn't mean those things I said. I'm a bastard, okay?

"I need you," he added softly. "For the first time in years, I looked forward to coming home. I've been so damned lonely for so long and when you weren't here. . . . Too much time to dwell on the past. Too much time to dwell on my mistakes."

He touched her cheek, his fingers trembling. "When Anna asked me today if there was anyone special in my life, I realized there was. You. I think about you constantly. A hundred times today I wanted to pick up the phone and call you. Just to hear your voice, steady as a rock. Then I would remind myself that I'm not some sweaty-palmed adolescent driven by rampaging hormones."

Grinning, he said, "Not that there aren't a few rampaging hormones scrambling around inside me. I want you like hell. Have since the minute I first saw you. But if sex was all there was driving me, I could get that with any of the women I've dated over the last few years.

"Regardless of what I said earlier, I admire the hell out of you. Your loyalty to Melissa. Coming here and putting your life in jeopardy to help her. Your ability to put the past behind you and start over. You're so damn special."

He slowly, tentatively lowered his lips to hers, brushed her mouth gently, his breath sighing against her, his fist clenching as if he were fighting the need to drag her into his arms, against his body.

"Please stay," he whispered, then backed away, taking her hand in his and tugging her along, to the coffee table where he picked up the wrapped present and offered it to her, his eyes eager, his grin boyish. "Open it."

She sat on the futon, stared at the gift on her lap, the pretty silver paper and the bright red bow. She tried to recall a time when anyone had given her such an exquisitely wrapped gift, far too beautiful to destroy in haste. She wanted to savor the moment, even as the hurt and anger she had experienced over his cruelty began to drain from her, allowing her feelings for Damascus to fill her up again. A pain more acute than his mean words. If she was smart, she could walk away now. Use his insult as an excuse to run again. Before there was no turning back . . . at least for her heart.

Carefully, she peeled back the tape, her heart squeezing and racing at once. Her eyes burned. Breathing was difficult. Her hands shaking, she opened the box and blinked with disbelief at the black dress, removed it from the wrapping as she slowly stood.

She swallowed and smiled, her gaze locking with his. "It's beautiful, John. The most beautiful dress I've ever seen."

"Put it on." He grinned his little boy grin and nudged her toward the bedroom. "Go on."

Nodding, Holly hurried to the bedroom, stood for a moment with the dress clutched to her breasts. From the living room came the sorrowful but romantic orchestration of "Unchained Melody." Dear God. How could he have known that was her favorite song?

For a moment, she closed her eyes, her hand stroking the dress as she whispered, "I hunger for your touch."

Holly removed her jeans and T-shirt and slid the dress down over her head. She stared at herself in the dresser mirror, tears rising to her eyes as she ran her hands down the form-fitting, sleeveless shift then along the modestly-cut neckline. She hardly recognized herself—this . . . lady.

A smile formed on her lips. She wanted a picture of this image, the woman she could have been had things been different, had her desperation and fear not sent her running into the night . . . and the streets for survival. Not for the first time, her heart ached with regret. The lady who stood before her, beautiful and demure, might have had a future with a man such as John Damascus.

John moved up behind her, laid his hand on her shoulder, his eyes dark with admiration. "Beautiful."

"It must have been horribly expensive. You shouldn't have—"

"You deserve to be draped in the finest clothes money can buy."

He turned her, slowly, and took her face in his hands. He lowered his mouth to hers, hesitated, sweet and brief, before gently crossing his mouth over hers, savoring her taste until she parted her lips, inviting him in. Their tongues flirted, warm, wet, slightly atremble with restraint. Her arms slid around him and she kissed him back, meeting each urgent thrust of his tongue with her own as his hands threaded through her hair, holding her fiercely, fingers twisting into the long black tresses that fanned over her shoulders and down her breasts.

They moved as one, turning slowly, their bodies pressed together. Each needed the closeness of the other, their pounding hearts an echo of the other's, their kissing suddenly hungry, a drowning man and a starving woman.

As they clung to one another, she memorized his scent, the feel of his thick hair in her fingers as she stroked his head in long, slow sweeps, making him shiver and moan like a man in pain. His hands slid down her body, caressing each curve, a sigh escaping his lips as he nuzzled her ear.

"Who are you?" he whispered, his words a ragged tear of desire that sluiced through her hot as mercury, warming her, making her weak in a way that caused her knees to tremble.

"Does it matter?" she finally managed, wanting no reminders of her past in that moment.

Looking into her eyes, he shook his head. "No. Nothing matters right now but us."

He slid the dress up to her waist, eased his hand down her panties, and parted her. His fingers stroked her until she felt hot and achy. She wanted him as she had wanted no other man. She felt it in her heart, which beat wildly as she became lost within the pleasure, the beautiful heat.

Vaguely she was aware that he lifted the dress up over her head, allowing it to float to a dark pool on the floor. Releasing her bra, he let it fall, stood before her as his dark eyes appraised her with an appreciation that made her body shake.

"Incredible." He smiled and cupped her breasts in his hands, easing his thumbs over her nipples so they hardened. She felt so sensitive as he stroked her that her breath caught. She was as nervous as a virgin. Ridiculous, of course, a woman with her past trembling for the first time under a man's touch. Then again, she had never known the pleasure of receiving, only the degradation of giving.

He lifted her in his arms and carried her to the bed, eased her down on her back. His body moved down over hers, his lips and tongue teasing, swirling round and round the little sapphire in her navel, then lower, his breath like fire as he pressed his mouth against the crotch of her filmy thong panties, his desirous groan like sweet music that made her heart sing. Her entire adult life, she had longed for a man to touch her in this way, with heartfelt emotion.

His hands tugged down the thong to her knees, letting it slide down her legs to her ankles. Then he nudged it away and straightened, his erection barely contained in the low-slung underwear that he discarded.

She was quite certain in that moment that she had never seen so beautiful a specimen as he. Tall and tanned, every muscle defined, his hair shaggy and spilling over his brow, his unshaven jaw shadow-dark, he looked savage. His eyes burned with desire for her.

The realization occurred to her, as he eased his body down on hers, that she had fallen in love with John Damascus. She had tried to deny it to herself, to her heart. They were strangers, two people with a past that had left them broken. Yet, it was there, squeezing her heart with such pain she wanted to weep. Wanted to run from his arms, into the hot and humid night and never look back. They had no future, after all.

Still, she opened herself to him, gasped as he drove his body into hers and kissed her, his tongue matching the rhythmic pumping of his body. Clutching him to her, she dug her fingers into his flexing back. Lifting her legs around his hips, she embraced him, pulled him deeper, matching each thrust with a lift of her hips. Their rocking caused the bed to bang against the wall. Holly buried her hands into the sheets as her body arched and her breath caught, a groan working up her throat.

On he drove, propping his body up on braced arms as he watched her face, his jaw working as he fought his own climax, intent on giving her pleasure for as long as she needed it.

Forever, her mind cried. She wanted it forever. She needed him . . . forever.

The tears rose, hot, to her eyes and streamed down her temples. He licked them away, kissed her mouth, tasting her tears as he loved her more gently this time.

So this was lovemaking. Tender, emotional, the pleasure a sublimity that made a brilliant happiness shine inside her.

Such sweet words he whispered in her ear. Words that seemed wrenched from his very soul. "So beautiful. So wonderful. I need you, Holly. I care for you. Love me. Please love me, Holly."

And then the exquisite climax came upon her, lifting her to a shimmering place that she had never known. Heaven.

And she knew in her heart that this night would—must—last her forever.

14

They were already late for the dinner party when they left J.D.'s apartment thanks to Detective Mallory's phone call advising them that the forensics team had found no evidence of foul play in Melissa's apartment. The luminal they had used to locate blood unseen by the human eye had exposed nothing, and once again Mallory had driven home to Holly that there was little they could do under the circumstances. He reminded her that Melissa was an adult and it wasn't uncommon for a prostitute to simply disappear without telling anyone. As if she needed any reminders.

The dress J.D. had bought looked like it had been made for her. She looked breathtakingly beautiful, with her hair swept back from her face and hanging in coils and curls down her back. She'd spent hours on it, fretting the entire time, though he told her she would look as lovely if she'd shaved her head bald and worn a crown of thistles.

To accentuate the dress, he had stunned her with a necklace that had belonged to Laura, a lavish diamond and pearl heart-shaped pendant on a gold chain. He assured her that there had been no real sentimental value to it. After a particularly nasty argument, he had splurged on the jewelry, hoping to make amends. Laura's only response had been, "I would rather have a divorce."

His decision to visit the cemetery on the way to his parents' was spur of the moment. He made a quick stop at Balloons To Go, bought a half dozen pink and blue glitter-covered helium balloons and laughed as Holly fought to control them as they floated wildly around her in the car.

He'd laughed a great deal in the last few hours, he realized, as he admired her flushed, smiling face that reflected the brilliant colors of the balloons. More than he'd laughed in years. Their lovemaking had been frantic, then tender, then hilarious. They'd eaten cold pizza and drunk warm wine. They'd slow danced to the heartrending piano of Emile Pandolfi on the stereo. He'd laughed when she'd botched his eggs Benedict and then he assured her they were the best he'd ever eaten.

And he realized he'd fallen in love with her when he found her curled up asleep on the futon with Puddin' sprawled across her head purring contently. For an hour he had sat in a chair watching her as Pandolfi quietly played "Unchained Melody" in the background, the words of his favorite song drifting through his head . . . "God speed your love to me."

For the first time in four years, he had felt the bleeding wound in his heart begin to heal.

He parked the car under the old spreading oak and together they walked down the path to his family's graves, she holding the bumping pink balloons, he holding the blue. She took his hand and squeezed it reassuringly. He smiled.

"I'm nervous," he confessed after taking a deep breath. "I've never brought anyone here."

Holly said nothing, just looked up into his eyes, her own sad yet understanding. How could he confess to her that the pain he experienced when he came here wasn't something he had ever cared to share with anyone else? He couldn't even explain it to himself. Just knew this was a part of his life in which he wanted—needed—to include her.

The balloons he had brought before were there still, deflated and storm beaten, hanging by their strings like faded, withered flowers. As Holly stood back, he removed them before anchoring the new ones to the children's headstones. Then he took her hand and they sat on the bench, shoulder to shoulder, silent but for the shifting of the leaves on the trees.

Holly took his hand in both of hers and gripped it fiercely. "Tell me about your children," she said softly.

"Billy loved soccer." He grinned. "He was very certain he would grow up to play professionally. He was surprisingly good for his age. I had planned to send him to soccer camp that next summer—as a surprise. He played the piano well. Had been taking lessons for three years. Not that he admitted it to his pals. They might have thought he was a sissy.

"Every night I would sit and listen to him practice and

he wouldn't quit until he got it perfect. Then he would go to his room and play computer games until I forced him into bed. His favorite food was macaroni and cheese. He refused to eat broccoli and thought girls were yucky, except for his sister who he considered tolerable when she wasn't fooling with his collection of soccer cards. Tall for his age. A bit on the thin side. Tried to convince his mother and me that if we fed him more Rocky Road ice cream he would muscle up a bit."

Swallowing, he tugged at the tie around his neck, which suddenly felt too tight for him to breathe.

"I guess every dad thinks his daughter is special. But Lisa *was* special. I knew it the first time I looked into her eyes. From the first day after we brought her home from the hospital, she slept all night. Never once cried from hunger. Much too wise for her young years.

"After Laura had given me a particularly hard time, Lisa would crawl up into my lap, take my face in her hands, and say, 'I love you, Daddy. I promise.'

"Her favorite book was *Goodnight Moon*, and I read it to her every night that I put her to bed. She wanted to grow up to be an angel so she could fly."

Holly slid closer and lay her head on his shoulder, her breathing a little ragged.

Looking up at the sky, J.D. watched the billowy white clouds dance across the sun. "Guess some of us actually realize our dreams."

Credence Clearwater blasted in Patrick's ears as he stood at the window in his grandparents' living

room, the earphones snug on his head. The words
pounded inside his brain as his anger mounted. "I hear
the voice of rage and ruin," he said as he watched J.D.
and his whore girlfriend move among the guests scattered
over the garden.

He had to admit, she didn't look much like a whore.
But the fact that his uncle had brought her here made his
stomach clench. How dare J.D. flaunt the bitch in front of
his mother, who had already excused herself to the bathroom and spent ten minutes crying? It was enough that
she and his dad had spent the morning yelling at one
another because of his expulsion from St. Michael's.

He turned from the window and wandered the big
house, stopped by the dining room where white-clothed
tables were lavished with immense bowls of boiled shrimp
on crushed ice, fresh crabmeat, and crackers heaped with
pâté that looked like mud. He opted for the shrimp, filled
a crystal plate with them, then slapped on a spoonful of
spicy red sauce that spattered on the white tablecloth like
blood.

Continuing down the hall, he paused outside his grandfather's office. He recognized his old man's voice along
with his father's and Senator Strong's. Bastards. All of
them.

Onward, down a short flight of stairs, into his grandfather's private quarters. Wood and leather. The scent of
tobacco both acrid and sweet. The walls were crowded
with animal heads. Deer and cougar, a snarling grizzly
anchored over the fireplace. A zebra hide was stretched
out over the wood floor like roadkill flattened by an
eighteen-wheeler.

These were only a few of his so-called trophies. Most he kept at his Colorado retreat. Big game from Africa. Illegal elephant tusks, a rare white leopard, stuffed monkeys, and a lion hide. Patrick had once heard the old fart brag that all he needed to complete his collection was a human head. Patrick had had nightmares for a month—about walking into the room to find his own head mounted over the fireplace.

He moved to the gun cabinet and gazed upon the collection of artillery. Military arsenal, mostly. The old man killed his prey with an Uzi.

Patrick took a cautious glance over his shoulder. Coast clear. He put down his plate, opened the cabinet, and reached for the M16A1 assault rifle, balanced it in his hands before raising it to his shoulder. He looked down the barrel, set the site on the grizzly head, and gently put his finger on the trigger. The weapon was his grandfather's pride and joy, capable of firing up to nine-hundred-fifty rounds per minute in full-auto mode. There was even a 40mm grenade launcher that could be attached that would fire spin-stabilized grenades over a distance of three hundred meters.

"Pow," he whispered, grinning. Bet those bastards at St. Michael's would regret expelling him if he showed up with this. Yeah, baby. Folks would sure sit up and take notice if he paraded down the streets with this. His old man could kiss his political aspirations good-bye.

Hitching the gun up under his armpit, he moved down the wall first to a collection of handguns, one of which he tucked into the back waistband of his jeans, covering it with his shirttail, then moved to the collection of knives of every conceivable size. Hunting knives, military knives, smooth blade and serrated. Ivory hilts. Turquoise and pearl hilts. Even one that had purportedly belonged to James Bowie during the battle of the Alamo. But it was the Rambo-style weapon that made him grin. Opening the glass door, he retrieved the knife, sliced the air with it, and imagined himself dressed in a loincloth battling terrorists in a jungle. Badass stuff.

Sliding the knife into his jeans waist, he eased out of the room, cast a cautious glance up and down the hall, then made for the back staircase, ascended swiftly, ducking into the first room he came to—his grandparents' bedroom. He hurried to the window overlooking the gardens and shifted aside the sheer curtains so he could see the guests milling below.

With the sunlight baking through the windowpanes, he began to sweat. His heart seemed to beat a hundred miles an hour and his head swam with an exhilaration that made his breathing loud in the room.

Positioning the gun firmly against his shoulder, he pointed it downward, squinted through the site as he slowly moved from one target to another, centering the crosshairs first on one forehead, then another, his hands slippery, his eyes burning with perspiration until, at last, he located his objective . . . Holly, standing under an oak tree with a drink in her hand as she spoke to his grandmother.

"Bitch," he said through his teeth, easing his finger over the trigger, pressure light, then firm, feeling the tension giving slightly as the idea occurred to him that the gun might, just might, be loaded. And if it was, the whore's head would explode like a melon. Gross, he thought, and chuckled as he bit down on his bottom lip, then squeezed the trigger.

J.D. joined Holly and his mother in the shade of the oak tree. He'd always been careful not to show annoyance at his mother—respect and love and all that—but since his and Holly's arrival, discovering the get-together was anything but a family affair, it had been cutting at his stomach like knives. His mother knew what was coming and she drew back her slender shoulders in anticipation.

"I thought this was supposed to be a family thing, Mom. Unless you've been burying half the population of New Orleans under the family tree, you lied."

"A mother's prerogative, dear. I wanted you here and I knew you wouldn't come otherwise." She smiled at Holly. "John has always had an aversion to my dinner parties."

"I wonder why." He glanced toward the house. "It's one thing for Dad to snub or insult me privately. It's another when he does it in front of the entire city."

"You're exaggerating again, John."

He looked at Holly. She was obviously uneasy and not just a slight bit annoyed. She hadn't wanted to come to the damn party in the first place. When she realized it wasn't a "family gathering" as his mother had pretended, she had all but jumped out of the car into traffic.

Had Beverly been behind this manipulation, the intent would have been obvious. To set up Holly for humiliation. But his mother didn't think like that. There wasn't a spiteful bone in her body. She simply had given no ponderance at all to the problem that could arise should Holly be recognized. The fact was, his mother had never been allowed to think for herself. Her actions had always been dictated to her by his father. Charles Damascus chose her clothes. Her friends. Controlled her every waking minute. Just as he had J.D.'s and Eric's.

"I was just telling Holly how lovely she looks," said his mother. "And how thrilled I am that she's joined us."

Grinning, he watched color flush Holly's face. "The most beautiful woman here, with the exception of you, of course. Now, you want to confess what this soirée is all about?"

"In time," Helen said as her gaze moved over the crowd, her eyebrow lifting. "Here comes Beverly. I understand the two of you had words."

J.D. moved closer to Holly, slid his arm around her shoulders. She felt tense, as if she would bolt at the slightest provocation. "She's been crying on your shoulder again, I take it." He grinned at his mother.

"Her sensitivities are very delicate. You know how she is."

"She'd better get over it."

Beverly moved into the shade to stand beside his mother. Her eyes were slightly red and puffy. She avoided looking at J.D. at first, as well as at Holly, and just zeroed in on his mother's smiling face as she forced a tight pleasantry into her voice.

"Everyone seems to be enjoying themselves, Helen. As always, you've done a marvelous job. The caterer informs me that he'll be ready to serve dinner in half an hour."

"Splendid. If the three of you will excuse me, there are a few last minute preparations." Her glance at J.D. told him in no uncertain terms to behave himself, then she marched away, leaving them standing in tense silence.

Beverly finally spoke. "Your mother is a remarkable woman."

"No argument there."

"She's been my rock these last few hours."

"I'm certain she had wonderful words of wisdom to impart."

Beverly finally looked at Holly, focused on the necklace, the color draining from her face. "That's Laura's pendant."

"Was Laura's pendant," J.D. said.

"I know. I helped you pick it out."

"Looks nice with the dress, doesn't it?"

Beverly forced a tight smile. "Lovely."

"So you want to tell me what this party is all about?"

"Eric is going public with his intentions to run for the Senate."

"Ah. He's passing the plate for campaign donations."

"I wouldn't be so crass as to call it that."

"Shake a few powerful hands, make shallow promises that he has no intention of keeping, just like Jack Strong. I take it the son of a bitch is here as well."

"What do you think?"

"Nothing like double-dipping into the voters' bank accounts." He drank his vodka and glanced over the crowd. "Shouldn't you be out there schmoozing, flashing that First Lady smile, and telling them what a wonderful husband and father Eric is and what an asset he'll be to America's families in this time of economic recession?"

"I'm not in the mood to espouse his humanitarianism."

"Better get accustomed to it, sweetheart," he said more gently. "As a politician's wife, you can be crying on the inside, but you gotta flash those pearly whites like you're the happiest woman in the world. Give Hillary Clinton a call. I'm sure she'll be thrilled to give you a few tips."

"I really don't appreciate your sarcasm right now, John. If you'll excuse me?"

As Beverly moved up the walkway, Holly pulled back, drawing J.D.'s attention to her eyes, which were not simply nervous now, but frantic.

"Look, I shouldn't be here, John. I've upset Beverly even more. . . . Take me home. Please. This is obviously meant to be a very special occasion and I wouldn't want to do anything—"

"Hey." He reached for her hand. "Relax. No big deal, honey. If I leave now, my mom will get upset—"

"Then give me the car keys and I'll go alone." She swallowed. "I can't stay here, John. I shouldn't have come in the first place. It was stupid of me. But I thought it was just a small gathering—just your family—"

"So did I." He frowned. Her hand had begun to tremble and there were tears in her eyes. "What's wrong, Holly? Tell me."

She searched his face, cupped his cheek with her hand, and appeared to be on the verge of speaking when someone called his name.

Before he could do more than give her hand a quick reassuring squeeze, he was surrounded by several men he had known when he worked for the D.A.'s office. Glancing over his shoulder, he saw Holly back against the tree,

her head down as she looked toward the car as if searching
for an escape route.

*He moves through the crowd, absorbing their energy, feel-
ing buoyant and slightly smug. What grand idiots they
are. They have no idea what he is, what he is capable of,
whose presence walks among them. He, the all powerful.
The giver of life and death. He could destroy any one of
them if he cared to. And he will. Oh yes, someday . . .*

*The woman is standing alone under the oak tree. He
can sense her distress. It shimmers like the heat in the air
around her, drawing him closer, a pull so powerful his
blood feels like a moon tide, accelerating his heartbeat,
his body heat rising, his penis growing so wonderfully
hard he feels euphoric.*

So beautiful and so vulnerable. A loner. Timid.

*Closer, he feels her panic. Does she sense him? Of
course she does. There is something in human nature that
detects danger. She is on the verge of running—deliber-
ates it as she glances toward the parked cars on the street.
He can almost hear her thoughts, clashing like a merging
of radio stations in her head. If he so much as breathed
on her now she would disintegrate.*

*He is tempted. So tempted. Just to watch the shattering
of the frail thread of composure she is struggling to main-
tain. But no. It's not the disintegration that compels him
to move behind the hedge of fragrant rosebushes and edge
nearer, but the fright he appreciates in her eyes that are
so wide and moving wildly, her gaze shifting among the
garden guests.*

Her perfume wafts to him, musky and floral in the heat.

The perspiration on her smooth forehead glistens like diamond drops. She bites her full lower lip and clenches her hands, shifts from one foot to the other, the high heels of her shoes puncturing the grassy earth. There is a tiny run in her hose, inching up the back of her shapely leg. Sexy. Very sexy.

His erection strains as he hears her whisper, "Oh God, I've got to get out of here."

Oh yes, she senses him. Sweet aphrodisiac, this ability to control her emotions with his presence.

This stranger makes him hunger for the absolution that he has not experienced in a while because the bitch Melissa no longer succumbs to her fear of him. Soon he will be forced to move on from her. Yes, soon, because she bores him, but not until he has made certain that he has caused her to suffer for her disrespect.

Perhaps then, this beautiful, exotic stranger could entertain him. Oh yes, she would do very nicely. Let the games begin.

As the group of acquaintances rehashed old times, J.D. continued to glance back at Holly, whose discomposure mounted by the second. He nodded idly as the men debated on court cases they had won or lost during his tenure at the D.A.'s office, and when Holly appeared on the verge of outright hysteria, he excused himself and rejoined her.

Her eyes wide and frantic, she grabbed his sleeve with one hand and declared, "Get me out of here. Please. Now."

"What the hell is wrong with you?"

Shaking her head, her fingers twisting more tightly into

his sleeve, she took a deep, shaky breath and tried to relax. "Look, it's obvious this is meant to be a very public and important occasion for your brother. I just don't want to put a damper on things, okay?"

Her meaning struck him then like the stab of a knife. As he stared down into her eyes, he felt his face, his entire body begin to burn, the truth sinking into his stomach like lead.

"You've recognized someone," he said through his teeth, hating his tone even as he said it.

Her gaze never leaving his, she swallowed and nodded. "Yes."

"Who is it?"

"It doesn't matter—"

"The hell it doesn't. Who is it, Holly?"

With a flash of her old fury and toughness, she set her shoulders and lifted her chin. "Look, Damascus, don't stand there and look at me as if I'm some damn nasty viral germ all of a sudden. Were you so dense to believe that if you parade me around among your friends that eventually we wouldn't run into one of my old tricks? I am what I am, John. You can dress me up like a lady so I'm presentable to your mother, but no amount of white-washing is going to change the fact that I was a whore. Now get me the hell out of here before something happens to disgrace your family."

"And just how am I supposed to do that without insulting my mother?"

Thrusting her hand at him, she said, "Give me the keys."

"J.D."

A hand slammed down on his shoulder. J.D. cursed

under his breath, turning to come face-to-face with a smiling Jack Strong, Eric at his side.

"You going to introduce us to the little filly hiding behind you? She's got this whole place buzzing about how pretty she is. Come on out from behind him, darlin', so I can make your acquaintance. Hell, I can't pass up the chance to shake the hand of a potential voter, can I?"

Holly slowly stepped around him.

The smile froze on Jack's face. "What the hell." His gaze turned hard and his cocky composure disintegrated into shocked disbelief.

"Hello, Senator Strong." Her expression stony, Holly stepped away from J.D.

"I take it you and Holly have already met." J.D. flung his cigarette to the ground and crushed it out with his shoe heel.

"Sure," Holly purred, her eyes narrowing and her lips curving. "The Senator and I go way back."

Turning on J.D., his sweating face so close J.D. could smell the bourbon on his breath, Jack said, "What the hell are you doin' bringin' that tramp to this function? Are you aware of who and what she is?"

"Sure I am, Jack. Her name is Holly Jones and she's my date. So I suggest, if you desire to avoid an ugly scene, you'd better remember that."

His eyebrows shot up. "Well, now, Eric. I thought your brother had sunk just about as low as he could get. But fraternizing with a hooker and a murderer to boot exceeds even my low expectations of him. You know who this woman is? Why this is Shana Corvasce, the bitch who blew away Carlos Cortez."

15

The sudden flood of cameramen advancing across the gardens would have been Eric's doing. Their mother despised the press and would never have allowed such a media event in her home, regardless of the auspicious occasion of her son announcing his plans to run for the Senate. No doubt he had made a phone call in the privacy of their father's office to let the voracious newshounds in on their little secret. By six P.M. his name and face would be blasted across every television screen in Louisiana and beyond.

So it was no wonder Eric glared at J.D. with a mounting sense of panic as the camera crews spread out over the landscape like an army of ants. But Eric's discomposure over Holly Jones, aka Shana Corvasce, was no greater than J.D.'s own. If one more revelation came out of the blue to further shock him, he was going to lose it. And if Eric didn't get out of his face, he was going to drive his fist into his teeth and to hell with the headlines and his mother's sensitivities.

His hand fiercely gripping Holly's arm, J.D. elbowed his way through the guests, who were more than a little alarmed at the horde of reporters surrounding them. Eric dogged him, growing more irate as J.D. ignored him.

Finally, Eric stepped before him, planting one hand against J.D.'s chest, feet braced apart and his teeth showing.

"What the hell were you thinking?" Eric said. "For that matter, where the hell is your head—getting involved with this woman?"

"Unless you want tomorrow's headlines to read that I punched out your lights, Eric, you'll shut up and get out of my way."

"Is this some ploy to ruin my chances at the Senate? Do you know what your association with that bitch will do to me? Have you gone brain-dead, John? Christ, Carlos Cortez was a drug lord, among other things. Don't tell me you didn't realize that. Her face was blasted across every newspaper in this country four years ago."

"Sorry. I was too busy mourning the death of my wife and kids to give much notice to current events."

Shoving Eric aside, hauling Holly behind him, J.D. fought his way through the crowd, the shouts of the reporters bringing back unwelcome images of his prosecutor days. With luck, the news crews would focus their energies on Eric and Jack and he and Holly could make a clean getaway without calling attention to their departure.

"Hey!" someone shouted. "It's J.D. Damascus!"

Ah hell.

Suddenly there were microphones shoved in his face, and as Holly did her best to turn her back to the cameras, a reporter cried, "Any comments regarding the return of the French Quarter killer, Mr. Damascus? What is your reaction to the news that the wrong man was apparently executed for the murders four years ago?"

The reporter stopped him in his tracks. He'd anticipated their line of questioning to be focused on his supporting Eric's candidacy, but obviously Anna Travelli, going public with the newest killings, had already hit the media like a tidal wave.

Quicker than he could formulate his "No comment," the reporters' interest in Eric shifted to him. Cameras were thrust into his and Holly's faces, whirring and clicking, bodies pressing, the shouts becoming a cacophony that made Holly cover her ears and bury her face in his shoulder.

"Mr. Damascus, how do you feel knowing that the man who slaughtered your family is walking the streets killing more women?"

"Four years ago, you went on record regarding your feelings about the Gonzalez conviction. Do you somehow feel vindicated knowing you were correct?"

"What are the legal ramifications to the state over this debacle?"

"It's obvious that Chief Killroy has kept a lid on the latest murders. What's your impression about why the FBI has become involved in this case again so soon? Do you feel the local police are incapable of finding this killer?"

As in the past, silence fell over the group as it eagerly awaited his responses. As Holly trembled against him, his arm hugging her close, he looked around the sea of anticipatory faces and replied, "No comment."

Not the wisest choice of words. He should have known better. His refusal to respond to their questions only whipped the reporters into a heightened frenzy, their voices rising as they jostled among themselves to move closer, stabbing at his face with their microphones.

Holly tore herself away, and with her head down, her hand up to shield her from the cameras, she elbowed her way through the press of bodies, out of his reach. The shouts became a blur as he plunged into the crowd after her.

At last breaking through the reporters, she ran toward the street, past his car, which was parked at the curb. Like hounds on a scent, the reporters followed J.D. to his Mustang, forcing him to move them aside, as politely as possible, as he wedged himself through the open door and into the car, doing his best to ignore their continued shouts and the camera lenses thrust up to the car window.

By the time he had managed a U-turn, Holly was out of sight. Carefully he pulled away from the frustrated reporters and floored the accelerator so the tires squealed. The car fishtailed before catching traction and hurling him down the narrow residential street.

Coming to a four-way stop, he glanced one way, then another, and spotted Holly walking swiftly along the sidewalk. Making the turn, he pulled up beside her and lowered the window.

"Get in!"

Her pace slowed. Then she stopped, her face down, one hand covering her eyes as her shoulders shook.

"Get in," he said more softly. "Please."

Her head turned and she looked at him. Mascara streaked her cheeks. Her hair streamed limply around her pale face. She had removed her heels, and her trek along the cement sidewalk had caused her panty hose to disintegrate.

He forced a smile as his hands gripped the steering wheel so tightly his knuckles turned white. "Come on, sweetheart. Before that pack of hyenas comes after us. I'm sure neither of us is up to that bombardment again."

As she moved slowly around the car, he leaned over and opened the passenger door. Once she was settled, her head resting back against the seat, and her eyes closed, J.D. continued to drive, taking cautious glances at her profile.

"I'm so sorry," she finally said, her tone weary and defeated. "So damn sorry about everything, John."

"Hey." He took her hand and gripped it hard. "I should be the one apologizing, Holly. I shouldn't have forced you to come along. I had no idea this was going to be anything more than a family thing."

Her fingers curling around his, she turned her face away and stared out the window at the passing countryside. "Sorry," she repeated.

"What happened between you and Jack in the past . . . it doesn't matter. None of that matters, honey. We're going to start fresh. Bury the history."

As the traffic light turned red, he stopped the car, leaned closer to her, took her face in his hand, and forced it around, searching her eyes, which were blue pools of distress. There was a tension in his body that made breathing next to impossible.

"All that other crap about your being Shana Corvasce . . . he was mistaken is all. He's confused you with someone else. I'll set him straight." He swallowed. "Right? He's got the wrong woman."

Her hard, unblinking gaze drove into his own. "That kind of self-denial didn't make you this state's most fearsome prosecutor, John."

Oh Christ. Oh no. This couldn't be happening. Closing his eyes, he sank back in his seat.

"My name *is* Shana Corvasce—"

"Shut up," he said through his teeth. "I don't want to hear it."

"I killed Carlos Cortez. Put a bullet between his eyes. The only thing that kept me from getting life or execution for premeditated murder was I turned federal witness. There are men doing time now because of my testimony against them. Disreputable, infamous, and powerful men. For that I was given my freedom and a new identity."

The light turned green. The car remained stopped, engine purring as J.D. stared out through the windshield, his chest swelling with an ache that made each breath an agony. A car horn blasted behind them. Still, he did nothing, forcing the frustrated driver to back up, then pull around them, flashing an obscene gesture.

"You might say I was Carlos's property. Tyron set us up. You know the routine. Big shot comes into town and needs a little companionship. I didn't work much in those days. I didn't need to. Tyron paid me generously to entertain his more influential clients . . . such as the senator and others who shall remain nameless. Problem was, I didn't like him. I despised him and everything he stood for. I wanted out. Desperately. But one doesn't simply walk away from a goon like Cortez. Eventually . . ."

She looked away, the old recognizable coldness returning to her voice. "I won't bore you with all the gruesome details. They'll only come across as excuses for what I did. Suffice it to say, I finally came to the conclusion that I would rather spend the remainder of my life locked away than allow an animal like that to continue victimizing the helpless.

"But murder is murder any way you look at it, isn't it, Mr. Prosecutor? I had no right to take the law into my own hands. You would have locked me away and flushed the key. Even now you sit there like stone, judging me, hammered by indignation, your justice shaking its fist in the face of my reasoning."

Her voice softened, became tremulous. "For what it's worth, I wanted to tell you, after I realized that something special was happening between us. But I didn't want to disappoint you. You've been hurt too damn much. I couldn't bring myself to see pain in your eyes again and know that I had put it there.

"I didn't expect us to grow so close so quickly. It was like a fairy tale. At least for me. For the first time in my life, I experienced just a little of what it was like to be just a normal woman doing normal things, falling in love with a great guy and hoping against hope that he might care for me, too.

"You just can't appreciate normal if you've never experienced it, John. What's mundane to you or Beverly,

like sewing on your shirt button, decorating your apartment, cooking you miserably failed eggs Benedict, and
watching you wolf them down with a grimacing smile,
has always been something enjoyed by other women. Taking care of you . . . you taking care of me. It was the first
time in my life someone actually gave a damn about me.
I didn't want to lose that.

"It was inevitable, of course. I knew that. But can you
blame me for wanting to hold on to that as long as I
could?"

He couldn't speak. Couldn't look at her. His eyes
burned and he turned his face away, stared through a watery blur out at the skateboarding boys on the sidewalk
who stopped to stare back at the car that remained in the
street, despite the blaring horns and the traffic zooming
by.

The car door opened, allowing the sound of traffic to
flood over him as well as the muggy heat of the sweltering
afternoon. Then there was a gentle close and click. When
he looked again toward the passenger seat, Shana Corvasce was gone.

The television anchored near the ceiling of the
pub replayed the afternoon's fiasco on the ten o'clock
news. No one noticed except J.D. Sitting at the bar, a
drink before him, a cigarette smoldering, he watched himself battle his way through the reporters, clutching Shana
Corvasce with one arm wrapped possessively around her
as she did her best to shield her face from the cameras.

Around him, life on Bourbon Street raged on. The side-

walks teemed with shouting, laughing men and women,
all on their way to inebriation. Music from a nearby jazz
club added to the cacophony as the photographs of murdered women flashed across the screen. Tomorrow, in the
throes of their hangovers, the revelers would take notice.
The women around him tonight, braless in their skimpy
tank tops and indecently short shorts, would read their
morning papers and shudder in shock and fear. They
would think twice this time tomorrow night about ac-
cepting drinks and a dance from a stranger. They would
regard their boyfriends with a niggling of suspicion.
Mothers would phone their daughters to beseech them to
lock their doors and stay away from the Vieux Carre.

Indeed, life raged on. It raged inside him, beating at his
temples, his heart, his burning gut.

Deep into his third Smirnoff, the numbness of disbelief
had begun to wear off. The events of the day had blasted
him with a reality that he had been too stunned to fully
appreciate when they had taken place.

First the confirmation that his girlfriend, a former
hooker, had serviced Senator Jack Strong. Not that Jack's
taste for the illicit distressed or surprised him for that matter. But the fact that it had been with the woman he had
grown to love did. That bare-fanged, gnashing anger and
jealousy—not to mention embarrassment, not just for
himself but for Holly—had been brief and inconsequential
compared to the news that she was the infamous Shana
Corvasce who had murdered one of the most notorious
drug lords in history.

He'd been willing to forgive and forget her hooker history. Having defended countless numbers of such women

in court, he knew that most shared a common bond. Abuse and neglect as children. Fighting for survival any way they could as teenagers. Bastards like Tyron Johnson sweeping them into a life that, in their innocence, seemed the only recourse. They sold their bodies and innocence for security.

But forgiving murder was something else.

At a quarter to twelve, he paid the bar bill and exited onto the street. Bumped and shoved by howling, drunken crowds of prowling young men, J.D. moved along the sidewalk, passed the blazing windows of tourist trap T-shirt and voodoo shops, his gaze wandering over the animated faces of the women he passed.

He didn't expect to find her there. Shana or Holly or whatever she might call herself next. She would be holed away someplace. Maybe his apartment, hoping against hope he would walk through the door and express his apologies for his behavior and assure her that the feelings he had for her couldn't be tarnished by this newest disclosure.

No, she wouldn't be there. Not the Holly he knew. She would be too damn proud to face him again.

When he at last reached his car, parked down a dimly lit side street, he sank into it and locked the door. Sliding the Pandolfi CD into the stereo, he laid his head back against the seat as the heartrending notes of "Unchained Melody" surrounded him. He didn't want to go home, back to the emptiness, the loneliness, the memories and wounds that, once again, had been laid open to bleed anew.

Of course Holly wouldn't be there.

He dug the cell phone from the glove compartment,

hesitated briefly before punching in his number. No answer. He called his voice mail, listened to message after message—all reporters wanting a comment. One from his concerned mother. Obviously Eric had wasted little time informing her about Holly. Then there was Beverly, who was more than eager to put their differences behind them if he would only allow her to be there for him. An irate chief of police. May with her usual agitated demand to let her know that he was okay and that he had not succumbed to a perforated ulcer.

No message from Holly. He wasn't surprised.

He drove with no particular destination, ending up at Lake Pontchartrain where he sat on the hood of his car and smoked until the pack was empty, enjoying the breeze, cooled by its rush across the water as it kissed away the sweat on his face. On his way back to the city, he stopped at a convenience store to buy more cigarettes, only to discover his wallet empty and the ATM burping back a tape that indicated he had no money in his account. He'd wiped out what little he had on the dress for Holly.

With the car parked under a vapor light swarming with frantic moths, J.D. turned up Pandolfi, laid his forehead against the steering wheel, and closed his eyes. The realization had finally hit him. He was a hypocrite. He, who had been on the verge of hunting down Tyron Johnson and killing him in cold blood, had allowed his old A.D.A.'s instincts to kick in. For that brief moment he had turned from Holly when she needed his understanding the most.

* * *

Jerry and Anna shared a house that was located exactly one residential block down the street from the house J.D. had lived in with Laura and the kids. As he leaned on the doorbell a third time, he glanced at his watch in the glow of the security lights. Four-fifteen.

"Who the hell is it?" Jerry shouted behind the door.

"Who the hell else would be ringing your bell at this ungodly hour?"

"J.D.?" The door opened slightly and a bleary-eyed Jerry peered out at him. "Christ. Hang on." The door closed as he fumbled with the chain lock, then opened again to reveal Jerry in nothing more than low-slung, baggy pajama bottoms, his hair straggling nearly to his eyes.

"Yeah, yeah, I know. I look like hell." J.D. stepped into the house to find Anna in the foyer tying a housecoat sash around her waist.

"That's putting it mildly, Damascus. Where have you been? Jerry's been trying to reach you for hours."

Jerry relocked the door and took a quick glance out the window. "I'd offer you a drink, but by the looks of you, I suspect you've reached your legal limit. How about coffee? Honey, would you mind?"

"Sure." She turned and barefooted her way down the hall as Jerry led J.D. into the living room.

J.D. glanced around. "Anna's done a nice job with the place. You never did have much talent for interior decorating."

"Nothing like a woman's touch to wring the bachelor out of a man. Christ, she even made me trash my voodoo priestess dolls and framed prints of bare-breasted Mardi Gras babes."

"Life's a bitch, right?"

"Right."

They exchanged sleepy grins, the memories tumbling in on them—wild college parties, the many nights J.D. had turned up on Jerry's doorstep to hash over problem cases during their stint as prosecutors.

"Make yourself at home. Are you hungry? Anna, bring those oatmeal cookies you made!"

"You got it!"

"Oatmeal cookies?" J.D. dropped onto the sofa. "I have a hard time imagining that tough-ass FBI agent toiling over a hot stove making cookies."

"She has her moments." Jerry eased down into a chair and propped his elbows on his knees, his gaze intense and assessing. "I caught the news. Sorry about all that."

J.D. shrugged. "I'm not. A small price to pay to force Killroy into doing his job. You must have had your share of harassment when the news broke."

"We've had to unplug the phones."

Anna joined them, placing a tray of cups and cookies on the coffee table. "The media was roosting like vultures outside throughout the afternoon. There wasn't much Jerry could say. He's in a bad place. If he was still the D.A., he would be forced to defend his position regarding Gonzalez. But since he's not . . ." She gave Jerry a sympathetic smile. "If he comes right out and admits that he was railroaded into the prosecution, heads are going to roll."

As Anna left the room to retrieve the coffee, Jerry relaxed into the chair, his gaze still locked on J.D. "So how's the practice going?"

"I suppose if I could get my act together I'd do okay. Too much pro bono work. You know me. I was always a sucker for the underdog. Justice for all and all that bullshit. Truth and fairness don't relate well when putting a price on it."

"I'm ready to expand my practice. I need a partner. Think about it." He grinned. "You have to admit, we were one hell of a team."

Anna returned and filled their cups, then settled on the chair arm next to Jerry, one slender arm draped around his shoulder. "I spent the day with Killroy. You can imagine how thrilled he was. Prick looks at me as if I'm a freak, among other things."

Her voice lowered to mock Killroy, she added, "If the FBI is gonna get involved in my business, they could at least send me a real agent and not a frickin' psychic."

"How's the investigation developing?"

"Same old story. The killer is meticulous. The CSI has turned up nothing. No witnesses, either. As before, the women were younger, fairly fresh in the business. I've requested a printout of all the men who fit my profile who were arrested and spent time in prison during the last four years, and whose release coincided with the current killings. Might explain why he simply disappeared for the last four years. We're also running a check through Quantico—cross-referencing similar killings across the country. If he's mobile, say his job relocated him for a time, it's likely that he continued his pastime in his new location. Although I suspect, if he's as bright as I think he is, he changed his signature. He wouldn't have wanted to call attention to the fact that the wrong man was convicted for his crimes."

"But now that Gonzalez is gone he can come out of the closet, so to speak," J.D. said.

"Goes deeper than that, J.D. He's into power, and how better to get off on his domination than to flaunt the state's screwup in executing the wrong man? He must be feeling very full of himself right now. And that could be good. Generally, when such a perp gets that carried away with his ego, he begins to take more chances. Not only does it takes bigger risks to feed his addiction, but he's so confident in his power and control that he begins to see himself as truly omnipotent.

"If this is the case, we can rattle him. Force his hand, hopefully. Challenge him. I've called a news conference for tomorrow at ten. I'm going to suggest that he's screwed up. Left evidence at the scene and we're focusing on a suspect. I'm going to publicly profile him just to make sure he takes me seriously."

"That's sticking your neck out, Anna. What if you're wrong?"

"She hasn't been wrong yet." Jerry laid a hand on her thigh. "She's the best profiler to come out of Quantico's Behavioral Science Unit since John Douglas."

J.D. put down his empty cup, rubbed his grainy eyes. "I've been giving a lot of thought to your speculation that Laura might have been involved with the killer."

"It's a place to start. There has to be someone—somewhere—who could give us some insight about that possibility. You know women. They have a compulsive need to confide in friends."

"She really didn't have any close friends. She and Beverly were friendly the first few years we were married, but that began to erode eventually. There wasn't much communication between them the last couple of years, except during family get-togethers."

"We'll subpoena your phone records. If she carried on conversations with some man, it'll be there."

"Changing the subject," Jerry said. "Who's the new lady in your life?"

J.D. blinked, confused for a moment.

"The one you were so valiantly attempting to protect during the media's barrage. A real looker, Damascus, although I suspect that if she's going to continue being involved with you, she'd better take a few lessons on gracefully dealing with voracious reporters."

Silent, the weight of the day's events crushing down on him again, J.D. stared into Jerry's eyes. Finally, he cleared his throat, though the words came out dry as sawdust. "Shana Corvasce."

The name obviously didn't register immediately with Jerry. Anna, however, was a different matter. Freezing in her steps, her head whipping around, she stared at him.

"Not *the* Shana Corvasce."

"One and the same."

"Oh my God. What the hell . . ." Anna turned on Jerry. "She's the gal who killed Carlos Cortez. What the hell is she doing? We buried her so deep in the Witness Protection Program that God couldn't have found her."

Doing his best to keep his emotions in check, J.D. spent

the next ten minutes explaining his relationship with Shana and what she was doing in New Orleans, how he had learned only yesterday her true identity.

Anna dropped onto the sofa and shook her head, grinning. "I'll be damned. I always knew the woman must have some big, brass balls hidden under her skirts, but I never expected she would have the guts to surface again. When she blew that bastard away, every FBI agent in this country stood up and cheered her. We'd been trying to nail that creep for years, but he kept evading us. The few times we thought we'd hammered him, he got off on technicalities or our witnesses conveniently disappeared. If we could have given her a medal and gotten away with it, we would have.

"Have you any idea—either of you—what that woman did, not just for the agency, but for this country? Thanks to her, we cracked the biggest drug ring in the United States, if not the world. And that's only the tip of the iceberg. There was gambling and racketeering—"

"And for that she would have gone to prison?" He glared at her.

"No way. Shana Corvasce would never have seen the inside of a prison. But we weren't above twisting her arm a little and making her believe she was looking at a stretch if it meant she would talk. It didn't take much, believe me. Hey, you and Jerry were the masters of arm-twisting, so don't look at me so sanctimoniously. You do what you got to do, or have the two of you become amnesiacs since you left the D.A.'s office?"

She shrugged and poured herself another coffee. "Getting her off would have been as simple as her declaring self-defense. If anyone deserved the right to put a bullet in Cortez, it was Corvasce. The stories she told us of his treatment of her would blow your mind, and even if we had contemplated the idea that she was making up his perversions to justify her actions, the proof she gave us obliterated our doubts.

"Unknown even to us, Cortez had established a very lucrative sideline. Prostitution. Not your typical hooker–call girl kind of thing. This might better be termed slavery. These girls were special, appealing to certain tastes. Children."

She stared down into her coffee as silence filled the room. "Kids," she finally continued in a tight voice. "He plucked them from the streets, from school yards, from mommy's backyard, smuggled them like stolen cattle out of the country where they were housed in bordellos throughout Mexico, Columbia, Germany, and the Philippines. They were used for sex and pornography."

Clearing her throat, she put down her coffee. "When Shana found out about it, she snapped. Not surprising, considering her own background."

Frowning, Anna shook her head, swung her gaze back to J.D. "Where is she?"

He felt cold suddenly, the impact of what she had told him slugging him like a fist. "I don't know."

"Well, we better find her. Once word is out that she's in New Orleans, Shana won't last twenty-four hours."

Dawn was just breaking as J.D. pulled his car to the curb outside his apartment. Anna and Jerry parked behind him and together they mounted the steps, J.D. hesitating as he discovered the front door ajar.

Anna stepped around him as she slid her gun from the holster, cradled it in both hands, and toed back the door.

"FBI," she shouted as she shouldered her way into the apartment, gun extended and prepared to fire if necessary. She made a sweep of the apartment before relaxing and allowing J.D. and Jerry to enter.

"Ah God." His heart climbing his throat, J.D. groaned as he appraised what was left of his apartment. The place was in shambles, furniture overturned, photographs and papers scattered.

Anna holstered her gun. "I'll phone the agency. Jerry, you call Killroy." Turning to J.D., she forced a reassuring smile. "Try to think positive, Damascus. Maybe Shana wasn't here."

"She was here," he said, looking into her eyes. "The cat is gone."

16

"Oh my God. Shana?" Honey's sunken eyes widened in shock.

"Surprise." Holly hoisted her purse higher on her shoulder, causing Puddin', his head jutting out of the bag, to meow pitifully and squirm with discomfort. "Got a cup of coffee for an old friend?"

"Yeah. Sure." Honey stepped back and opened the door, her gaze still reflecting her bewilderment to find Shana Corvasce on her threshold.

Shana moved into the cramped, unkempt efficiency apartment and put down her bag so the cat scrambled for freedom. The air smelled heavily of incense and the dozen or more burning voodoo candles lent a yellow glow in the predawn darkness.

"Like, I thought I was hallucinating when I saw you on the news. I thought, no way. That ain't Shana with Damascus. No way would you blow your cover, much less come back to New Orleans."

Shana needed no reminders of the precarious situation in which she now found herself. Since the airing of the six o'clock news, she'd spent the last long, frightening hours loitering in alleyways and looking over her shoulder, expecting to discover Tyron or one of his bullies prepared to sweep down on her—or worse. Indeed, Tyron's threats seemed almost inconsequential compared to Cortez's associates, who put a bounty on her head after her testimony not only royally screwed their drug business but also put many of them in prison for the rest of their lives.

Shana moved to the kitchen alcove and shifted aside the cluster of canned soups in the cupboard until she located the coffee. "I'm looking for Melissa."

"You and everyone else. Tyron is major pissed. You know how he gets when one of his girls takes off."

"I was hoping you might know something. Maybe you saw her or spoke to her?"

"Nope. Not since a couple of days before she disappeared."

"She give you any indication that she might be leaving town?"

"Right. Like she would be stupid enough to risk Tyron finding out." Honey moved up beside Shana and leaned against the countertop, her overly thin arms, bruised from needle marks, crossed over her chest. "So what were you doing with Damascus?"

Shana's chest constricted. She wished Honey hadn't brought up J.D. Damascus. The ache was too keen each

time she recalled the pain and disillusionment in his eyes
when she confessed her identity. She didn't want to think
about the idiotic little fantasies she had harbored while in
his arms—fantasies that had disintegrated like her heart
when he turned away from her, shadows of his reputation
as the by-the-book and to-hell-with-justification prosecutor he once had been.

But not only that. She may have put his life in jeopardy
as well. The men who had put a price on her head would
stop at nothing to find her, even if it meant nailing Damascus.

"We're . . . acquainted," she said. "Let's leave it at
that."

As Shana filled the coffeemaker with water, she glanced
at Honey, her gaunt face and hollow eyes smudged by
deep purple discolorations. The woman's entire body
trembled.

"You hurting?"

Honey averted her gaze, hugged herself more tightly as
she nodded. "Things are a bit tight right now. Hey, you
wouldn't have a few bucks on you, would you? I'll pay
you back."

"I'm busted."

"Johns have been scarce lately. They take one look at
me and run."

Shana lay a compassionate hand on Honey's arm, a
dreaded realization making her heart skip a beat. "You
sick, sweetie?"

Her eyes tearing, Honey looked away. "I told you. I'm
hurting."

"That's not what I meant. Are you HIV positive, Honey?"

"Is it that obvious?"

Shana swallowed, her voice growing tight as she asked, "How bad?"

"Full blown. Doc gives me six months."

"Oh God. I'm so sorry. You're under treatment, right?"

"What's the point? If AIDS doesn't kill me, the heroine will."

Honey moved away, raking one hand through her lank hair. "I called my folks when I found out. You know, just wanted to make peace just in case. . . . Wanted to apologize for all the pain and embarrassment I've caused them. Mom hung up on me."

"I'm sorry."

She shrugged. "Doesn't matter." Forcing a smile, Honey turned back to face her. "Hey, you look great. Obviously, the straight life suits you."

"Life's good. Or it was." Shana retrieved a coffee cup from the cupboard, noting her hands were trembling, the old fears looming and settling in the pit of her stomach. "I blew it big-time coming back here."

"So you go back to the agency. They'll take care of you, right?"

"I'm not going anywhere until I find Melissa."

"Guess you heard about Tyra and Cherry." Shuddering, Honey sank into a chair. "Maybe I should be grateful the dudes want nothing to do with me. Girls are freaked. I mean, like, how are we supposed to work when there's some creep out there wanting to cut off our heads? The freakin' cops are doin' nothing about it."

"That's going to change now."

"Yeah, like they put away the wrong guy the last time. So where are you hanging since you've been back?"

"Here and there. Melissa's place occasionally, but that's too risky. By now I'm sure that Tyron is aware I'm in town. Melissa's would be the first place he'd look for me. I thought . . . maybe you'd let me crash here for a few days, until I can think of what to do next."

"Here?" Honey shrugged, her gaze intense as she regarded Shana. She hugged herself as she was racked by a fresh onset of pain. "Why not?" Honey finally replied. "Just like the good old days, huh?"

"Yeah." Shana glanced around the shabby apartment, the memories tumbling over her like a load of bricks. "Just like the good old days."

Tyron was fully aware that he was risking pissing off DiAngelo by coming to his knockoff Graceland. While DiAngelo tolerated Tyron's presence at the Lucky Lady—after all, Tyron's laying down a smooth ten thousand dollars a month for the Lady's penthouse was enough to make even the dead Elvis shake, rattle, and roll—DiAngelo didn't care to be associated with Tyron in public, must less having his top pimp seen visiting his home.

Since Damascus had come a gnat's ass–hair close to convicting DiAngelo of racketeering, among other things, he'd become greatly paranoid of doing anything in this city to raise eyebrows. Not that the chief of police was going to bust the fat little bastard when he was one of

Tyron's and DiAngelo's most esteemed clients—along with Jack Strong and every other elected official in the state.

Therefore, Tyron had begun to sweat profusely as he paced the Jungle Room, waiting for DiAngelo to join him. He had convinced himself that this meeting was necessary, and if the mountain wouldn't come to Mohammed, then Mohammed was forced to come to the mountain, although Tyron was certain that the mountain hadn't been decorated with life-sized velvet portraits of Elvis. The King stared down at him from every wall, as did posters of every movie Presley had ever made—all autographed, of course.

"What the hell are you doing here, Tyron?"

Tyron spun around to find DiAngelo entering the room.

"You seen the news?" Tyron asked.

DiAngelo curled his lip. "I seen it. What about it?"

"Then you seen Shana."

"Is that what this business is about? Shana Corvasce?"

"She's back."

"Stupid bitch."

"I wanna find her."

"So find her."

"I need your help, Mr. DiAngelo."

"Look, I already told you, Tyron. I ain't stickin' my nose into this Corvasce business."

"My brother is in prison, thanks to her."

"I repeat. That . . . ain't . . . my . . . problem."

"She was with Damascus. Somebody on the force has got to know where she is."

"Try askin' Damascus . . . real nicely." He chuckled.

"I went to his place early this morning. He wasn't there and neither was she."

. "Obviously or you wouldn't be here now, would you? Which brings me to the matter of your bein' here at all. What have I told you about that, Tyron? Hey, haven't I helped you in the past—stuck out my neck for you when I shouldn't have?"

"Just a few phone calls. Maybe put a few of your men on it."

"Why should I?"

"Because . . ."

"Because why? She ain't nothin' to me."

"Just because."

"That ain't no reason. Because."

"Think of it this way. . . . That bitch has got a price on her head that would put the Lucky Lady in the black for the next year even after splittin' it fifty-fifty with me. There's a lot of influential men who would be very grateful. They might start lookin' at you with new respect."

DiAngelo's eyes narrowed as he contemplated. Good. No better way to pique the squat bastard's interest than the idea of him rising in the ranks among the mob bosses who considered him little more than a pissant.

Finally, he nodded. "Maybe you ain't as stupid as I thought, Tyron. Maybe you're on to something. Tell you what. You get out of my house and I'll think about it and let you know."

Hefting himself out of his chair, he started toward the door, paused, and looked back. "One more thing. If you ever show your face here again, I'll cut off your nuts. Understand me, Tyron?"

"Right. Sure, Mr. DiAngelo."

Tyron stared after DiAngelo as he left the room, the smile melting from his lips. "Fat prick," he sneered.

Tyron drove back to the Lucky Lady at breakneck speed, Snoop Doggy Dogg blasting from ten stereo speakers while a pair of fuzzy purple dice gyrated from the rearview mirror.

He formulated his plan and stewed as he thought of DiAngelo's calling him stupid. Yeah, well, the pudgy little gnome was in for a surprise. A big one. He was going to realize very soon just how unstupid Tyron Johnson was.

DiAngelo had greatly underestimated Tyron. Had underestimated his craftiness and desire to get somewhere in this world. No way was Tyron Johnson going to split that bounty with anybody. Soon as he got his hands on Shana Corvasce, he was going to do two things. No, make that three.

First he was going to make that two-faced little bitch regret the day she was born. She was going to suffer for what she had done. Big-time suffer. Not just for fingering his brother for his involvement with Cortez's prostitution ring, but for breaking Tyron's heart. He had loved Shana. Actually loved her. Even promised to let her out of hooking if she would marry him. But no. Thought herself too good to marry him. Even laughed in his face. Nobody laughed at Tyron Johnson.

Then, he would enjoy himself a little. Take pleasure in her body, and when she least expected it, *whack, slam, kapooie*.

He would rough her up a bit. Maybe even carve up her pretty face a little. Make her beg for mercy.

Finally, he would take care of DiAngelo. Pop him right between the eyes with a bullet. As DiAngelo's number one man, Tyron would easily step into DiAngelo's shoes and take the necessary measures to turn over Shana and collect the bounty. There wouldn't be a mob boss in the country who wouldn't respect Tyron for his slick method of connivery.

"Stupid, huh?" Tyron cranked the stereo up a few more decibels. "We're gonna see about that."

Chief Killroy's face resembled raw, red meat as he crushed out his cigarette then gulped down cold coffee, his bloodshot eyes furious as he looked at Anna and J.D., both sitting in chairs before his cluttered desk. Playing on a small television in the corner of his office was a video of Anna's earlier press conference. A horde of reporters shouted questions while Anna remained unperturbed and matter-of-fact as she discussed the ongoing investigation.

"Fuck me sideways, Travelli. I've already received an irate call from the mayor and Senator Strong, and you're in here wanting a favor from me? You're lucky I'm even allowing you to step foot in my office."

"I'm not asking you for a favor, Killroy. I'm telling you. I want an APB put out on Shana Corvasce. The FBI wants her found. Now."

He cut his gaze to J.D. "Imagine. John Damascus cozying up to Carlos Cortez's bit of stuff. Once upon a time you would have minced her up like ground beef and slam-dunked her so deep into a state prison cell she wouldn't have seen the light of day for fifty years."

"Don't talk to me about the company I choose to keep, Killroy, considering the bullet hole in your shoulder."

They glared at one another as Anna looked from one to the other. "Am I missing something here?"

As Killroy rubbed his shoulder and sank back in his chair, J.D. shook his head. "You're going to put out an APB on Shana, not because you owe me big-time, Killroy. But because you owe it to this department and yourself. For the last four years you've gone to hell personally because you've been so full of guilt you can't stand to look at yourself in the mirror."

Leaning forward J.D. jabbed one finger toward Killroy. "The trouble you're in now is going to be nothing compared to what you're going to face if you refuse to cooperate in finding Shana Corvasce. If anything happens to her, I'm going to dog you for the rest of your life. You won't have a pot left to piss in after I finish with you. Then I'll represent your wife in court when she divorces you for adultery. You'll have to take a part-time job as a night guard just to pay the damn child support I'm going to ream out of you."

A knock at the door interrupted them. An officer glanced first at Killroy, then at Anna. "We've got the information you requested. The printout on the released cons coinciding with the recent killings—cross-referenced to those matching your profile of our unknown subject."

Anna left her chair and took the file from the officer, flipped it open, and studied it a moment before nodding. "These characters should be checked out. Where they're living. What they're doing. Put a car on them if you have to. I want to know what they're up to every minute."

As the officer turned to leave, Anna slammed a hand down on his shoulder, stopping him in his tracks. Looking back at Killroy, she said, "Do it, chief, or I will."

Killroy said through his teeth, "Just who the hell is in charge of this department anyway? The NOPD or the FBI?" He glanced from Anna to J.D. "Hell, put an APB out on Shana Corvasce. She's to be taken into protective custody and notify myself or Agent Travelli as soon as she's picked up."

J.D. joined Anna in the hallway. "Thanks."

"Not necessary. I love castrating asses like Killroy." She smiled sympathetically. "You okay?"

"I will be as soon as we find Shana." They moved together down the corridor. "I spent most of the night at Melissa's, hoping Shana would show up. I've called her cell phone and she's still not picking up."

"Jerry and I want you to stay with us tonight. It's safer until I can arrange with the agency for you to have protection."

"I can take care of myself."

She stopped. "I don't think you quite get my drift, Damascus. Your photograph with Shana has, by now, sent every drug provider in this country scrambling to find her. The last I heard she has a two-million-dollar price on her head. The troops crawling their way to New Orleans would put Operation Enduring Freedom to shame."

"Hey, you're preaching to the choir, Anna. I've been forced to carry a gun on me since I worked as prosecutor. I know how to watch my back."

"I'll have you locked up in police custody if I have to."

He flashed a glance at Killroy's closed door. "I'd be safer on the streets."

"Travelli!" Detective Mallory lumbered down the corridor, a half-eaten burger in one hand, a file in the other. "Fax in from Quantico on my desk. Damascus, we got a witness who says she saw Melissa Carmichael on the night she went missing."

As Mallory entered his office, Anna and J.D. followed. Mallory tossed the file onto his desk, beside a stack of onion rings swimming in ketchup and piles of loose papers. He shoved the fax toward Anna and sank back in his chair, the springs squeaking from his weight.

"It's bedlam in this place. We've had to bring in off-duty uniforms to handle the calls since you went public this morning about the killings. Three nuts have already confessed. Everybody wants their fifteen minutes of glory, I guess."

He ripped off another bite of burger and chewed, his gaze locked on J.D. "Some hooker named Belinda says she spoke to Melissa on her way to meet her john. Mentioned she was concerned. Some dude on a bicycle had been tailing her for a while. Would never approach her."

J.D. frowned. "Shana mentioned to me once that she was being followed by a biker—when she was staying at Melissa's."

"Maybe thought she was Melissa."

"Or maybe our UNSUB's form of transportation is a bike," Anna said, redirecting her gaze from the file on her lap to Mallory.

Mallory nodded. "Would explain why he doesn't relocate the bodies when he's done with them."

She shook her head. "He wants the bodies found. No doubt about that. Part of his power trip. A bike gives him better ingress and egress. No traffic problems. Parking problems. No plates to ID him."

Sitting back in the chair, her long legs crossed, Anna fell silent, her eyes growing a little dreamy, her gaze fixed on the wall above Mallory's head. "He'll reside close," she said, her words breathy. "Maybe a five- or ten-minute bike ride to the district. He's not a student. But dresses the part while prowling—to blend in. He'll carry a bag of some sort with him. Maybe a backpack—something easy to transport while biking. He carries his necessities there: knives, wire to bind her ankles and wrists, maybe a change of clothes. After he's decapitated the victim, he tucks the head into the backpack and rides off into the night."

Mallory had ceased chewing as Anna spoke. His cheek bulged and his eyebrows appeared frozen in high arcs on his forehead as he stared at her.

She blinked, took a deep breath, and relaxed. "Advise your officers on night duty to investigate any bikers thoroughly. Get names and home addresses. Knock on their doors, and if they won't admit the officers, then attain search warrants because they've obviously got something to hide."

J.D. frowned. "So you believe Melissa is his newest victim?"

"She doesn't match the usual M.O.," Mallory said. "He always kills his victims in their apartment."

"Not always," J.D. reminded. "He murdered my family in a park."

Anna nodded and gave him a sympathetic glance. "But we both know there are possible extenuating circumstances in that instance."

Anna left the chair and paced. "Melissa was on her way to meet a john. It would help if we knew who she was meeting and where."

J.D. and Mallory exchanged looks.

"I know the john," J.D. said, his gaze still locked on Mallory, who tossed the remainder of the burger down in obvious disgust and irritation. "And I know where she was going to meet him."

Anna stopped, hands on her hips as she stared and waited.

"It was Chief Killroy."

"You're kidding me, Damascus." Anna laughed, then looked at Mallory, whose bulldog face showed no amusement. "Killroy?"

"Melissa was to meet him at a warehouse. She'd left a message on Shana's cell phone describing where she was going. She was nervous, obviously, since she was already aware that she was being stalked. When Shana arrived in town, she went there immediately—only to discover that Melissa hadn't made her appointment. She hung around a while, then the john showed up. Killroy. Seems our illustrious chief of police is into kinky Darth Vader fantasies."

Anna rolled her eyes and bit back a smile before focusing her thoughts again. "So Melissa never made the appointment. Something happened between her apartment and the warehouse."

She moved to the wall where photographs of the murdered women stared back at her. Her gaze roamed their faces, but J.D. knew Anna well enough to realize that her mind, once again, was formulating the scenario. Melissa walking the dark street, perhaps cutting down an alley-way, taking a shortcut to meet her john, glancing back over her shoulder nervously.

"He was following her again," Anna said. "Instead of running this time, she decided to confront him. After all, where could she run? If he was on a bike, he could obviously catch up to her quickly. She ducked around a corner and waited. When he approached, she stepped out to meet him, face-to-face."

She closed her eyes and rubbed her temple. "Confrontation. A struggle." Turning slowly to Mallory, she said, "Melissa's not dead."

"Yeah? What makes you think that?"

"No body." She moved to his desk. "He wasn't prepared to kill her that night. He was enjoying the sport of stalking her. Making her afraid. Once he overpowered her . . . She has to be close. In the immediate vicinity. It's not like he could take her far on foot."

Mallory gave a grunt and looked at J.D. "There's a shit-pot full of supposition flying around this room all because a couple of hookers were followed by some jerk on a bike."

He fingered an onion ring then licked ketchup off his thumbnail as Anna and J.D. stared at him in silence. "So what makes you think he didn't haul her butt off some-place and cut her up?"

"Maybe he's waiting. Allowing the tension to build. Remember, it's the power issue with him. He enjoys the game. Puts him in control. Or maybe he's getting his rocks off on the drawn-out torture."

Planting her hands on the desk, she leaned in close to Mallory. "Now that he has the public's attention, and fear, he'll be ready to play his hand. I want officers combing every vacant building between Melissa's apartment and the warehouse where she was to meet Killroy."

"That covers a lot of territory, Travelli."

"Then you better get on it, Mallory."

He scratched his head. "I gotta run this by the chief first."

"You do that. And if he gives you any grief, just tell him I was never a big Darth Vader fan."

17

Tyron wasn't pleased to find Honey outside his door, looking like a half-drowned mewling cat. In fact, he felt royally pissed about it. He had plans to make. The last thing he needed to interrupt his train of thought was a used-up old hooker who was obviously in the throes of a meltdown, judging by her shaking body and sweating face.

But what the hell. Now was as good a time as any to give her the goods. The cocktail DiAngelo had delivered him would put her out of her misery and he could get on with the business at hand. Not that he particularly cared to do it himself, but the man gotta do what the man gotta do, and by God, he was the man. If he was gonna step into DiAngelo's shoes, there was no better way to start than with Honey.

Crouched on the floor, her knees pressed against her scrawny breasts, Honey rocked and looked up at him with raccoon eyes. "Where the hell have you been, Tyron? I've been waiting here two hours."

"Takin' care of bisness, bitch. What the hell do you want? As if I didn't know." He slid his key-card into the door lock.

"You promised you'd fix me, Tyron."

He shoved open the door and gave her a thin smile, stepped aside as she scrambled into the penthouse on all fours.

"Damn, woman, you're a mess." He gently closed the door and locked it.

"I'm hurting bad, Tyron."

"No joke." He laughed and stepped over her. "What you got for me, Honey?"

"You know the johns won't touch me. How am I supposed to work like this?" She stood unsteadily, her thin arms clutching herself. "A couple of hits, and I'll be fine. That's all I need. Just a good bang, and I'll be good as new."

"You're already into me for three grand. Why should I spot you for any more? Specially lookin' like you do. Ain't no way I'm gonna see my investment back."

He went to the kitchen and poured himself a V8 and topped it with a dash of Tabasco sauce.

Honey moved up behind him. "I got something better than money, Tyron."

"Bitch, there ain't nothin' better than money."

"I got Shana Corvasce."

He slowly lowered the drink to the countertop, then turned, looking down into Honey's tortured eyes. "What did you say?"

Honey lowered her face, covered it with her bony hands, and began to weep so hard her shoulders heaved.

"God, oh God, I can't believe I'm doin' this."

Tyron grabbed a handful of her greasy hair and jerked her head back. "What do you mean you got Shana?"

"Ow! You're hurting me, Tyron."

"I'm gonna do more than that if you're bullshittin' me, Honey."

"I ain't. I swear it. You fix me, Tyron, and I'll tell you where she is."

"How about you tell me where she is first or I'll break your stupid neck."

"You show me the stuff, and I'll tell you."

Gritting his teeth and trying to keep his excitement in check, Tyron shoved her away. "If you're lyin' to me—"

"I ain't. I swear it."

Tyron deliberated a moment. Stupid bitch would do anything for a fix, even lie.

He moved to the refrigerator and opened the freezer, extracted a Ziploc bag containing a small, black ball of tar, waved it in front of her face as her eyes locked on it and her body shook even harder.

"You wanna ride on the horse, baby? Here it is. Got your name written all over it. This stud will take you right to la-la land. I'll even shoot it for you. But first you gotta tell me where Shana is."

Honey backed away, chewing her lower lip so hard blood began to ooze.

Tyron followed her, knowing in that moment that Honey wasn't lying. No way would she back away from the horse unless she was struggling with her conscience. His heart beat double-time as he grinned, thoughts ricocheting from one side of his brain to the other. He couldn't believe how easily his plans were falling into place. The risk of DiAngelo getting his hands on Shana first and cutting him out of the deal vanished, filling him with glee.

"I—I can't do it," she wept, shaking her head. "I thought I could—"

"Sure you can, baby. You can and you will. Just think how appreciative I'm gonna be. I'm gonna forgive you for bein' such a miserable failure. I'm gonna take care of you, Honey. Gonna get you back on your feet. Maybe even take you off the street. Set you up in someplace nice. You'll be my number one girl. Save you for the money johns. Class all the way."

"You're lying, Tyron."

"No I ain't, baby. When have you ever known me not to reward my girls for a job well done? You know I'll take good care of you if you deserve it."

"I don't trust you."

Her resistance was beginning to erode his patience. "Okay. I'll mix it myself."

He retrieved a razor and a spoon, extracted the tar from the bag, and shaved it, the dust falling in fine particles onto the spoon into which he added water. Then he took up a lighter and held it beneath the spoon as Honey watched, her willpower evaporating as he prepared the pure heroin. This sweetheart would send her to la-la land all right. She would never know what hit her.

He opened a kitchen drawer and took out a syringe and

an elastic band, which he tossed to Honey, eased the fluid into the syringe, flashing Honey a wide, trust-me smile as he thumped it to remove any air. As if it would matter, but best to assure her.

"All ready, baby." Holding it up before her face, he waited.

Her resistance collapsed like a house of Lucky Lady cards. Hands trembling, she tied the elastic band around her arm so tightly the skin blanched, causing the old needle mark bruises to stand out like blotches of purple paint.

He gripped her arm, positioned the needle against the thin thread of a dark blue vein. "Where is she?" he asked softly.

"My place," she replied in a dry, defeated voice, her gaze locked on the needle.

"You know if you're lyin' to me, you're gonna suffer."

"I ain't lying." Her shoulders shook as she wept. "God, I'm sorry, Shana."

It occurred to Tyron, as he slid the needle into her vein and looked into her eyes, that she knew she was a dead woman . . . and didn't give a damn.

News about the hooker murders hadn't affected business much along Bourbon Street, but J.D. could sense a difference. Women clustered together—they were safer in numbers. Their occasional glances at prowling men were more cautious. They dressed more conservatively, jeans instead of shorts, despite the miserably hot night.

He cruised the Mustang, top down, into the district where the streets were virtually empty. The men who normally frequented the area looking for hookers were sparse. The news of the murders would affect them as well. The last thing a john needed was to be hauled in by the force as a potential suspect. This, of course, would not sit well with Tyron. No doubt the son of a bitch was biting his nails over his financial losses.

As black-and-whites cruised the area, J.D. spotted just as many unmarked cars parked in the alleys, as well as the occasional undercover cop loitering in the shadows.

Again, J.D. reached for his cell phone, checked his voice mail, frustration mounting that Shana had not returned his many phone calls. There were several messages from Anna and Jerry, who were not happy because he hadn't shown up at their house as directed.

He had taken the necessary precautions. Phoned May to cancel all his client and court appointments, directed her to shut the office down and take a few days off. He had spoken to his mother, assuring her that he was fine; he'd even gone so far as to lie to assuage her worry by telling her that Anna and the force had assigned him protection. That would come, of course. Anna would see to it, but tonight he would utilize what privacy he had left to continue his search for Shana.

There were calls from Beverly. At least every half hour. He would call her back, eventually, but not now. Considering everything, the last thing he wanted was to listen to her "I told you so's." She would use this stinking mess to insinuate herself into his business, just as she had for years. Not that she was totally to blame. He had allowed it. His using her as a crutch to lean on had encouraged her unfairly.

J.D. parked the Mustang along the curb and glanced up into the rearview mirror as he sank deeper into the seat, listening to the stereo music drift into the humid night air. A full moon hung over the dilapidated buildings, its bright white light casting shadows like black fingers over the streets.

He waited, his gaze locked on the mirror.

A car slowly turned the corner and eased toward him, lights on dim, engine purring. He reached for the gun on the seat beside him, sank lower into the seat, finger sliding over the trigger in preparation as he held his breath, sweat rising to his brow, heart beating in his throat.

The Camry drew close, eased alongside him, the driver glancing his way briefly before moving on. J.D. slowly released his breath, glanced back over his shoulder before exiting the car and sliding the gun into the waistband of his jeans.

The group of apartments where Honey resided was in bad need of demolition. Most were vacant, some occupied by the homeless. There was a murmuring of voices in the night as he moved down the black alleyway to Honey's place—not for the first time. Twice since Shana had disappeared, he had come beating on Honey's door, hoping she might have heard from Shana—to no avail. Again, he banged with his fist, the sound echoing along the long corridor.

"Honey, are you in there?" he shouted. "It's Damascus. Open up."

Nothing.

He banged again, his anger mounting as he imagined the woman strung out and too paranoid to respond. He thought briefly of kicking the door in, but instead, sank one shoulder against it and sighed in frustration.

Now that her cover was blown, Shana wouldn't hesitate in searching out her old acquaintances. She could be anywhere, holed up in one of her old haunts.

So what was he supposed to do now? Nothing? Close himself up with Jerry and Anna and simply wait? For what? News that Tyron Johnson or the mob had taken Shana out?

Christ, this was all his fault. If he hadn't pressured Shana into accompanying him to his mother's dinner party, she wouldn't be in this predicament. If anything happened to her . . .

The thought made fresh fear rush through him and pain stab through his stomach. He wouldn't survive losing her. He wouldn't want to.

"What the hell are you doing? You act like a man with a freaking death wish, Damascus. I was just about to call the cops."

Anna glared at him while Jerry poured J.D. a drink. "Back off him a little, for Christ's sake. You sound like a damn FBI agent or something." Jerry gave her a warm, warning grin. "Can't you see the man is on the edge? Jesus, have a little compassion, Anna."

"Compassion, huh? Let's see how you feel when your friend shows up in an alley with his head blown off."

Jerry handed J.D. the drink. "No luck, huh?"

He shook his head and dropped onto the sofa. "I don't know where else to look."

"Good." Her hands propped on her hips, Anna glared at him. "Maybe now you'll lay low and let the cops do their job."

"Right." He took a deep swallow of his drink.

Anna sank down beside him. "Sorry. Look, I know how you're feeling right now. We both do."

"No, you don't. You can't possibly know, Anna. I didn't think my nightmares could get any worse. For four years I've partly blamed myself for my family's murder. Had I been more attentive. Had I not stayed out of town longer than necessary. Now, because of me, Shana is out there somewhere. . . ."

J.D. swallowed, then cleared his throat. "It's been a hell of a long time since I last felt this way about a woman. Maybe never. I cared for Laura. But I never loved her. Not like I should have. But Shana . . . I can't explain it."

He shook his head. "I've tried to convince myself that I have to be crazy. She was a hooker, for God's sake. She killed a man in cold blood. Killroy was right. Once upon a time I would have dragged her pretty butt into court and crucified her. But none of that matters. Not what she was or what she's done. All I know is that when I looked into her eyes, I saw vulnerability, desperation, and fear. And for the first time in years she made me forget my own misery. I wanted to . . . save her."

"We're going to find her, J.D." Anna allowed him a reassuring smile. "Up to a little detective work? I got your phone records. Preliminary, but a start. Just a breakdown of the incoming and outgoing calls. You might want to have a look at it, if you're up to it. Look for anything that stands out from the ordinary, and we'll do a trace back to the caller. Hey, it's a start, right? You never know."

"Sure," he said. "Why the hell not."

Shana curled up in the bed, her arms around Puddin', who slept contentedly, purring in the silence. She cried softly.

God, it had been difficult to restrain herself from flying to the door when J.D. came knocking. She had placed her cheek against the door, wanting to call out to him, wanting to be as near him as possible. Knowing he would once again chase the fear away and protect her.

But she couldn't—wouldn't—risk his life by doing so. He would be in enough jeopardy as it was.

Stupid, stupid, stupid to have agreed to join him at his parents. But she had allowed her feelings for him to overpower her better judgment. But more than that, she had yearned to bask in familial camaraderie, to experience and share that most personal aspect of Damascus's life. With John at her side, she could have held her head high and pretended, just for a little while, that she was respectable.

But she wasn't respectable and she had been crazy to delude herself.

The intense night heat pressing down on her, Shana rolled to her back, her gaze moving around Honey's apartment, lit only by the dwindling glow of black candles. She was reminded of just how far from respectable she was. Hard to deny all the old memories when surrounded by the shabby evidence of her past. Granted, she had never been forced to work the streets long like Honey, thanks to Tyron who felt she was "too fine" to spoil. She was better suited to big money. Power players. Like Senator Jack Strong.

Bastard. If his voters only knew. How many times had she been tempted to go public with his filthy little perversions? But if there was one thing she had always avoided, it was calling attention to herself. As if she wanted the entire world to know her as somebody's whore.

What irony that she had done just that by killing Cortez. But better to sacrifice herself than allow him to continue his sick foray into victimizing children. If she somehow saved one innocent child from facing the pain and humiliation of "the life," then the consequences of her actions were well worth it.

What now?

She couldn't simply remain here, and as hard as it was to accept, she had finally come to grips with the reality that she wasn't going to find Melissa. There really was no choice in the matter. She would turn herself in to the agency and let them worry about it. Once again, she would be given a new identity, and Holly Jones and Shana Corvasce would cease to exist. She would spend the rest of her life floating from town to town, afraid to form relationships because how did one keep her past a secret forever—especially to loved ones? And she sure wasn't going to risk again feeling the pain she had experienced upon looking into Damascus's eyes and acknowledging his shock over her killing another human being, regardless of how despicable the human being had been.

A key scraped at the door lock.

Shana rolled to face the wall. She would pretend to be

asleep. Looking into Honey's haunting eyes had broken her heart these last couple of days. Shana didn't want to witness again the inevitability of her old friend's future, not tonight when her own regrets were weighing so heavily on her.

The door closed, just a gentle click in the quiet.

The cat stirred, wiggled against her, the gentle purring becoming a growl in its throat.

And Shana knew, even before the cat yowled and sprang for escape, that it wasn't Honey who had moved up beside the bed. Her body stiffened, heart climbing her throat as she rolled to look up into Tyron's grinning face.

"Long time no see, bitch."

He sat down on the bed beside her, his smile widening, sweeping her back to that sultry afternoon years ago: she and Melissa, hungry, frightened, sleeping in alleyways and desperate for a friendly face. So desperate. Tyron had flashed them that trust-me smile that could seduce the most jaded of souls.

"Lookin' good, baby. Just like always. Did you miss me?"

"Honey told you."

"What did you expect? That she actually gave a bigger damn about you than she did over gettin' a ride on the pony?" His hand slid up her thigh. "Damn, but you always had the best set of legs of any bitch I've ever known."

"Get your filthy hands off of me."

He laughed. "Still got attitude, huh? As I recall, I slapped that attitude out of you a time or two."

"Lift a hand against me again, and I'll kill you, Tyron."

Eyes narrowing to a recognizable glitter, he clenched

her thigh hard enough to make her gasp. "Me and you got a little unfinished business to address. Like what I do to bitches who turn on me and my brother."

"I didn't turn on you. You're the one who set me up with Cortez. I wanted to come back. He wouldn't let me."

"Yeah, yeah. Sure. As if you would walk away from the high life. You always did think you was too good for me."

She gave an incredulous laugh, the pain he was inflicting on her leg making her grit her teeth. No way was she going to give him the pleasure of acknowledging the discomfort. "You're a lousy stinking pimp, Tyron. A worm is too good for you."

"Ain't we got all uppity since you been gone. Or maybe Damascus rubbed a little class off on you when he was crawling between your legs."

He stood and unbuttoned his trousers, the erection straining his pants appallingly evident.

No way. Not again. Shana kicked out as he fell toward her, missing his crotch but driving her foot hard enough into his gut that the wind left him in a rush. She did her best to scramble from beneath him, shoving at his shoulders and driving her knee into his ribs. But he grabbed her hair and yanked so hard tears sprang to her eyes.

Somehow she managed to get her feet to the floor and throw herself backward, dragging him from the bed as he attempted to loop one arm around her waist. They tumbled hard on the floor, the impact of his body on hers driving the air from her lungs.

Tyron slammed one knee against her chest, pinning her to the threadbare carpet. She had managed to draw blood

from his mouth. It bubbled on his lips and smeared his
teeth as he sneered at her. "Alive or dead, bitch. It don't
matter to me. You're worth two million one way or the
other."

He slapped her.

She threw up her hands to claw his face, vaguely feeling her nails sink into his cheek. She heard him howl like
a kicked dog before he drove his fist into her face. The
impact sent shards of pain through her head and she felt
the strength flow out of her body before blackness came
rushing in to consume her.

The pain roused her, little by little. Tyron's
voice drifted to her, each syllable he spoke driving
through her face like a spike.

"Mr. DiAngelo. Tyron here. I got good news. Yes, sir.
I understand. I ain't supposed to call you at home, but
this is important. I got Shana Corvasce. Yes, sir, you
heard me right. The bitch is right here. On the floor. I
whacked her a good one. She's gonna be out for a while."

Puddin' licked her face, sniffed at the blood running
from Shana's nose. Opening her eyes slightly, she peered
through her lashes, focusing on Tyron's feet, so close she
could smell the leather on the soles of his shoes.

Tyron gave DiAngelo Honey's address, his tone cocky.
"I'll be waitin', Mr. DiAngelo. You bet. See you in fifteen
minutes."

He hung up the phone, then squatted down beside her,
knocking the cat aside. Shana closed her eyes.

"You're gonna be my ticket out of this place, Shana.

You're gonna buy me respect from the big dogs. No more slummin' it with a bunch of stinkin' whores. No more takin' orders and insults from that fat prick. In another twenty minutes, DiAngelo is gonna be singin' 'Blue Suede Shoes' with the King himself. All the sons of bitches who did me wrong over the years are gonna suffer. Like your boyfriend Damascus. With my new influence, I'm gonna take 'em all out. Just on principle."

Tyron stood and moved to the kitchenette, opened the fridge, and began to rifle through the collection of beers and sodas, mumbling to himself about his high aspirations and what he intended to do with two million tax-free dollars.

Shana opened her eyes, her bleary vision focusing on her purse under the bed. Her cell phone lay beside it. She reached for it, fingers brushing it, her body sweating. She managed to grip it with her fingertips, tug it up under her body, and slide it down into her panties as Tyron slammed the fridge door.

Returning, Tyron dropped onto the bed, one foot planted on either side of her as he popped the top of a beer can, then set it on the floor.

The deep grooves Shana had clawed in his cheek burned like hell. Didn't matter. He'd suffered worse. Well worth the investment, he thought as he blotted away the blood with his coat sleeve.

He still couldn't believe his luck. Good fortune had surely smiled on him this time, just as it had when he had first hooked up with DiAngelo in California. DiAngelo's plucking him off the streets had been a big turning point in his life. But this . . .

He had been destined for big things, but this was mind-blowing. The potential of it made him heady. Made him sweat, more than he already was. From now on, things were going to be different. No more kissing anyone's ass. Others were going to be doing the kissing from now on.

He slid his gun from under his suit coat, then dug the silencer out of his pocket, snapped it into place, then fingered the barrel with awe and a touch of nervousness. It was one thing to put down an old hooker with bad smack, but it was another thing to blow out a man's brains. That much blood and gore was liable to make him a little queasy.

What if he missed? The silencer was good for only one quiet pop. After that, every worthless bum within a block would hear the shot. There was only one way out of Honey's apartment. A fired gun, followed by his dragging Shana out to the car, was going to call attention to himself. Obviously.

No problem. He wouldn't miss. As if he could miss the fat little bastard. It would be like shooting at the side of a barn.

He looked down at Shana. There was plenty of time to enjoy her. He'd waited years for it. A little while longer wouldn't matter.

Just looking at her caused his penis to hurt. There wasn't another woman in existence who affected him physically to such a degree. If he thought he stood a chance at winning her heart, he might have second thoughts about collecting that bounty.

Nah. No bitch was worth passing up two million. Especially since she had spread her legs for Damascus. That alone would contaminate her.

Still, going at her just to spite Damascus would be fun. He would even drop the prick a note detailing the pleasure he had taken in her body.

Maybe he should just go ahead and kill her. Get it over with. Before she woke up and he was forced to look again into her incredible eyes. It was those damn eyes that had always turned him inside out. They had a way of looking at a man that made him want to change his life.

Once upon a time he'd even considered getting out of the pimp business just to win her over. She'd made him regret his life. Made him want to go legit. Get a stupid job doing stupid stuff like office work or pumping gas. Even made him want to cut her loose from her work—give her the money to start over and apologize for victimizing her innocence.

Oh well. Too late for that now.

Right. Kill her now and do her a favor . . . while she's unconscious. Suffocate her with a pillow. Quiet and painless. Because what the mob bosses would do to her wasn't going to be painless. They would make her suffer, then they would tie a concrete block to her and sink her into the deepest part of the ocean—Hoffa fashion.

He reached for his beer, took a long drink, checked his gold and diamond Rolex. The prospect of killing Shana squirmed inside him, unnerving him even more than blowing away DiAngelo.

Calmly as he could manage, he put down the gun and beer, picked up the pillow, and gripped it in both hands.

Damn, it was hot. He hadn't noticed the stifling heat of the unair-conditioned room until now.

Swallowing, he stared down at Shana, her long black hair spread around her. He felt regret over the swelling on her cheek—as he always had anytime he had been forced to slam her. It was the dignity with which she had tolerated his abuse that had most irritated him, because it had forced him to respect her.

As if she wasn't worthy of the discipline he administered to the others who thought to defy him.

Damn the bitch, always gnawing at his conscience from the first day he had picked her and Melissa off the street. Two wide-eyed, frightened teenagers, desperate for help. While Melissa hadn't had much going for her, Shana had been different. Given different circumstances, she might have been worthy of an ass like Damascus. Leading the privileged life. Good things handed to her on a silver platter. Kids. She loved kids. She would have made one hell of a mother. He'd known it from the way she nurtured the other girls, took care of them, protected them.

Like Melissa. Shana had risked her life in coming back to New Orleans to help her friend. Now she was a dead woman herself.

"Damn." He tossed the pillow aside, his shoulders slumping. He couldn't do it—kill her. Besides, if he killed her, how would he collect his bounty? It wasn't like he'd brought around a stupid camera to take a picture of her corpse as proof of his doing her in.

A knock at the door sat him erect, grabbing for his gun and sliding it under his coat. Do or die time. Jesus, he was shaking.

Shana opened her eyes, watched as Tyron moved cautiously to the door. "Who is it?" he said.

"DiAngelo, stupid. Who do you think it is—Avon calling?"

Think. She rolled her pounding head and looked toward the bathroom.

Tyron opened the door, allowing DiAngelo in.

Honey had once mentioned that her 'panic room' was there, in the bathroom. But where?

DiAngelo crossed the floor and stood beside her. "So this is the bitch?"

"That's her." Tyron's voice sounded sulky and shaky.

"Is she alive?"

"What difference does it make?"

DiAngelo nudged her with his foot. "She don't look so good, does she?"

"This ain't no beauty contest. Alive or dead, she's worth two million."

DiAngelo bent down beside her, grabbed her face so hard Shana gasped.

He chuckled. "Playing possum, Miss Corvasce? Maybe thought you'd make a quick getaway when we weren't looking? Look at me, bitch."

He shook her again, the pain in her cheek crucifying as her eyes flew open and she stared up into DiAngelo's smirking face.

"I might not kill you, Miss Corvasce, but I can sure make you wish you were dead. I suggest you behave yourself. Understand me?"

She nodded, too immobilized by the grip on her swollen cheek to do anything else. Then she saw the grip of the gun flash beneath his suit coat, saw his hand slide around it as he began to stand, to turn toward Tyron.

"Gun!" she tried to shout, but her jaw was locked tight, the bones in her face grinding together like shards of glass.

The muffled pop of Tyron's gun made her jump, and DiAngelo staggered back, the gray shirt beneath his coat turning dark across his belly. As he sprawled back on the bed, arms and legs akimbo, he made a loud wheeze, like air escaping a punctured tire. Shana heaved herself up on all fours, trying her best to lift her heavy head as she crawled toward the bathroom, Tyron too focused on DiAngelo to notice.

"Jesus, oh, Jesus," he shouted. "I did it. I shot the fat bastard!"

18

He has basked in the moon's heat for an hour *before joining Melissa. The power of it has infused him with a headiness that makes him slightly dizzy. Even dizzier than the pleasure he received watching Anna Travelli announce to the entire world that he is back.*

Yes, yes, he is back. Gloriously back and more brilliant than ever!

How incredibly sweet to walk the streets and feel the electricity of the people's fear. To stand among them, hearing their whispers, watching their cautious glances toward strangers. And there he stands, smiling into their eyes, passing within a knife's slice of their throats. He yearns to kill them all. One by one. Blondes, brunettes, redheads. He has dreamed about it. Imagined himself going down in history as the greatest killer of all times. More notorious than Jack the Ripper, Ted Bundy, or Jeffrey Dahmer.

Impossible, of course. He cannot kill all of them. But he is destined for greatness, regardless. His next killing will streak his crimes across the country in bold headlines. Perhaps even the entire world. Then, perhaps, he'll retire. He won't need this bloody little hobby to arouse him. Soon the entire world will adore him. Oh yes. The arms of this country will embrace him. Trust him. And in one last brilliant stroke he will destroy them all.

He smiles at Melissa, strokes her hair, and looks into her distant, glazed eyes, running his fingertip along her bruised cheek, his erection wondrously painful as he contemplates this incredible turn of good luck.

"Remember Holly Jones?" he asks softly, thrilling at the spark of surprise and fear that replaces the dead acceptance that has dimmed Melissa's eyes these last few days. "Of course you do." He chuckles. "She's here, Melissa. Looking for you. Or should I say Shana Corvasce?"

He sits down beside her, crosses his legs, and trails his finger over her breasts, circling each nipple before lowering himself to kiss each one. Resting his head on her chest, he closes his eyes and listens to her rapidly beating heart.

Oh yes, she can pretend that she no longer fears him, that she welcomes death, but the heart doesn't lie. Her terror expands inside her chest, and with each frantic thud of her heart against his ear, the anticipation of what is to come sluices through his groin like the knife at his fingertips, its blade glistening in the lantern light.

"This finale will be even grander than the last one, the killing of Laura and the children. I hadn't planned on killing them. But she left me little choice. I couldn't have everyone *know about the affair, could I? She was an idiot to bring them along. What was I to do when they saw me?"*

He hums to himself, reminiscing in his mind about Laura, her pale hair and remarkable body. It had begun as a game. He does so love the game. Luring her in. Tempting her. Crumbling her resistance with his sweet words of endearment and understanding. Unloved Laura. Unappreciated Laura. Lonely, lonely Laura. A shame she had become too demanding. Stupid woman for threatening to reveal their affair.

He speaks softly, his lips brushing her nipple, her heartbeat causing his blood to pulse in his temples, to warm him, the sweat of sweet anticipation beading on his brow.

"Killing her was . . . bittersweet. And yet—the fear I saw in her face was magical. Dying at the hands of someone you know intimately must be the ultimate in horror."

Sitting up, he yawns and leans back against the wall, flips open the little black book—Melissa's book—and holds it closer to the candle flame. He laughs. So many familiar names. Friends. Acquaintances. Family.

"I had almost forgotten about the book," he says, glancing down into Melissa's face. "Would you like me to remove the tape from your mouth? I will if you promise to be nice. No more insults about my masculinity. Naughty girl."

She nods and he reaches for the duct tape, peels it away from her mouth, slowly, because he enjoys the drawn-out discomfort.

"Better?" He smiles.

"What are you going to do?" she asks in a dry whisper.

"Explain?"

"With the book."

"Ah." He nods and runs his finger down the page. "Opportunity knocks. And I have never been a man who locks the door to opportunity. Since I was informed about Shana's mission here—to shepherd you away from this unseemly existence—I pondered on just how I could use her. But first, I would have to get my hands on her. Not an easy task, considering. Then I remembered the book."

Taking a deep breath, he briefly closes his eyes, the anticipation humming in his blood almost too much to bear.

"And there she is. Black on white. Right there. Holly Jones. Home and cell. Imagine killing you both at once. The infamous Shana Corvasce and the whore Melissa. Not that anyone will give a damn about you, I'm sorry to say."

Tears rise to her swollen eyes as she pleads, "Don't. Please, don't."

He reaches for Melissa's cell phone, his smile growing. "Would you like to call her, sweetheart? Or shall I?"

J.D. lay on the bed, the phone records scattered beside him. He'd been too damn tired to do much more than glance at the hundreds of numbers that had blurred before his grainy eyes. Jerry had convinced him to get some sleep before poring over them, marking any suspect numbers with a yellow highlighter.

Besides, he was much less interested in a serial killer at that moment than he was in finding Shana. He was tempted to climb into his Mustang again and cruise the streets, looking for Shana. But it would do no good. She would lie low for a while, until she realized that her only hope of surviving this nightmare was to turn to the FBI. Anna was right about that.

So why hadn't she already done so?

Unless Tyron had already gotten his hands on her.

"Son of a bitch." He rolled from the bed, stumbled through the dark to his clothes, dragged on his jeans, and snagged his shirt as he headed for the door, coming face-to-face with Anna in the hallway.

"Where the hell are you going?"

"Tyron's."

"Over my dead body."

"That can be arranged, Anna."

She grabbed his arm. "Killroy has put a car at the Lucky Lady. If Tyron so much as sticks his nose out of that joint, we'll know about it."

"Are you certain about that?"

"I don't get you."

"Christ. Killroy is Tyron's client. The last thing the chief wants is for Tyron to go down. Why the hell do you think Johnson hasn't been busted already? His list of clients probably consists of half this town's elected officials."

"That's a damning accusation, Damascus."

"So is the bullet hole in Killroy's shoulder."

She nodded. "Okay. Give me a few minutes to call Mallory. We check out your suspicions before we do anything. Did you have a chance to look over those numbers? No? Then give it a shot while I make a couple of calls."

As she headed for a phone, J.D. returned to the bedroom and collected the phone records, sank onto the bed, and did his best to look them over as he tried not to think about Tyron Johnson getting his hands on Shana. He rubbed his eyes.

The computerized series of numbers had been broken down into incoming and outgoing calls—compiled into listings of repeated numbers. Most were to clients he had called after business hours. There were calls to Billy's school, to May, his office, Jerry's old number. His parents. His brother's house. Many from his brother's house. Odd. The last couple of years of her life, Laura had avoided Beverly, and she Laura.

J.D. rubbed his eyes again.

"Hey."

J.D. looked up at Jerry, who was buttoning his shirt.

"Seems you were right. Killroy didn't put a car at the Lucky Lady."

Standing, his gaze locked on Jerry's troubled expression, J.D. said, "You know something. What's happened?"

Jerry briefly closed his eyes and sank against the doorjamb. "Mallory's at Tyron's now. Seems a security guard noted his front door was ajar and stepped in to check things out. He found a body. A woman."

"Relax," Anna told him. "It isn't Shana."

J.D. stepped around her, to the kitchen threshold, and looked down into the woman's open eyes. Around him the CSI were snapping photographs of the body and waiting for the coroner to show before the body could be moved.

Malloy stood near, jotting notes, glancing at J.D. "You can ID this woman?"

"One of Tyron's girls."

"I'd say she got a kick from a bad horse," Anna said, stooping beside Honey's body. Beside her lay the syringe. The elastic band was still wrapped around her arm. "Poor kid didn't know what hit her. I take it Tyron's her supplier."

J.D. nodded and turned away.

"Figures. Keeps his girls dependent on him." She stood. "Any idea why he would want to take her out like this?"

He moved into the living room, caught between relief that the corpse hadn't been Shana's and sadness over Honey. Another soul lost. What a damn shame and a waste. But that wasn't what troubled him the most at that moment. Not by a long shot.

Anna followed. "Whatever the reason, he was apparently in a big hurry if he didn't hang around long enough to dispose of the body."

J.D. walked to the plateglass window where the drapes were open. He focused on the river, the bright neon lights of the casino reflecting off the murky surface. Anna moved up beside him.

"What are you thinking?" she said.

"I'm thinking that he's already got her." He removed his cigarettes from his T-shirt pocket, lit one as he continued to stare down at the river. "I'm thinking that Shana went to Honey for help . . . and Honey was desperate enough to sell her out for a hit." He blew smoke through his lips. "He'd like nothing better than to get his hands on her,

Anna. Not simply for revenge's sake, but for that bounty."

"So we take a drive to Honey's place. Check it out."

He nodded, but didn't move. "There's one more thing, Anna." He swallowed and, with his wrist, wiped the sheen of sweat that had risen to his brow. "I think I know the identity of Laura's lover."

Patrick tiptoed past his father's office. The door was closed, light filtering beneath it in a slant of dim yellow. He made his way quietly up the staircase, slowing as he noticed his door was open.

His mother sat on the bed. Around her, the room was in shambles, the mattress shoved partially off the box springs, the drawers to his desk open and emptied, the books and CDs scattered on the floor as if she had raked them off the shelf in a frantic search.

The sheets atangle around her ankles, she looked up at him, her face white and her mouth pursed. Tears streamed down her cheeks.

"Where have you been, Patrick? It's three hours after your curfew."

He moved into the room, his face burning. "What the fuck have you done?"

"I got a call from your grandfather this evening. He's missing a gun. Do you have it, Patrick? And don't lie to me," she said through her teeth. "I'm sick to death of your behavior and don't intend to tolerate it a moment more. Did you take Granddad's gun?"

"What makes you think that?"

"The maid saw you in his den the day of the party."

He shoved his hands into his jeans pockets. "No."

"I don't believe you." She stood and moved toward him. Only then did he notice the articles in her hand. "Where did you get these?"

He focused on the small black books she thrust at him. Lowering his gaze, he shrugged.

"Look at me."

Patrick turned away, moved to collect his earphones and CD player from the floor. Here it comes, he thought. Rage and ruin.

He wanted to smash his fist into the wall, his fury over her searching his room as raging as his need to spew all the filthy secrets out in the open, regurgitate them like bad meat. Maybe then she would understand. Maybe then the pain and disappointment she felt over his behavior would be forgiven. But, as always, he couldn't do it. Couldn't destroy her that way.

His mother grabbed a handful of his hair and yanked it back so hard he stumbled and let out a yowl of pain and surprise.

She shook him, the pain bringing tears to his eyes. "Answer me, you young ass!"

"Ow!" He struggled, grabbing her wrist and shoving at her. "You're hurting me, Mom. Stop it!"

"Where did you get these books, Patrick?"

"What difference does it make? I found them, okay?"

"Where did you find them?"

"None of your business. Jeez, it's just a bunch of hookers' phone numbers. What's the big deal?"

"The big deal is they belonged to murdered hookers, Patrick."

Rubbing his head, he stared at the books, then into his mother's eyes. Jeez, she looked crazy. Looked like a zombie from his favorite movie, *Night of the Living Dead.* Face white as death and eyes wide and glazed. She didn't look like his mother. Didn't sound like his mother—no hurt, confusion or anger in her voice. Just pure panic. And fear. Her body shook with it as she repeated, "Murdered hookers, Patrick. Slaughtered by a serial killer."

He backed away.

"I called your father, Patrick—"

"You told him?" He yelled it, his voice so tight in his throat he sounded like a ten-year-old. "Oh, Jesus. You told him . . ." He moved toward the door, hands fisted, throat convulsing as angry tears flooded his eyes. She was staring at him like . . . like, oh Christ—"You think it's me? You think I killed those hookers?"

"We'll get you help, darling. We won't allow anyone to harm you—"

"What did Dad say? What did he say?"

"To remain calm. He's leaving Baton Rouge immediately. He'll take care of everything."

He squeezed his eyes closed, dug the knuckles of both fists into the sockets. "Stupid," he groaned. "You should'na done that, Mom."

"We'll all go together to the police—"

His face burning, he began to cry. "I wanted to tell you. Please, believe me, I wanted to, but I couldn't—"

She looked, for a moment, as if she might shatter, the books falling from her hands. "Oh, Patrick. Oh dear God."

"I found them in Dad's office. And those magazines, too."

Her grief-stricken face froze.

"I've followed him. Okay? The sick son of a bitch is into hookers. How could I tell you that? How?"

Her hand flew up to cover her mouth as she backed away, shaking her head.

"I wanted to tell you. I couldn't hurt you. And there's his stupid political career. Hey, they're just a bunch of hookers' names and phone numbers. That's all."

"Oh my God."

"And he isn't in Baton Rouge. All those nights he said he was with the senator. He wasn't. He was with them. Just like tonight. I followed him to the old Redman Market warehouse. I think he must be meeting them there—"

"Eric? You're telling me it was Eric—"

"He hasn't murdered anybody!" Fists clenched and shaking, Patrick lunged at her, shouting, "He's a sick pervert but he hasn't killed anybody!"

Patrick ran from the room, desperate to flee the look of horror in his mother's eyes, more desperate to escape the implications of her words. Down the stairs, stumbling, bumping his way through the dark, into the kitchen and out the door into the garage, gulping air, and feeling like he needed to puke.

He stood in the dark, panting, eyes squeezed closed. The anger that had eaten him up these last few weeks was boiling up inside him.

Not his dad. His dad was a sicko, but not a killer. Coincidence. That's all. Those damn hookers had simply serviced him. Maybe he stole their books. Maybe, maybe, maybe—but not a killer. Oh Christ, not his dad.

Bastard. Lousy, stinking bastard.

His mind scrambled. The memories of following his dad through the dark streets, watching him enter hookers' apartments, following him these last few days to the warehouse district, sitting in the night heat, simmering, his anger and hate for his father building inside him, fighting the need to sneak into that warehouse and confront him in the act—

He covered his ears with his hands. Conversations between his mother and father, his mother and grandmother these last few days. Holly Jones. Shana Corvasce. Dead hookers and missing hookers. Melissa something. Shana Corvasce was in New Orleans looking for her friend Melissa. . . .

"Bastard," Patrick ground through his teeth, then dug under the tattered green tarp covering the fishing equipment that had grown dusty from lack of use, threw open the tackle box, and withdrew his grandfather's gun.

19

Holly scrambled on her hands and knees for the bathroom. Almost there—almost there. The room ahead appeared miles away through her blurred vision. At any moment Tyron would snap out of his momentary mania over killing DiAngelo and notice her. Don't think about the pain. Concentrate. Don't lose consciousness again. Focus. Almost there. Tyron was still howling and babbling like a lunatic. He wouldn't kill her. He wouldn't.

Oh God. Her head. Felt like a ton weight. Face on fire, every movement excruciating. Her left cheek felt as if it was disintegrating, bone by bone. She couldn't breathe through her nose. Too much blood. Now she could taste it in her mouth, like old copper.

Move. Move. One hand in front of the other. Don't stop. Don't try to look back. Focus on his laughter. He hadn't noticed her. Not yet. Too full of himself for killing DiAngelo.

At last! She reached the bathroom, her hands slipping in the blood that drained from her nose and onto the tiled floor. She slammed the door, the sound drawing Tyron's attention from DiAngelo. Clawing her way onto her knees, she fumbled with the lock as Tyron's footsteps thundered toward her. Her fingers wouldn't work. Too stiff. Too bloody. They kept sliding off the lock—

It clicked into place as Tyron's weight hit the door, jarring the floor, the walls, the sound like an explosion whose impact drove through her face so forcefully she felt momentarily frozen, bolts of lightning-hot pain splintering through her.

Tyron kicked the door. "Stupid bitch, come out of there!"

She shuffled back, away from the door. Think. Where was Honey's panic space? Room too small. No place to hide. Had she misunderstood Honey? Maybe it was in the kitchen—like Melissa's. No, no, that wasn't it. The bathroom. She was certain of it, but—

"I'm gonna beat the hell out of you again, Shana, if you don't open this door. I'm gonna smash in your whole face—"

She remembered the phone, tucked into her panties. No time. Where the hell was that escape room?

The shower? Toilet? Sink? No, no, no—dirty clothes closet?—

"There won't be enough left of you, Shana—"

She yanked open the small door, spilling soiled clothes onto the floor. She flung them aside, clawing her way toward the back of the little cubby. There! Oh God, there, just a latch and small exit—

Tyron kicked hard enough to fracture the doorknob. Too late, too late—

Suddenly, the door exploded inward, wood shattering. Shana sank onto her back, stared up through her swollen eyes at Tyron as he stood over her, wide smile as if painted on, eyes as hard and cold as the gun barrel he pointed at her.

Breathing hard, he flipped on the light, the sudden assault on Shana's eyes making her wince and weakly raise one shaking hand to shield her face.

Tyron shook his head. "I'm surprised at you, Shana. I'm sensing a certain amount of disrespect from you— again, and you know how that pisses off the man. Your brains leaked out your nose or what?"

He stooped beside her, nudged her with his gun. His white face shone with sweat and his body trembled. "Hey, I killed him. DiAngelo. How about that, huh? I really did it. Bet you thought I wouldn't have the guts." Cocking his head to one side. "You saved my life, baby. Maybe you care for the man more than I thought. Maybe you're regretting now all the times you spurned me? But guess what? That's just too damn bad.

"Now you and me are gonna leave here quietly. Gonna go someplace nice and secluded while I make a few phone calls on your behalf. And maybe while we wait, we'll get . . . reacquainted. Know what I mean, bitch?"

Standing, he tucked the gun into his trouser waist, bloody hands flexing into fists.

The sudden gunshot erupted through the small room like a nuclear explosion, causing Shana to jump and scream, her gaze riveted on Tyron's face that began to disintegrate as if in slow motion, replaced by a wall of blood that rained onto her in a hot wave. His body lurched forward, fell onto her with a dead weight that drove the air from her lungs.

Can't breathe, can't breathe. She beat at the body, shoved at his shoulders, trying her best to heave him away. Then DiAngelo was there, looming over them, one hand clutching his belly as he struggled to stand upright, the other gripping his gun. His mouth opened and closed like a gasping fish as he looked into her eyes. Dead man walking. He was dying and fully intended to kill her—

She slid one hand between Tyron's body and her own.

DiAngelo sank against the wall, slowly raising the gun.

Her fingers slid around the butt of Tyron's gun. No time to think, no time to second-guess, he was going to kill her—

With all her strength, she heaved Tyron aside, drawing the gun and raising it, flashes of Cortez's face streaking through her mind's eye as piercingly as the pain through her face.

She fired. Once, twice, again, again, squeezing her eyes closed, pumping, pumping, unable to distinguish one shot from the other until the only sound in the tomblike silence was the frantic *click, click, click,* of the emptied weapon.

Arm collapsing to her side, Shana opened her eyes.

Oh God. She looked away, too weary in that moment to move, the rush of adrenaline numbing the pain in her face. Think. Police. Call the police. Call J.D. Someone help her. Please.

A sound then. Beep beep. Her phone. Yes. Oh yes, thank God. Please be J.D. Please.

Frantically, she pulled it out of her panties, swiped blood from her eyes as she focused on the caller ID: M. Carmichael.

Melissa?

A sound escaped her—agony and relief. Hands shaking, she punched on the phone and clutched it to her ear.

"Mel," she wept through her teeth, the word ripping through her head like a bullet.

"Shana?" Soft laughter. "Shana Corvasce?"

Confusion. Shana shook her head.

"Would you like to see Melissa again, Miss Corvasce? I have her here. Right here. Would you like to speak to her?"

A noise. A whimper. A sudden terrorized screaming of Shana's name.

"Mel?" Shana cried, climbing to her knees, dragging herself up onto the toilet seat.

Then he was back with soft laughter. "She's a bit distressed right now, as you can tell. Can you guess what will make her feel better? Of course, you can. She wants to see you. As do I."

Shana closed her eyes, breathed through her mouth. "Who—" She tried to speak, but the pain was back, spasms clenching her teeth together as she listened to his calm voice drone on.

"I want you here in five minutes. If you're one second late, I'll kill her. Just like that. Just like all the others. All your whore friends. I'll send you her head in a box wrapped in a pretty pink ribbon. And don't think about calling the cops. If I even sniff a uniform, I'll kill her."

"Go to hell," she ground through her swollen lips.

"Ah, very good. Just as I thought. You're going to be very . . . stimulating, I think. Make you a deal, Miss Corvasce. I'll trade Melissa for your company. She's really rather boring, while you, on the other hand . . . The corner of Poland and Rampart Street, Miss Corvasce. Five minutes. After that . . . I start cutting."

The phone went dead.

No. Oh, no. Not now.

She began to cry, her head hanging, each sob like a drill bit grinding through her face. The sick bastard had had Melissa all this time. Dear God, she had tried to tell them—the police. Why hadn't they listened?

Think. He would kill Melissa, regardless. He would kill them both if she went there.

She climbed to her feet. The room tipped and swayed, forcing her to grab the sink edge as she sidestepped around Tyron's body, refusing to look down, focusing straight ahead, careful not to slip in the blood.

DiAngelo had slumped across the threshold to the living room. Don't look down. Keep going. Only then did she realize she was still gripping the empty gun in her hand. She flung it away, hearing it clatter on the tile floor and stepped over DiAngelo. Don't faint. Focus. Don't think about the pain. Think about Melissa. Only Melissa. One foot in front of the other. Time was slipping away. No time to waste. Poland and Rampart Street was only two minutes by car. No traffic now. Streets deserted this hour of the morning.

She fumbled with the cell phone. Punched 911.

"Nine-one-one, what is your emergency?"

"Help me. Please."

"Hello, hello, I can barely hear you. This is the police, what is your emergency?"

"Kill her—"

"What? Is someone trying to kill you?"

"Melissa."

"Is your name Melissa?"

"Help Melissa!"

"Ma'am, are you alone in the house? Is someone trying to kill you now?"

"Don' understand. Not me . . . lis'en . . ."

"Please give me more information, are you injured? An officer is on his way. Try to calm down and tell me what's happening. What is your name?"

"Rum'ar Street—Killer—Shana—"

"Your name is Shana?"

"Umm—Street—go—Rum'ar Street."

"Shana, is Melissa with you? Is she injured? Shana, are you bleeding? Just yes or no. Now, have you been shot or stabbed or—"

"Corvasce—call FBI."

"Shana, an officer will be there any minute, you'll hear the sirens, now tell me—"

"Lis'en t'me caref'ly, killer has M'lissa. Cut off her head . . ."

"Shana, who is Melissa? Is she there with you? Has someone cut off her head?"

Shana threw down the phone. No time. No time.

She turned too quickly. The room spun around her. She stumbled toward the bathroom, focusing through the red haze in her eyes. Red everywhere. The floors, the walls, her hands—

Think. She needed keys. Car keys. Tyron's pocket. Time was running out. Carefully, stepping over DiAngelo, crossing to Tyron, turning her eyes away, she dug into his suit coat, grasping his keys.

Gun. She needed a gun. Where the hell had she put her gun?

Back into the living room, easing to her hands and knees, she reached for her purse under the bed. How long since he had called? One minute? Two? No time to dress.

She stumbled out of the apartment, clung to the banister as she carefully descended the old steps to the alley. A pack of stray dogs digging in the garbage scattered as she ran in bare feet toward the fog-shrouded street.

The flashing lights of the patrol cars signaled trouble.

As Anna pulled her car to the curb, J.D. jumped out. Christ, oh Christ, he was too late.

He heard Anna shout his name. Don't stop. He ran into the alley where he was met by a pair of cops who reacted instinctively the moment J.D. attempted to bulldoze his way between them. He hit the ground hard, face ground into the slick brick pavement as the officer wrenched one arm behind J.D.'s back.

"Back off!" Anna appeared through the fog, her shield raised. "FBI. He's with me."

The officer moved aside, allowing J.D. to his feet.

"Get a grip, Damascus," she said, stepping between him and the steps leading to Honey's apartment. "No way am

I letting you into that apartment until I know what's happened." She glanced at the officer, waiting.

"Two dead."

"Male? Female?"

"Not sure."

J.D. made a move toward the stairs. Anna set her shoulder into his chest and said through her teeth, "One more step and I'll have these officers lock your ass in that squad car."

Sirens screamed as an emergency vehicle pulled up behind the patrol cars, several EMTs jumping from the van and rushing down the alley.

"Relax," the officer shouted. "DOAs."

"Who is the responding officer?" Anna demanded.

"That would be McGowan, ma'am." He looked around at Honey's open door just as an officer exited the apartment. "That would be him."

As McGowan moved toward them, Anna said, "Travelli, FBI. What have you got?"

"Two dead—"

"Male? Female?"

"Male."

J.D. sank against the wall, swallowed back his groan of relief.

"Names?" Anna asked.

"Tyron Johnson and Marcus DiAngelo. Ugly stuff."

"Who was the RP?"

McGowan reached for the flashlight on his belt, clicked it on, and focused the beam on his notebook. "Call came in at approximately three-fifteen. A one-eighty-three in progress. Reporting person was female in obvious emo-